SWEET

by

AMBER JAMESON

CHIMERA

Sweet Punishment first published in 1997 by
Chimera Publishing Ltd
PO Box 152
Waterlooville
Hants
PO8 9FS

Printed and bound in Great Britain by
Caledonian International Book Manufacturing Ltd Glasgow

New authors welcome

SWEET PUNISHMENT

Amber Jameson

CHAPTER ONE

Jonas Fairweather gazed at the girl, his manhood filling and lengthening in his tight buckskin breeches. It pressed painfully upwards, almost reaching the scarlet sash at his slim waist.

She was a picture of grace; slender but gloriously voluptuous. Full scarlet lips were temptingly moist and parted as if expecting a kiss to be planted by an unknown lover.

Jonas frowned and drew himself up to his full height. At six feet he towered over his companions. His shoulders, too, were strong and broad, unlike the man to whom he spoke.

"Doesn't look like slave material somehow," said Jonas. "The skin is too light, too smooth, too free of blemish ..."

Somewhere there must be a father, a husband, a lover who would seek her out and rescue her, he thought. There was something about her which spelled trouble. Bad trouble. But then again, she was so gloriously beautiful any red-blooded male would take a risk for her - wouldn't he?

Jonas set his jaw and planted his booted feet squarely apart as if making a firm decision.

The girl's facial bones were delicately carved, and this was enhanced by the full generous mouth. With high exotic cheekbones and skin glowing with golden undertones she looked like the daughter of an ancient pharaoh; haughty and aristocratic.

The dress the girl wore, he mused, now that was something else! Fine sprigged India muslin caught under the breasts with a thin golden chain. The globes were full and firm, the nipples dark and all too evident through the light cloth. His big hands itched to cup the pliant flesh; to tease the dark aureoles to hardness. His thick length in the well-cut breeches stirred further.

He cast his periwinkle-blue eyes towards the slave ship, the Don Cortez, bobbing at anchor out in the bay. The thought of the lovely creature they discussed being laid, end to end, with the rest of the miserable beings in the hold turned his stomach more than he cared to admit.

Harry Dawkins, one of Fairweather's subordinates, chuckled as he looked up at the tall young fellow. He rubbed his groin vigorously, his own interest evident. "Believe me, sir, the wench'll make a willing slave, and we're short of the fancies."

The other men murmured agreement. They were anxious to leave the West African port. The longer they stayed the greater would grow the stench in the slave decks, and these were already almost full.

"Approach her," whispered Harry, rubbing his breeches again. The bulge at the crotch was growing, pressing hard against the worn material.

The girl was lovely, thought Jonas. She had an air of innocence and a bloom of freshness upon her tawny cheeks. She sat so straight and proud in the barouche, her features shaded by a twirling parasol. The white sprigged muslin dress barely covered her full breasts, and the globes burst lusciously from the flimsy material.

Only this, the low cut dress, gave any hint that her body might be for sale. She glanced towards Jonas and he gasped. Her dark fringed, huge eyes beckoned him sensuously.

"Now do you believe me?" Harry clapped Jonas on the shoulder in a familiar manner and chuckled evilly. "That girl is for sale! She knows what she's about, hanging around the port like this. Deserves everything she gets!"

The men surrounding them again murmured agreement, whilst shuffling their feet impatiently.

"Carry her to the ship!" cried one.

"Strip her!"

"A touch with the lash won't go amiss!"

"We'll take her one after the other!"

Harry cuffed a few heads and the men fell silent, except for an occasional murmur of dissent.

The look the girl gave Jonas had bewitched him. Must've done. His cock was thick and throbbing, butting hard against his breeches. In the slave-hold or out of it, he vowed, he'd have her body before the roughness of his men got to her.

"Right!" said Jonas firmly. "We'll take her!" He'd take her if only to spare her the worst of the torture.

The slave trade sickened him. This was his first and, he hoped, his only experience of it. By being first mate to the captain of the Don Cortez he was working his passage to the West Indies, where a legacy from his grandfather - a sugar plantation and all it entailed - awaited him.

Slaves, he thought. Yes, he'd have to deal with slaves. Hundreds of them. Hopefully, his grandfather's workers would remain loyal and the plantation would still be working smoothly.

His gaze was drawn back to the girl. He would need a housekeeper, someone who would relieve the loneliness which he knew he'd experience far away from England's green and pleasant land. Perhaps ...

Jonas allowed a smile to soften his hard and chiselled features. Perhaps the girl would suit his needs very well.

The soft beckoning eyes were tortoiseshell; neither brown nor gold, but a pleasing mixture of both. The glossy black lashes fluttered as she stared at him from the barouche.

The vehicle was white, decorated over-lavishly with gold and red. Harry was right, thought Jonas - it wasn't a lady's carriage at all. It was one such as a whore might use to bring attention to her plying of her trade.

Suddenly, eager and erratic as an African storm, Jonas strode forward. The stench of the continent rose up from the unpaved streets to greet him and he wrinkled his aquiline nose, but the smell was nothing to what they would experience during the coming days and weeks at sea.

"I knew you would come," said the girl as Jonas reached the carriage.

The voice was rich and husky with a hint of a tremor. He felt it like a kiss, brushing lightly over his balls. He felt the lips soft as velvet, the tongue warm and moist with the tiny pink tip brushing the length of his cock until it reached the moist pinnacle.

A slight flush, like an African fever, made roses bloom on the tawny cheeks, and the captivating eyes were bright and hot.

Had she no idea how sensuous she was, asked Jonas of himself, the effect she had on a man? It took every effort of will to control his urges.

"Have you come to rescue me?" The question was asked in the same tremulous whisper, the same husky breathiness which Jonas found so engaging.

He felt the big muscles in his upper arms tighten as he imagined folding her into his embrace; feeling the pliant body against his, bending to his will. He shuddered in the blistering heat.

"Rescue you?" Jonas shook his head questioningly. "From whom?" He clenched and unclenched his big fists, driving his short nails into the fleshy pads of his palms, trying to still his own urgency.

The girl looked at the broad back of the driver of the carriage and Jonas saw fear in the tortoiseshell eyes. The driver had not moved, but it was more than evident that he was listening to the exchange.

"The emir." The girl merely mouthed the words and Jonas was fascinated by the full redness of her lips, the sensuous way they moved, and it took no effort to imagine them fastened about his cock. Such a mouth was made to service a man; give endless pleasure and swallow copious issues of semen. He licked his own lips, lapping the tip of his tongue around the width of his mouth, eager to taste the soft beauty of her flesh. It would be sweet and clean, but once on board ... he shuddered again; it would become tainted by the stench of the cargo.

"My master," she added, glancing up again at the driver. "The emir is my master."

These last words had an even more profound effect upon Jonas. "Master," he repeated, half to himself and half to the girl. Yes, he thought, such a one would belong to a powerful man, a master, one who would invade her flesh without waiting for invitation. The mastery would be total as she submitted willingly to the forceful taking.

"Is he cruel to you?" he asked. He felt his cock rise even further as his thoughts ran riot in his head. He felt the girl's skin, cool and smooth as he stroked the perfection of her curves.

The thought of her being naked and at the mercy of some African potentate was a delightful vision. It stirred the heaviness in his loins yet more. He felt his balls draw up as they tightened. The muscles of his flat belly drew

9

together, making him take a deep breath. The girl had conjured an image which he could not shake off.

The girl lowered the lushness of the glossy lashes and Jonas watched, fascinated as, with one dainty lace-mittened hand, she raised the gossamer fineness of the muslin gown to reveal slender but shapely thighs. The limbs glowed as if burnished like precious metal as she parted them.

"My dear girl ..." Jonas began, looking around anxiously. If any of his companions should see her actions they could easily be mobbed and the girl raped where she sat. But the native passers-by were disinterested, and his shipboard companions could not see the movement of the girl's hand nor her open thighs below the sill of the barouche.

"Please ... release this!" her soft but urgent whisper directed his blue eyes to her spread limbs.

Jonas grunted at the sight which she revealed to him. He felt his breathing quicken and his cock twitch ever more urgently in his breeches. At first he saw what the girl revealed as some kind of jewelled decoration upon the plump flesh of her femininity. At that first glance he saw the glint of precious stones, rubies, emeralds and sapphires set in thin curved struts of gold and silver. The struts formed a cage, pear-shaped, to cup and confine the girl's sex. It was held in place, so far as Jonas could see, by a soft leather belt strapped vertically over the tiny swell of her belly and around the slender waist. The leather, too, was garnished with jewels, glinting in the African sun.

"A chastity belt," he murmured. "The emir wants no one to have you but himself and, in truth, I cannot blame him." He gave the girl a smile of admiration. His pale blue eyes darted over the tempting fullness of her breasts, the smooth slenderness of her waist, and the gentle swell of her hips.

He turned away, his mind saddened by the loss of something which could never be his.

"Touch me," she whispered to the turned broadness of his back. "Touch the cage."

He spun on his heel to face her. The tortoiseshell eyes were limpid, begging him to feel the flesh beneath. She reached out with one hand and lightly grazed his wrist; beckoning and persuading.

The lace-covered fingers traced each of the struts with infinite slowness.

To see the glory of her flesh and not be at liberty to touch it made his head reel in the blinding heat. Sweat beaded his forehead, dripped from his lashes, and stung his eyes. The ache at his groin became intense with longing.

She peeped at him from beneath her own lustrous lashes. The gossamer of the muslin fluttered enticingly about the exposed tawny skin.

Jonas was torn by strong emotion. On the one hand he wanted to lift the girl from the barouche, hold her close against his chest, and spirit her away, protecting her from all harm. On the other, there was a part of him which was full of inexplicable fury; wanted to drag her to the filth of the street, tear her clothes from her and strike her with the bullwhip.

"Please," she murmured. "The emir has trained me ..."

Jonas breathed harshly, barely able to speak. "Trained you to what?" he asked hoarsely. The terrible images which she conjured up were surely a touch of madness on his part.

"To please men ..." she whispered, "... to entice them to his palace."

So Harry was right, he thought. She was a trained whore. Maybe she could make the journey to the Indies less tedious. He licked his lips, tasting her flesh. She could bunk in his cabin. He could already feel the curves of her body moulding against his; could hear the flap of the sails and the whisper of winds in the rigging above her murmurs of pleasure.

He frowned, questioning her words. "His palace?" He knew he was repeating her words, but his imagination was flying high.

"But I wish to leave this hell-hole ..."

Heart leaping for joy, Jonas smiled and leaned into the barouche, trailing his fingers along the golden smoothness of her arms. He could feel the sudden quickening under his touch. She would be willing enough, he was sure.

"I'm a slaver going to the Indies," he said irascibly. He sensed danger; danger for the girl and danger for himself and his crew, and yet he could not prevent himself from tearing hell for leather down the treacherous road which beckoned.

The muslin fluttered downwards and Jonas felt his cock still throbbing thickly with the knowledge of what the flimsy sprigged gown barely concealed.

"I don't care," said the girl. "Please take me with you. Anything would be better than my life here with the emir."

"He's cruel to you? He whips you?" asked Jonas. His blue eyes blazed in the ruggedly handsome face, so lightly bronzed by sun and wind.

The girl, surprisingly, shook her head. Stray curls shook loose from a bonnet fashioned to match the muslin gown. "If only he would!" she gasped. "To feel the kiss of a lash upon my naked flesh would ease the burning desire which this thing creates within me!" She looked down at her lap and then up again to Jonas. "The lash upon my bare buttocks would be a pleasure by comparison, kind sir."

Again Jonas felt his loins become heated and painfully full. The thought of a lash cracking about the sweetly rounded buttocks and the slenderness of the shapely waist was enough to send a strong man crazy with desire - and here was this dear girl pleading for such treatment.

He frowned, puzzled beyond measure.

"I beg you!" The girl suddenly sounded frantic and unconcerned about the silent driver. "Again! My pleasure rises again! Look!"

The tawny skin was flushed about the cheeks. The soft full lips were parted, and Jonas could hear her breathing quicken, becoming more harsh. The lace-covered hand trembled as she again lifted the gossamer skirt. The jewels shimmered in the blinding light of the West African sun.

"He has fitted a phallus, you see!" said the girl in her soft tremulous voice. "I cannot remove it. It vibrates within me; thick and fast, filling me and making my juices flow."

Between the gold and silver struts Jonas could see strangely coloured pubic curls glinting with the sheen of moisture being produced by the girl's flushed and swollen sex flesh. The precious metals seemed to tighten about the puffy mound, cutting into the delicate flesh with cruel bites.

A slick of moisture caused the girl's pretty features to shine as her excitement increased. Her breasts heaved above the low-cut gown, and Jonas saw the darkness of tautened nipples peeping above the muslin.

"Ah, there you are, Humility," said a deep and rasping voice.

Although the English was perfect, thought Jonas as he turned towards the speaker, he could hear the guttural inflection of Arabic.

Humility, he thought, casting his blue eyes back to the

girl. The tortoiseshell eyes were glazed with passion, and she made no attempt to adjust the gown which was now revealing more than it covered. The name suited her. She was born to be used by men, and to meekly accept whatever they required.

Jonas turned again towards the Arab who was borne on a cushioned litter upon the huge shoulders of four slaves.

"I most humbly beg your pardon, young white sir," said the emir - for Jonas was quite sure that this was he. "The young lady insists upon offering herself to sailors ..."

"No," hissed Humility, her wide lips still soft and moist from the pleasure brought by the devilish contraption which tormented her. "He sends me out like this."

Jonas was surprised at her boldness, but then he argued with himself, if she hated her life so much, what had she to lose?

The emir smiled and, leaning into the barouche, lifted the muslin and gazed at Humility's sex. He chuckled, snaking a long finger between the golden struts to stroke the swollen labia. He tutted in mock disgust. "The young women of today ..." he said, allowing his voice to trail away on a note of censure. "No modesty, you see. That is why I must truss-up her female parts." The finger continued to stroke and Jonas noticed a flush of colour return to Humility's tawny face.

"As I touch her female bud," said the emir, "she shudders into paroxysms of ecstasy." He smiled, showing perfect white teeth, snowy against the duskiness of his face. With smooth olive skin stretched over high cheekbones Jonas saw a cruel beauty in the hawklike face. Even with the smile the thin lips had a cynical twist.

Jonas felt a chill trickle of sweat down his backbone; it was not a face to be trusted.

"But I delay you, young sir," the emir said, the smile fading. "You have business in our humble town?" His black eyes narrowed and became hooded like the mountain eagles which Jonas had seen circling over the barren terrain of this godforsaken territory. The eyes roved lazily out to the bay where the Don Cortez bobbed at anchor on the mirror-smooth blue water.

"Filling our holds, your highness," said Jonas with a respect he did not feel. "Filling our holds."

"A black cargo perhaps?" The emir did not look at Jonas but continued to lean into the barouche to pinch and prod the swollen flesh cupped by the jewelled cage. "A living cargo?"

Something made Jonas look at Humility. Her tortoiseshell eyes flashed a warning. The full pliant breasts pressed hard against the muslin, the nipples darkly erect. What message was she trying to convey?

"Perhaps I could help you." The emir sat straight in his litter, his hands stilled from their quest of Humility's sex and tucked in the wide sleeves of his white robe. The huge slaves holding the crude vehicle remained impassive, although Jonas knew that the emir's continued fidgeting must cause them great discomfort.

"Very kind of you, your highness." Jonas gave a slight but obsequious bow as his gaze was again drawn to the beautiful girl. Now fear, stark and vivid, glittered in her eyes. Was he about to fall into a trap of some kind? Or perhaps it was just that she wished desperately to leave Dakar and all the gentle tortures she must endure there.

"My palace," said the emir, gesturing vaguely into the hills, "is overrun with slaves. You are most welcome to take your pick. You may peruse my excess at your leisure, and I should be delighted to extend my warmest hospitality." The invitation was given in a friendly enough manner, and yet ...

The emir lifted his robe to display the dark rigidity of his penis. It speared up from his hairy groin. He tapped its pinnacle with a gentle index finger and held out the digit to Humility. Jonas watched as she dutifully opened her lovely mouth and snaked out the daintiest, pinkest tongue he had ever seen.

Looking deep into the emir's hawklike eyes she curled the pretty tongue about the offered finger, tasting the salt of his issue.

Jonas was suddenly very aware of his breeches chafing his sweat-slicked thighs. His highly polished calf-length boots pinched. The billowing lawn of his shirt tickled his arms and chest. All of his senses warned him of the trap and yet, he knew, he was powerless to resist.

"My companions and I planned to leave on the morning tide," excused Jonas, trying to look away from the intimate scene before him.

"Ah," murmured the emir, his harsh features expressing deep regret, "such a pity. Humility would be so delighted to entertain you. And you can, I'm sure, see the quality of the entertainment." The black, hawklike eyes glanced at the jewelled cage, hinting of sexual diversions as yet unknown to Jonas.

The girl gave a slight shake of her head, but cleared the tortoiseshell eyes of all emotion.

"In that case," said Jonas, "I cannot refuse." He placed one of his big, capable hands upon Humility's shoulders, giving her a silent warning to agree with his decision. "My companions will accompany me, of course."

An angry darkening of the emir's features was gone in a flash, to be replaced by an hospitable, welcoming smile.

The emir's palace was a startling sugar-white against the

reddish dust of the desert. It was set high on the rocks, perched precariously upon a rugged cliff. It taunted them, like a mirage, many uncomfortable miles away.

"But why, Jonas?" Harry Dawkins was fidgeting uncomfortably on a borrowed camel, his ruddy face redder than ever as they traversed the steep and parched landscape. "Apart from the girl, we already had all the slaves we needed. Why did you agree to this stinking journey to buy more?"

Jonas shrugged. "Profit, Harry," he said tersely. "What else? If the emir is virtually giving slaves away, we'll make a good profit on the voyage and you and I will get the promised bonus." He clapped his friend on the shoulder, almost unseating him, and laughed at the grimace of fear which shadowed the older man's face.

Ahead there was the curtained litter in which Jonas knew sat Humility. As they prepared for the journey he had watched, fascinated, as the girl was stripped of her European finery. The muslin gown was torn roughly from her slender figure, baring the full mounds of her breasts and the shapely curves of her waist and hips. Barefoot and wearing nothing but the jewelled chastity cage, she was made to walk ahead of the emir through the stinking lanes of the town ...

The sight of the girl's total nakedness was more lovely than Jonas could have imagined. It made his head spin and sweat soak the billowing fullness of his shirt. The tawny glow of her skin was enhanced by a gloss of perspiration under the blazing sun. She glided, straight and proud, unmindful of the hisses of hatred from the native women who spat at her as she walked.

Walking beside the emir's litter, Jonas frowned. "Why do they hate her so much?" he asked.

The emir curved his thin lips in an enigmatic smile. "Human nature, young sir," he said, his tone sharp and cynical. "The women here have so little, you see, and they see Humility as having so much. They are envious."

Degraded in the extreme, thought Jonas, and the native women were envious! What must their own lives be like?

Jonas looked at the perfectly rounded globes of Humility's buttocks, cleaved by the leather strip of the chastity cage, and saw only her total subjugation by the emir.

"But she is your chattel," he pointed out.

The litter swayed as one of the slaves bearing the emir stumbled in a pot-hole in the uneven dirt road, but he righted himself immediately. Like lightening a whip was cracked across the slave's broad shoulders, drawing a thin stream of blood.

"Dolt!" hissed the emir, but at the same time he turned to Jonas to give him a smile of agreement. "Quite correct, young sir," he said. "She is indeed my chattel. She is neither wife nor concubine, but a mere vessel; an urn into which I can plunge my penis at will."

Jonas saw the black eyes narrow unpleasantly as the emir allowed his gaze to linger on Humility's slender waist flaring out into shapely hips.

"Have you owned her for long?" asked Jonas, in a tone he hoped was casual.

The emir laughed and turned his gaze upon his young white companion. "Are you hoping, perhaps, that I may soon tire of her pampering?" He prodded Humility with the handle of the whip, tapping her smooth upper arms none too gently. She seemed to know immediately what was expected of her, and she placed her hands upon her head, causing her magnificent breasts to thrust out.

"You see how she tempts with a sway of her bottom,"

18

whispered the emir. "The tawny hillocks so delicately parted by the strip of leather ..." He touched the tail of the whip across first one bronze globe and then the other. It was a teasing tickle, no more than the flutter of an insect's wing, but it caused a reaction.

Humility, her hands clasped hard upon her head, bent at the waist. Her thighs parted to reveal moist puffy labia, glossed with the dew of her permanent excitement. Between the struts of the cage Jonas could see flushed folds of flesh, glinting like the jewels which adorned it.

"She offers herself, d'you see?" pointed out the emir, leaning forward himself and using the handle of the whip to probe at Humility's rear orifice. "Not satisfied that I give her pleasure with the vaginal phallus, but she seeks more!" He sighed mockingly. "A greedy little creature indeed!"

"Would you consider parting with her?" asked Jonas. Humility was still posing her bottom, wriggling the tawny hillocks, offering the dark crease. "At a price, of course," he added, his voice becoming more husky by the minute.

The tip of the whip flicked again, and Humility was once more upright and walking ahead of the little caravan.

"Do you realise how long it has taken to train this girl to such a high standard?" The emir was obviously making it plain that Humility was almost beyond value. "There are very few girls who can be brought to this degree of excellence."

Jonas nodded his understanding gravely. "But all men become weary of the same girl in time," he said. Could he ever tire of this glorious creature? Could he ever tire of holding the fullness of the glorious breasts or kissing the tempting lips? He doubted it. Her very submissiveness would be delight enough.

"And what would you do," questioned the emir,

inclining his turbaned head to the side, "if you became tired of Humility?"

Jonas felt his cock lurch with renewed interest. He dared not look down for fear of seeing the tell-tale bulge lifting his breeches. He licked his wide lips and clenched and unclenched his big hands, feeling already the silky skin of the girl in his arms.

"Well, young sir?" prompted the emir as Jonas gasped for air at the thought that such a thing could come to pass; that he could ever be lucky enough to actually hold her close.

"If I should have the good fortune to possess the wench ..."

The emir laughed, tossing back his head and chuckling hugely. "Wench!" he exclaimed. "I like this word for my Humility."

Jonas saw the girl's naked shoulders straighten, her high firm breasts pout upwards, her caged sex arch forwards. What had he said to upset her? Upset she was, there was no doubt in his mind about that.

"She is a princess!" chuckled the emir, flicking at the plump buttocks in a playful manner. Jonas watched as the highly trained girl displayed her rear for their entertainment once more. "It's not often you have the opportunity to have such a revealing view of a princess, eh, young sir?"

"A princess!' Jonas surveyed the pouting bud of the girl's rose-hole, already feeling his cock tightly clamped into the taut flesh.

At the end of the town, Princess Humility, after another pleading glance at Jonas, was placed in the curtained litter in preparation for the journey into the mountains ...

"This heat!" complained Harry, swaying uncomfortably

on the camel and bringing Jonas out of his reverie.

Jonas laughed. "Be thankful you're not chained in the stinking hold with our cargo!"

Harry fell silent, lulled by the heat and the sound of the mountain wind, leaving Jonas to muse upon Humility's body, naked behind the silken curtains of the litter.

CHAPTER TWO

Princess Humility stood at the entrance of the huge banqueting hall. She displayed the same demure shyness which Jonas had found so engaging at the marketplace. Her head was bowed, her eyes lowered to the stone floor. Her small hands were placed at the back of her head.

Jonas allowed his eyes to rake boldly over her, wanting her badly, craving her. He desired to run his strong fingers through the lustrous strands of her hair. It was like a misty halo about her head; light palomino brown with frosty wisps escaping the jewelled combs which held it back from her beautiful face. He loved her expression. It was one of calm acceptance of her fate, and it made his heart reach out to her. The soft full lips managed a smile as she looked towards him, and he felt he would drown in the depths of dewy tortoiseshell eyes.

Allowing his gaze to flicker away from Humility for a moment he saw other girls, also naked, standing behind her. They were prodded and pushed by huge black slave guards. Their slender bodies trembled and they whimpered, pleading to be released.

They were lovely, but, thought Jonas, Humility was the loveliest of all.

The emir leaned forward on his cushions, his hawklike

face turned companionably towards Jonas. "See how she stands, young sir!" The words were growled hoarsely. "Always so proud, no matter how I try to degrade her." He placed a finger to his lips, as if in deep thought. "She is a trial to me. A trial, young sir."

The potentate smiled at Humility, pride of possession blatant upon his strong features. "Only this morning I had her in the kitchens. Made her kneel among the rotting vegetables and spilled broth as she offered her rump. As I pumped my semen into her bottom the kitchen slaves delighted in pelting her with produce."

He laughed coarsely, plucking a ripe grape from the platter of fruit beside him and popping it into his wide mouth. One of his concubines lay at his disposal, her belly lifted by a satin cushion, and he flicked the erectness of one of her nipples, making her whimper in pain before she mewed with joy at the stroke of the cool grape on her clitty.

Jonas turned away, sickened by the emir's behaviour and his crude description of Humility's suffering. What he would give to be alone with her!

"She is very beautiful," he managed. "Gloriously beautiful."

He could still imagine vividly the feel of her smooth skin under his fingers, the silky mounds of her breasts, the dip of her waist, the arch of her hips.

"The other girls are totally untrained, I'm afraid," said the emir. The hawklike eyes glinted and the thin lips lifted in a knowing smile. "But some of them are virgins," he added evilly.

A growl of excitement rumbled around the big room and Jonas felt warning spasms of alarm as he watched his crew sit up expectantly, turning to each other to grin and pass a comment.

"I must apologise for their lack of training," went on the emir, "but I am sure you will all be accommodated very happily."

He clapped his hands and Jonas could only watch as Humility walked forward, her lovely face calm and impassive. He sipped his wine, trying to slake his parched throat as he watched the girl glide gracefully across the vast stone floor.

Even though her eyes were still lowered, he knew her gaze was directed only at him. The slight sway of her full breasts seemed, to him, to be only for him. Was this merely his imagination? She was, after all, still owned by the emir.

The point of the toes was so graceful, thought Jonas. Each step was so measured and yet her whole demeanour was so gloriously slavish.

His head ached! The banqueting hall was noisy and crowded. The heat and the smell of roasting food was overwhelming. The noise echoed and re-echoed about the vast stone chamber.

Jonas had to rearrange his long legs upon the cushions to accommodate more comfortably the fullness at his groin. Humility glanced at him, her eyes wide, but almost expressionless. What was she thinking? Her nearness made his senses spin.

"Look at those tits!" he heard. "Lovely handfuls! So heavy and rounded."

"And connected by a chain!"

He longed to cuff the heads of the crew members who looked at Humility in that way, but he knew he must bide his time.

Two gold clamps were fastened to Humility's nipples, making them swell further as they hardened. Attached to the clamps were small bells which tinkled as she breathed and walked. It was an insistent, irritating noise to Jonas and he wondered how it affected the girl. The fine chain swayed across her ribs, tickling and stroking. Would it, he wondered, make her belly soften and her sex open? His eyes swept down to the gleaming triangle of curls at the join of her shapely thighs. It seemed to pout out to him, to spread, offering itself.

With a great effort he dragged his eyes to the other girls who were not so adorned. It was obvious that they had all been thoroughly paddled on the bottom. The rounded little cheeks were swollen and scarlet from long exposure to cruel slaps.

"Something in her navel!" Jonas heard, and his eyes turned quickly back to Humility. He saw her sigh, a soft drawing of breath between parted lips. All eyes were upon her now. The room was suddenly quiet, waiting for something to happen.

The dozen girls who trailed miserably behind her huddled together in little groups of two or three. Jonas could see their naked breasts trembling, one against the other. Some gave tiny moans as they looked fearfully at his crew. Some hid their faces altogether against the smooth necks of their companions.

Jonas gazed back to Humility. A jewel was fastened by the tiniest of clamps and pressed deeply into the pit of her navel. He was sure it must feel quite as invasive and hard as the phallus inserted into her earlier. Why did the emir seem to devise and reserve the cruellest of tortures for her?

Her ears were studded with lines of jewels with long pendants clamped to the lobes. They swayed against her neck at every elegant step. She allowed her thighs to part further as she moved closer to Jonas.

Was she aware, he wondered, of what she was doing?

A vibrant chord was plucked within him. It pulled at his guts; an intense pain which was also intense pleasure. The heat cloaked him. His breathing was harsh and laboured. His cock was turgid, urgent to be released from the restrictive confines of his breeches.

He could see the fresh adornments between her legs. Was it an unwitting action on her part that she pouted the slight swell of her belly? She arched her mound towards him, of that he was certain. It seemed to swell with pride as she drew closer. He swallowed hard as he gazed at the dainty pad of pliant flesh dusted with palomino curls.

He felt his broad shoulders heave as he breathed. Again he forced himself to look away from Humility to the other girls. A mixture of colours, they were pretty enough. Some were dark, almost ebony, and some were fair with pink and white colouring. On these the inflamed bottoms were painfully obvious although on the darker girls the heated flesh glowed purple.

"Dance!"

The single word was a command from the emir, ripping through the heated air, guttural and cruel.

"Oh, yes! Will ye look at that? Between her legs!"

She's got bells on her nether lips, me laddos!"

"Dance!" echoed a crew member. The word was urgent and eager this time - excited.

"Sway for us!"

"Show us! Show it all!"

Jonas swallowed hard and cupped his manhood with one of his big hands, adjusting the bundle. It was big and hard, thick and long. His blue eyes were drawn back to Humility's beautiful face. He saw her lick her lips slowly and sensuously. She knew how she was affecting him; how she was affecting them all.

The emir clapped his hands again and one of the guards,

huge and strong, stepped forward and bowed to his master.

"Hands to feet!" ordered the emir, gesturing to Humility's waiting body. "And carry her round the room. Allow my guests the pleasure of a touch in the most intimate of places."

Huge slaves stood against the cool white walls of the big room. At another signal from the emir they stepped forward, moving amidst the other girls, prodding them and slapping them into action.

Whimpering and cowering, holding their little bottoms against further punishment, they began to dance. It was slow at first; stilted. Jonas could see that they were embarrassed by their nakedness, and some were stiff and awkward, while others slowly began to enjoy their display; opening their young limbs and gyrating the puffy mounds with their little bunches of curls.

As the dance progressed some of them deliberately turned their backs to the audience, splaying their thighs and upending their bottoms, all glowing and soft. They showed their pretty pubic lips with sweet tender folds and nubbins coyly hiding.

The big slave especially chosen by the emir lifted Humility easily and slowly bowed her body, arching her spine around his thick neck.

Jonas could see the graze of his tightly curled hair against her rounded bottom-cheeks, irritating the crack. He wondered if she could feel the pain of tension upon the clamped flesh at nipples and nether-lips. He was sure that she could, although she gave no sign. Her expression was as impassive as ever. The hall had become silent, expectant, waiting for whatever the emir decided to instigate next.

"Bring Humility to our English friends," he eventually said.

At last, thought Jonas, his cock jerking painfully. I shall touch her, stroke her, even kiss her. Fuck her.

The bells tinkled at the big slave's every step, and Jonas watched eagerly, aching for her approach. The jewel at Humility's navel invaded the softness of her belly and the tiny clamps which held it in place pulled lightly on her skin, enhancing the sense of invasion, he knew that as surely as if he felt the sensation himself. He saw her close the soft tortoiseshell eyes. He wondered what she was thinking. That they were joined together, his cock piercing the soft moistness of her flesh?

"Can I?" asked an eager but rough voice. "Can I truly?"

Jonas saw Humility open her eyes to view the speaker. It was a young sailor, perhaps eighteen, a similar age to her own, and his fresh pink cock was in his hand, hard and throbbing. Jonas felt his heart sink.

"One of the other girls?" The young sailor sounded nervous. He wiped his forefinger across the bursting fullness of his swollen globe. His eyes were feverish with desire and his breathing was harsh and rapid. He looked at Jonas fearfully.

"No!" the emir rapped out the negation, allowing the word to hiss through his narrow lips. "Humility, her mouth seems very ready," he said with a chuckle. "It's open and the lips are parted and moist. See how the tongue snakes from the opening ready to curl about your cock."

Obediently, Humility allowed her tongue to snake around the fullness of her scarlet lips, opening her mouth fully in invitation. She kept her eyes averted from Jonas, and the action caused him considerable pain. He heard the young man groan, heard her bells tinkle loudly as the big slave knelt to allow her to accommodate the young guest.

The sailor, perhaps over-eager, prised his fingers into

Humility's mouth, forcing her lips further apart. The soft beauty of her face was stretched, distorted. Jonas snarled angrily as he saw the fingers force over her tongue. Two fingers, then three, and finally four slithered to the back of her throat. She cosseted the fingers, almost swallowing them.

"She's good, lads!" complimented the sailor, wriggling the fingers as he tested the fullness of the space behind her lips. "You can tell she's good!"

Jonas sat tensely, his blue eyes cold as ice, his handsome features a mask of fury. A dark girl knelt before him, all shyness gone, dispelled by her own growing excitement. She shimmied, sinking her little bottom on her heels, her soft young breasts shaking gracefully, making the skin glow with highlights in the flickering candlelight, but he waved his hand, dismissing her.

The girl frowned, looking to the emir for guidance. Her dark nipples were as hard as little stones, peaked upon the shaking mounds.

"You can resist this lovely girl's charms, young sir?" sneered the emir sinisterly. He stroked the open folds between the young thighs, sniffing the perfume of the musk with evident enjoyment. "My own cock rises at the prospect." The dark eyebrows raised in mock surprise.

Jonas said nothing, his resentment making bitter gall rise in his throat as he watched the young sailor wipe the silkiness of his globe about Humility's soft lips.

He clenched his fists as he watched his other men, impatient for their turn, twist the clamps at her nipples and press the glinting jewel at her navel. Jonas could only imagine the quivers of pain which these attentions might bring her. He wondered whether the arching of her body about the big slave's neck would make every sensation greater than before. Every clamped part of her body must

28

be under stress. He imagined the tiny darts of pain she must be experiencing, and bit his lip in sympathy for the lovely girl. But to Humility, with her trained and sensitised body, could the pain become shudders of soft pleasure?

His own body writhed on the silken cushions, trying to feel what Humility was feeling. Of course, he could not begin to imagine a male organ in his mouth. He could not imagine how the thick coolness would feel between her warm, soft lips; the veins twining along the length, throbbing in the moist depths of her throat. He did not notice the emir watching him from the corners of his glinting eyes.

He heard the sailor groan and seemed to feel Humility, as she had been taught, slowing her pampering, making his pleasure last.

Startled, Jonas was jerked from his ponderings as to how Humility must feel by the guttural voice of the emir. "Come now, gentlemen," cajoled the monarch, "is no one going to investigate her most intimate part? Her thighs may be clamped together but her flesh is very available."

Helplessly wrapped around the slave's neck, her mouth engaged in giving the young sailor pleasure, Humility, thought Jonas, must be all too aware that her pussy mound pouted eagerly, waiting for another of the emir's guests to plunder its ready moistness.

Jonas watched every movement and every remark with growing hatred. His cock was much plagued by the sights and actions going on around him, even though he found some of it distasteful. He wanted the girl for himself. He wanted her in his arms. He wanted to be alone with her.

A pretty blonde girl pampered his long legs, kneeling at his feet in supplication. She stroked her cheek against his thigh, purring like a cat. Her small fingers danced lightly over the buckskin, hovering about his crotch. He kicked her away impatiently.

"How much?" he groaned.

The emir chuckled, glancing at the girl with the shimmering blonde hair flowing about her pale shoulders. "For the pretty thing you tossed so lightly aside?" he asked cynically. "Look at her! So forlorn! One of the freshest and loveliest things in my new collection!" He tutted in mock disgust. "And you toss her aside for that young hussy, Humility! I despair of you young men."

Humility's lips were still busy about the young sailor's penis, for she was managing to prolong his delight to the point of agony.

"How much?" echoed the emir with more of his pretended dismay. The hawklike face expressed disbelief that such a question should have been asked.

"I'll take the Princess now," croaked Jonas, "and, if we left now, we could still catch the morning tide." His blue eyes looked sadly across the room and gazed into the golden, topaz depths which gazed so longingly at him.

He felt wretched, but, at the same time, furious that he should fall into the trap so neatly set to raise Humility's price.

He saw her slither her lips more quickly up and down the sailor's thickness. Jonas held his breath. Her actions excited him and, at the same time, made him sick with envy.

He could only imagine the first splash of semen upon her palate. He knew that the crewman's issue would be copious with his extreme youth, and he was right! He watched it spilling from her mouth to drool in pearly trails on her chained breasts.

"As you can see, young sir," said the emir coldly, "she is beyond price, and it would be ridiculously foolhardy to try the mountain path at night. Even with the path lighted by sconces men have fallen to their deaths over the cliffs." He shook his turbaned head. "No, I would not consider you taking such a chance."

Jonas hardly heard the cautionary speech. He watched another sailor - older and uglier than the first - tug at the bells at Humility's nether lips, taking the tiny clamps from them. Eagerly he opened her out with his coarse fingers, exposing the inflamed skin and the erect bud of her clitoris. With a light kiss he pampered this last, making her squirm with the sensations which radiated through her. Grinning, he faced the crew. With a finger and thumb he opened her further, exposing the scarlet opening, shining with dew in the light shed by the thousand candles spread about the banqueting hall.

"Feel," he offered, as though Humility was his to offer. "Feel the hot wetness." His slender hips pumped at another girl who was kneeling between his parted thighs caressing his scrotum with her tongue. His dark eyes lit up, spying the pearly droplets spilled upon Humility's breasts by the young sailor. He scooped them, one by one, examining the collected juice upon the tips of two fingers. He held them aloft, delighting in the show, and as quickly plunged the dewy fingers into Humility's opening.

It was too much for Jonas. "I must have her!" he cried, rising to his feet.

His head span; unwittingly, at some time during the evening, he, or the blonde, or one of the other girls, must have unfastened his breeches and released his cock. Somewhat dazed, he looked down at the thickness in his hand, straight and rigid. He thumbed the pre-issue, polishing his swollen and naked globe.

The emir opened his palms in a bemused shrug. "No one will stop you using my vessel, but you cannot have her for your own."

The hawklike eyes stared fondly at the young sailor who played with Humility's sex so intimately.

"But you hinted in the marketplace -"

The emir frowned. "Did I?" The short question was asked with such an air of pretended innocence. "My memory, young sir, is not what it was."

The older sailor was slavering upon Humility's swollen outer labia. He teased each puffy lip before diving his tongue between the silky folds to pamper the urgent tip of her clitoris.

Humility mewed softly.

"Her pleasure is upon her!" snarled the emir.

"Stop this!" Jonas flung himself to the spot where Humility was held so helpless. "For pity's sake, leave the girl be!"

Laughter, coarse and cruel, echoed through the huge chamber.

Jonas flung out his hand, clutching her upper arm, making the gold and silver bracelets fixed there, dig into the flesh. He tore her from the big slave's neck. His anger was a scalding fury, and he pulled her roughly, violently, to him, raking her beauty with his blazing blue eyes.

"You're mine!" he hissed, his breath whispering across the velvet of her cheek. The halo of palomino hair flared about her head. The tortoiseshell eyes gazed at him wonderingly. The slime of spillage was chill on the hot flesh of her cheeks and breasts.

"Yes," she murmured, the wide scarlet lips curving into a soft smile.

He loved the way she straddled her tawny thighs in mute invitation. She seemed to be spellbound by the silky warmth of his cock sliding between her parted thighs. It quivered powerfully, spearing up from his groin, butting her warm moistness with the globe. It was huge, purple, and so shiny it might have been polished. With gratitude he heard Humility sigh with longing. He was vaguely aware of shouts of encouragement from the other guests as they held each other close.

Together they sank to the floor with the scattered debris of the banquet. With long tawny legs drawn up and shapely knees spread outwards she beckoned him into her. Jonas was only aware of his own desires.

"Fuck the bitch!" crowed Harry Dawkins. "She's begging you, Jonas!"

The young crewman who had already enjoyed the pleasures of her expert mouth, stood at her head, his cock in his hands once more, rubbing vigorously, aiming at her upturned face. This it seemed was a signal for the other men, who also bared themselves and masturbated their flesh.

Jonas knelt between her open thighs, his blue eyes glazed with passion, his penis throbbing as he positioned it at her entrance.

"The woman is a temptress, young sirs!" The emir taunted the men harshly, persuading them to take their turn after Jonas. A soft sigh of acceptance escaped Humility's lips, and Jonas realised how her master loved to degrade her.

Buckskin brushed softly against the tenderness of her inner thighs as Jonas slowly pushed into her. He felt his thickness peel her open.

"See how she arches her body so wantonly, gentlemen!" gloated the emir. "Her belly and mound yearn to press against the young master!"

"Yes!" The other men chorused the affirmative and Jonas was aware how they closed in upon them.

"And her breasts!" continued the emir. "She teases her own breasts! Her greed is unimaginable, is it not?!"

The gathering men leaned over Jonas and Humility, all quite oblivious to the girls who entwined their naked bodies in and out of their straddled legs. Without exception the crew held their cocks in their hands. They rubbed vigorously as Jonas pumped into her. At each inward thrust he chafed the erect bud of her clitoris, and Humility whimpered in agonised ecstasy. The sweet sound made her seem even more vulnerable and it made Jonas pound into her more viciously.

"That's it, Jonas, me lad!" encouraged Harry Dawkins.

Humility caressed his thickness with pampering movements of her moist walls, and he could tell that she was thinking only of his pleasure and satisfaction. Jonas heard the rumbling of his men's voices; the groans as they began to reach their peaks. The first splash of issue was from the young sailor.

Arching her neck as she was taught by the emir's women, she offered her face to the fast spurts of creamy semen, hot and silky on her skin. The other men jostled for position, ready themselves to despoil her beauty with their outflow.

"Oh, Humility!" gasped Jonas, his buttocks pumping furiously. "Always be mine!"

Willingly she accepted the copious heat of his stream. Her hands grasped the hardness of his muscular buttocks, encouraging him to shoot into her.

"Humility!" The emir's voice cut through the sensual atmosphere of the banqueting hall, and Jonas felt her tremble at its tone. Something had angered the monarch.

Jonas, finished as he was, slowly rose to his feet, leaving her splayed and used amid the debris. He saw semen trickling over her hot face; down her forehead, her nose, between her lips. Tiny streams of it seeped through strands of her hair, darkening the fairness.

"Punishment position to the cells!" rapped the emir.

Immediately Humility curled her lithe body until she was on her knees while Jonas watched, horrified. Her forearms were flat upon the stone floor and her bottom was held high.

He looked upon the swollen love-lips which had been so recently his. They looked inflamed and greatly used. The sight aroused him further. They were so puffy and glossed with her dew as well as his. Jonas shuddered, directing his gaze to the wetness upon her inner thighs, and gloried in his use of her.

"Crawl!" hissed the emir. "And you girls ..."

Jonas heard the soft padding of bare feet as the girls hurried to gather round their master. They looked so dainty and cowed while Humility, even kneeling so humbly, managed to look serene.

"Smack her as she makes her way ..."

"This is too much!" said Jonas.

The untrained girls, delighting in their task, gathered close to Humility. They pinched the tender skin on the inner sides of her thighs. Crouching before her they pinched the soft fullness of her breasts, tweaking the hardness of her erect nipples. A very bold one parted the firm globes of her bottom, seeking out the flushed tightness of her rose-hole. She made Humility sigh with longing as her sensitive places were sought out.

Jonas could take no more. He leapt forward, his blue eyes blazing with anger. "What are you doing?" he snarled, kicking out with his highly polished boots to scatter the girls, hither and thither. Some of them whimpered and some hissed like wildcats, their dainty fingers clawing at his legs or at the air.

"Seize him!" The emir's voice no longer pretended to be welcoming. The order rent the air like a sabre; cold as tempered steel.

Humility flashed a warning with her eyes, but all too
late. Jonas was already imprisoned in the huge arms of
the emir's awesome guards. She could only watch as he
struggled in vain, straining over his shoulder at her as he
was walked, stumbling awkwardly to the punishment
cells.

Why didn't his friends jump to help him? Cautiously
she looked around the shadowy hall and understood; more
girls had entered and were keeping the sailors beautifully
occupied. She winced as two of the girls began to slap
her bottom with vicious little smacks.

"Kneel up," she was ordered by a soft, bell-like voice.
It was the girl who'd been so cruelly scorned by Jonas.

Perhaps, thought Humility, she was slow to obey, or
perhaps the girl was merely seeking revenge. Whatever
the case she was pulled upright and not only was her
bottom smacked by several pairs of hard little hands, but
her breasts, too, were slapped, making the soft flesh
shudder with the force of the blows.

"My dears!" called the emir, making the girls turn, wide-
eyed, to his reclining figure. "We must not waste this
opportunity."

The pretty little blonde, with lips as pink as sugar icing
and eyes as wide and blue as a china doll, pouted and
frowned. She had full and very mature breasts and, almost
absently, she fingered the rose-buds of her nipples. "What
do you mean, highness?" she asked in her tinkling voice.

"Yes, highness," added the very dark girl. "We don't
understand you."

"Nor will you if you neglect your duties!" snapped the
emir, pointing to Humility. "She waits to be slapped."

Both girls hastily set about smacking her sensitised flesh
again, and she felt the glow become a stinging pain, but

36

nevertheless, her soft open cunney yearned for more.

"What is it you wish us to do?" asked the girl who was the colour of dark chocolate. She was turning her attention to Humility's navel, slapping the jewelled belly until the poor girl thought she would swoon with the strange sharp sensations which were neither pain nor pleasure, but a mixture of both.

"Kneel up, the both of you," ordered the emir, legs astride. "Enjoy the attentions of Humility's tongue. She is an expert."

Giggling, the two girls, Loa and Therese, positioned themselves as the emir wished.

"The rest of you, continue to smack Humility's bottom as she attends to the two little beauties."

Humility watched the emir settle himself comfortably, his voluminous robe hitched about his thighs. His dark penis was thick and rigid in his slowly moving hands.

Her tortoiseshell eyes almost closed, her lashes fluttered. She parted her full lips to allow her tongue the freedom for the task ahead.

CHAPTER THREE

The emir's eyes were hooded moodily. Humility knew that he was studying her intently, and the message in those dark eyes was undisguised.

"Oh, my darling, Humility," she heard. "How I love to see the quite obvious delight you show in these situations." The emir sighed contentedly and, from the corner of her eye, she saw him settle himself more comfortably on the pile of richly hued cushions. The voluminous silk gown fluttered upwards - whether by accident or design Humility had no way of knowing - and exposed the darkness of his slim loins.

He was fully erect. Sable, noticed Humility; the turgid skin was sable in colour, stretched fine and smooth. The veins knotted the darkness of the upright staff. The flesh throbbed under the gentle caress of his own hands.

"Now, now, Humility!" purred the emir indulgently. "I know full well how much you would adore to have this ..." with a dark fingertip he touched the swollen smoothness, glancing across the smeared silkiness of the tip, hesitating at the tiny pulsing pore, "... within you. So much more appealing than the pale insipidness of your white admirer!"

He waved airily in the general direction of the cells and Humility shuddered. Tears filled her eyes. It was so unfair to speak of Jonas like that. The emir had arranged the entertainment as he always did; had almost thrown her at Jonas and forced their intimacy.

"But you fail in your duties, my darling." He spoke in a voice which was low and endlessly seductive.

What had she done to fail him? She dared not frown in puzzlement, for fear of angering him further.

Her skin glowed from the peevish slaps of the untrained girls. The side and underswells of her breasts smarted from the pinches of nipping fingers. The flesh about her jewelled navel felt swollen from the unfair onslaught. The tender inner sides of her thighs, too, stung and felt greatly heated by the irritation administered by the newer girls.

"You look so incomparably lovely, straddled as you are upon the floor," sighed the emir. "I love to
have you at my feet, and I know you love to pay homage to me."

A deep flush suffused Humility's cheeks. She knew that the hawklike eyes were focussed intently upon her open thighs; that they drank in the pout of her secret place, frosted so lightly with the palomino curls. Perhaps, she thought, he rested those eyes upon the scarlet nubbin which she knew was greatly swollen from the activities of the evening.

"Position her," whispered the emir, "so that I may lean down and stroke the swell of those delicious breasts."

With tears meandering hotly down the flush of her cheeks, Humility felt herself drawn across the flagstones. The hands which held her, for all that they were small and soft, were cruel in the grip they pinched on her arms. They dragged and stretched, and put a tension upon her slapped breasts causing sharp pains to dart out from her tense and tortured nipples; hard as little stones in the centres of the full mounds. A barely audible whimper was drawn from her lips. The sometimes gold and sometimes dark tresses of her tumbled hair spilled in a silken mass over the perfection of her shoulders and the arching beauty of her breasts.

"You look so lovely splayed helplessly at my feet," the emir sighed. "So truly lovely."

Humility watched him stroke the bared tip of his cock, paying homage to her as he did so.

"How could I have ever considered letting you go, Humility?" he asked of her, placing a thoughtful index finger at his neatly bearded chin. "How could I have ever considered giving you away to that white wretch? He would not cherish you as I do. You do know that, do you not?"

With wide tortoiseshell eyes, made more lustrous through a film of tears, Humility looked at him hopelessly. What was the use of denying him anything?

Loa gave her outstretched arm an extra little pinch, making her wince and try to pull away from this spiteful new pain.

"And it seems that the more Loa and Therese taunt you," he said with a sardonic chuckle, "the more lovely you become!"

The two girls, taking this as an invitation to torture their victim all the more, arched her body cruelly until the great mass of palomino curls brushed the plump up-slopes of her buttocks, and her breasts were offered tautly to the emir.

"Ahhh," he sighed slowly. "Yes, that is how I want her; always ready for me - offering herself to me." He turned to the two girls. "When you are trained, perhaps you will be as willing." He stirred a little on the mountain of satin cushions and flicked first one breast and then the other. "You see how passive she is, Loa?" he said, turning to the young ebony beauty. "Do you see? That is how I want you to be one day." He leaned further and used all fingers of one hand to close about the fullness of a breast, pressing only sufficiently hard to enhance the pain left there by the little slaps she had endured earlier.

"You see how she loves my touch, Loa?"

There was contempt in the silken voice, noticed Humility, as well as lust and passion - and even love. It was true; she did love the caress of the emir's hand, but then, hadn't she been trained to love the touch of all male hands? Hadn't she been trained to the point where her cunney seeped juices at the slightest stroke of the most inexperienced of young men? This was how she'd been prepared ever since the age when a girl becomes receptive.

"Look between her thighs," continued the emir. "Both of you, look between her thighs."

He sank back happily, his penis once more in his hands, the hawklike face content to watch the entertainment he'd devised so cunningly for himself.

Already degraded by her treatment at the hands of the untrained girls, Humility sank her head to the stone floor, allowing her hair to spill over her outstretched hands. She felt the cold strike up to the flushed flesh of her breasts, but the relief was short-lived.

"No, no, Humility!" The cry was angry, and yet there was a trace of cruel laughter in it. "Head up! I want to see those lovely breasts and, perhaps, a hint of that pretty little belly, decorated with the jewels I gave you! Up! Up!" He was leaning forward again, anxious to miss nothing. "And you girls! Spread her legs wide and examine her!"

There was nothing she could do. Her sex was gloriously ripe, she knew that. The thought of the two untrained girls peeping at its fullness and probing the folds made her flush deep crimson with humiliation. She held her head high, but the wonderful fall of hair clothed her crimson cheeks and partially covered the swell of her punished breasts.

"Oh, master," she heard Loa whisper. "What shall we do to her?"

Humility felt the soft hands stroking her calves, tickling unbearably, and it made the plumpness of her already ripe sex swell yet more.

The emir chuckled, looking down into Humility's fear-widened tortoiseshell eyes, teasing her unmercifully, glancing at the golden curls winding around the taut pegs of her uplifted nipples.

"Whatever seeps into your wonderful imaginations, my little ones!" The all seeing darkness of the onyx eyes slanted wickedly. "Anything!"

He slipped comfortably deeper into the heaped cushions, one hand cupping the raven darkness of his heavy balls and the other sliding up and down his spearing shaft.

A frightened quiver ran through Humility, knowing how the untrained girls loved to steal a march upon the queens and princesses of the harem; princesses like herself, who'd been favourites for years past. She knew, young as she was, that the emir was tiring of her and might quickly replace her with fresher flesh.

She heard Loa and Therese giggle excitedly. She felt her thighs pulled sharply apart, and this increased the ripe feeling at the very apex of those shapely limbs.

As if it was beyond her power to prevent it, she felt her slender pelvis tilt, lifting the heated fullness of her buttocks and offering the plumpness of her sex. The two girls giggled again, and Humility felt the soft but cruel hands driving into the tender flesh of her inner thighs, tugging them ever wider. She looked up pleadingly at the emir, but he merely smiled confidently.

"Can we bite?" panted Loa maliciously.

"You may not," said the emir firmly. "Remember, she is still mine, and she is extremely valuable in an undamaged state. Keep her that way."

"But master -" protested Therese.

Humility felt one of the girl's - she couldn't tell which - open her labia with a finger and thumb, and she felt a fresh flush of colour suffuse her cheeks. She knew that the erect little button of her clitoris was quite clear of the slick, pink bed of her sex.

"Do not question me ...! You may lick her all you like," permitted the emir, allowing his hands to spread away from his genitals in a magnanimous gesture. "You may let the soft little tip of your tongues flicker up and down each fold and around the base of her tiny stem. But you may not bite her!"

His mellow baritone was sharply edged with control, Humility noticed, trying desperately to still the tremor of her outspread limbs.

"Humility would not be Humility," he continued,

42

"without that beautifully sensitive tip to her clitoris.

The threat was there! Her throat ached with the fear of it. Although, in words, he had denied her the pain of circumcision by these peevish minxes, he had clearly placed the suggestion in their minds!

Her arms ached with the strain of keeping her head raised and her breasts proudly visible. they also trembled fearfully, and she pleaded, her soft lips parted in mute supplication, that her master would not have her mutilated.

"How I spoil you, Humility," he sighed, relenting, sinking back upon his pillows once more. "No, my loves," he purred, wagging an admonishing finger at the two little torturers. "I have decided. You must not circumcise my dear Humility!"

A shudder of sheer relief ran through her. She could again bear the pain of her strained arms and she managed the tiniest of smiles; the merest curve of her sweet lips as the emir brushed his fingers once more across each of her offered breasts.

She could imagine Loa and Therese pouting darkly in disappointment. She felt another pinch on the fullness of an outer labium, but stoically, she held back the murmur of pain which hesitated in her throat.

"Her juices seep very copiously from her opening, master," supplied Loa, her disappointment well hidden.

"Of course," exclaimed the emir. "She is fully trained, despite the fact that she is barely older than you two."

A fingertip, cool and soft, rimmed about the wetness of Humility's opening. Trying so very hard not to do so, she felt herself urging upon that little tip, moving slowly and sinuously from side to side.

"She cannot be still, master," murmured Loa's bell-like voice.

"Then make her!" said the emir severely. "Smack her

upon her naughty buttocks. You are in charge, are you not?"

The two girls murmured that they were indeed in charge, and the probing finger delved uncomfortably deeper. Two firm but dainty hands commenced a rapid tattoo upon the upraised flanks, making the already punished flesh become increasingly heated.

Humility whimpered afresh, although she felt her clitty jerk with fresh pearls of love dew. How could the emir allow this? She had been in his patronage for so long, and yet he was allowing such humiliation from two new and untrained girls. Her beautiful face flamed.

"Ah," he sighed. "I see that you have the good grace to blush. Yes, I am very pleased to see that. Very pleased indeed." His dark face held no humour. The eyes were slitted cruelly. The hooked nose was pinched, the nostrils drawn in. The wide mouth was compressed, the lips hardly visible. The expression was one which Humility had learned to fear.

With arms trembling she hardly dared to look at him, and allowed her head to droop, her hair to curtain her flushed features. Loa, or perhaps Therese, taunted her sex unmercifully. They pinched the moist flesh and invaded her depths. Her parted buttocks flamed from the beating.

"Your young white friend ..." said the emir, leaving the words hanging in the air; a threat of something yet to come.

Humility's eyes filled with tears afresh. The handsome man called Jonas had, indeed, invaded her heart. The thought of him suffering in the punishment cells was more than she could bear to imagine. Would he survive to sail away on the ship? She dared a quick glance at her master. His countenance was thunderous; a symbol of yet worse impending cruelty.

"Look at me, Humility! You have him to thank for this

present degradation!" hissed the emir, leaning forward and stamping a foot to make his point. His voluminous robes spilled over his erection, hiding it from her view. But it was there, and she knew he would use the magnificence of it upon her before the evening was out.

She began to quiver as fearful images built up in her mind. Jonas was so handsome. Why did he come into her life, disturbing the serenity of her slavery to the emir? Why did he try to interfere? Didn't he understand how men like the emir were all-powerful - were omnipotent?

"Now, you girls," The emir suddenly sounded playful again, but Humility knew this was nothing more than an act, and she felt chilled. "What mischief are you designing for my Humility?"

She was spread open. Her labia were peeled back, fully exposing the flushed underlying skin. How she longed to let her head droop again; to close the lustrous tortoiseshell eyes; to sink wearily upon the unyielding flagstones.

"Her nubbin is so hard and long," sighed Loa. "It is such a lovely toy!"

"Mmm," agreed Therese. "How wonderful to play with one so ready and so tutored."

Humility was unable to withhold her embarrassment any longer. She felt two flaming spots of colour burn on her high cheekbones. To be examined so intimately by these audacious girls was awful, but she could not, no matter how hard she tried, hold back her underlying excitement.

The emir relaxed once more, his penis again bared and throbbing. Humility watched his tongue slither slowly around the full perimeter of his thin lips.

"Then take it into your sweet little mouth, Loa," he purred. His voice, deep and sensual in the extreme, was like a caress upon the very nubbin about which they spoke.

"But gently, mark you!"

The hawklike eyes glittered above Humility, both loving and threatening at one and the same time.

Soft lips enclosed the throbbing length of that nubbin of sensitive flesh. Humility tensed and held her breath, making her clitty bob in the knowing little mouth.

"Does it feel nice?" whispered Therese.

So it was Loa who sucked her sex so urgently, thought Humility. She could expect no mercy from that little madam! A shudder ran through her, making her silky little peg pulse between the cosseting lips. If Loa decided to bite, Humility knew she would have no chance of preventing the mutilation.

Oh, please ... Humility mouthed the words silently, lifting eyes which portrayed both stimulation and fear to her master. She knew her shapely hips snaked, oh so very slightly, from side to side. Unable to prevent the sinuous movement, she gave a little hiccup of apprehension.

"Tsk!" hissed the emir. "What noise is that? Not a sound I wish to hear coming from one of my young ladies!" Humility saw him make a gesture to Therese. "Punish! Punish! Punish! Slap her bottom for such rudeness!" He tutted again and wagged a finger before Humility's face.

Lips, slippery with saliva and Humility's own silk, rubbed rhythmically at her clitoris, baring the sensitive tip. Her body glowed with the stimulation, and she knew her pleasure peak was close.

"Can I use the whip?" asked Therese. Her voice was tart and cruel, but she crouched at the emir's feet, looking up at him with sweetly coaxing eyes.

Close to her climax, Humility knew that hand or whip flailing upon the heated and tender flesh of her bottom would tip her into the beautiful void of a climax. She squirmed, pressing the burning of her sex closer still to

Loa's mouth. She felt sharp teeth scrape upon the sensitive stem of her captured bud.

"She's so naughty, master," gasped Loa, bobbing up from between Humility's trembling thighs. The dark girl flung herself at the emir's feet and looked at Humility with undisguised longing in her brown eyes.

With arms aching from the tension of her stance, and with a sex which hungered for fulfilment, Humility collapsed upon the stone floor.

"Indeed she is," agreed the emir. "Now none of us can enjoy her. How selfish she is, lying so flat and limp, and hiding every interesting part of herself from our view; spoiling our fun!"

"I'll drag her up, shall I, master?" offered an eager Therese. "And get the whip?" This last was said in an appealing tone and, with barely raised eyes, Humility saw Therese pick up the whip she'd flung there earlier.

The emir laughed, but there was a tightness about his eyes which spoke of impatience. And his lips were thinner - more cruel. Humility shuddered, dreading the outcome of this ordeal.

"Throw her over a chair," he said evenly.

Humility was pulled roughly to her feet. She hardly dared wince at the pinching fingers about her upper arms; hardly dared murmur when her bare toes stubbed the harsh floor as she was dragged to an upright chair.

"But, on second thoughts ..." considered the emir, "... place her here, across my lap."

"But, master," protested Therese. "You said she needed slapping - whipping." The younger girl pouted, her lower lip full and petulant.

"And I didn't yet bring her to a climax!" spat Loa, her dark eyes fiery with anger. She pushed Humility away so fiercely that the latter almost fell once more to the floor.

Her small hands were planted squarely upon her shapely hips. The crisply curled pubis was thrust out in a sensual but belligerent manner.

The emir displayed remarkable control by quelling his surge of rage at their undisciplined outbursts with little visible effort. He leaned forward and snaked out his long fingers to caress the silkiness of Loa's sex. "We can all enjoy ourselves," he said, rubbing back and forth about Loa's cleft until the girl bore down happily upon the probing digit. He quickly became bored and reached for Humility, much to Loa's chagrin.

"My very own, Humility," he purred. He looked at her adoringly. "I think you know what I wish you to do now?" It was a question, and he tilted his head to one side to emphasise his point.

Kneeling at his feet, she placed her soft hands upon his dark and naked thighs, and humbly dipped her head between them, her tongue sneaking between her parted lips.

"Oh, no, Humility." There was a cruel chuckle in his voice. "Not my penis - not yet. You do not deserve it yet."

The lustrous eyes widened quizzically. 'What would you have me do, my master?' Humility wanted to ask, but the words were captured in her dry throat.

"You see these pretty little feet?" The emir pointed to Loa's and Therese's.

Humility's eyes remained upon the emir, pleading and questioning. Her hands caressed his muscular thighs, as if this might persuade him not to humiliate her further.

His powerful hand suddenly lashed out, making Humility's hair swirl, and whipping her shocked features first to one side and then to the other. She fell, her hips twisting, to present her buttocks foremost to the two girls. The unexpected blow made a flutter of sensation enervate her extruded clitty.

"Kiss them prettily. And do it until I command you to stop."

Humility obediently lowered her head, her eyes wet with tears, her long hair brushing the girls' feet and making them snigger and cling together with mischievous enjoyment.

"Her lips feel so warm and soft," purred Loa.

"She kisses beautifully," confirmed Therese.

"Indeed," agreed the emir with a satisfied sigh, "she has expert lips. I taught her myself from an early age."

Humility couldn't resist but smooth the silkiness of her shoulder against her master's naked calf. Her tongue ached from her efforts, as did her hungry sex; longing for appeasement.

"Enough!" rapped the emir. Humility was abruptly hauled to her feet again and, just as quickly, forced down over her master's lap.

She felt the silky warmth of his penis against the curve of her hip. It throbbed delightfully and she pushed gently against it, longing to feel it inside her. She could feel, too, the heavy muscularity of his thighs beneath her belly; could feel the whiskered coarseness of his leg hair tickling her.

"Turn her round," he ordered hoarsely. "Straddle her legs across my lap and -"

There was a sudden groan of disappointment from Therese. "But master, you promised that I could slap her."

"Do not fret!" snapped the emir. "I keep my promises!" He stroked Therese's fair cheek in warning to complain no more, rolling Humility against his manhood as he did so. She was forced to bite her lip to suppress a murmur of delight at the firm touch of his male flesh.

"Spread her," he suddenly ordered. "Bottom-cheeks to

face me and cunney fully open. That way I can take my pleasure while you, you little minxes, can slap or whip her as you please."

The two girls grinned with wicked delight. Humility, too, could hardly contain her secret joy as she was positioned over the emir's penis.

It was Loa who made sure the great man fully impaled Humility, skilfully guiding the magnificence of his swollen globe to her entrance. Humility knew he could see the darkness of her bottom cleft, her shy rose-hole, the silky wetness of her female opening, and perhaps her urgent little bud. She felt hands at the back of her head, and she was urged forward, bending and lowering from the waist. Her breasts swung freely, and the girls cheekily took the opportunity to squeeze and weigh them. With a click of the emir's fingers a large slave was summonsed to stand in front of Humility's vulnerable face. Another click and his loincloth was lifted aside to display his penis. It was large but still soft. Without any further instructions he cupped her chin in one large palm, and then paused. With a mischievous grin the emir stabbed his own erection deep into her, and as she groaned and her lips peeled open, the slave fed his penis into her warm mouth. He clasped her head tightly and worked his hips until his penis slowly unfurled and stretched her lips wider and wider.

"The lash!" rasped the emir quite breathlessly. "Use the lash on her upper back, Therese!"

The effect was immediate. The lash bit across Humility's shoulders, snaking around the side-swell of one perfect breast.

"And you, Loa," panted the emir. "Tend to her bottom. Slap those perfect globes hard, and if you tire, intrude a dainty finger into her rose-hole!"

Humility, breathless herself with the passion brought

about by the emir's fucking, could not resist sliding back and forth on the two rigid columns and raising her bottom, posing it for the punishment she knew would come thick and fast.

CHAPTER FOUR

Fear twisted around Humility's heart like icy fingers. When the emir had finally dismissed her she'd run from the huge dining-hall, leaving Loa and Therese asleep, curled like kittens at her master's feet.

She was now wearing one of her muslin gowns. She had found it laid upon her bed; placed there by one of her laundry-maids. It was caught tightly under her delicious breasts by a narrow thread of gold. It skimmed into the dip of her waist and followed the contours of her shapely hips and buttocks. She'd quickly scrubbed and freshened herself, and now her glorious hair tumbled loosely about her shoulders. She padded along the narrow and damp passages to the cells.

She had to find Jonas.

In her haste she hardly noticed the soreness of those beaten places; the swellings; the heated weals.

Cold air made her shiver. The smell of the dungeons was dank - musty. The passage was ill-lit. Guttering sconces were placed only at the curves of the winding narrow way from the main part of the palace to the cells.

Her mind was deeply troubled. Worries gnawed at her consciousness. Why had the emir imprisoned Jonas? Did he fear losing her so much, or was there some other sinister motive? She knew of one possible motive - but banished it from her mind as rediculous.

The cells were not so much a means of punishment, Humility knew, but rather the emir's playroom. This part of the palace was the place where her master came when he was bored. Fearful tortures perpetrated by the huge and cruel eunuch, too terrible for most to imagine, were carried out in the dark, shadowy rooms.

Her bare feet felt leaden as she was drawn into the deeper regions of the dungeons. Although her conscience told her not to tarry, her slender legs moved slower and slower. It was as if they were becoming entangled in the gossamer fineness of her gown.

Fearful though she was and satiated by the stimulation given by the emir and the three slaves, her sex felt ripe and full. The plump labia caressed the very tops of her smooth thighs. Her clitty was hot and hugely irritated, peeping beyond the tautness of its fine little hood. As she walked she felt the slickness of juices, warm and smooth. They seeped from the folds to gather in tiny pearls on the curls of her sex hair.

Perhaps fear itself freshly primed her body for further excitement.

Sounds: the crackle of fires, the ominous clicking of the rack, the crack of whips and the cries of victims, reached her listening ears. She breathed in quick shallow gasps. An ice-cold knot formed in her stomach and her nails drove into the flesh of her perspiring palms. Her gown, cut low in the bodice, bared the top slopes of her heaving breasts. Their smoothness puckered in rough gooseflesh, making the tawny skin appear as pale as old ivory. Had she looked down she would have seen the darkness of her taut nipples, drawn to prominent nubs which thrust tightly against the gossamer of the muslin.

Suddenly, a sconce guttered out and a chill black silence, interrupted only by the occasional drip of distant water, surrounded her. Humility whimpered.

The darkness disorientated her and she whirled around, seeking the solidity of the rough wall; anything to help support her trembling legs. The enveloping darkness was broken as suddenly as it descended, but with the light came a greater fear.

"Is this what you're looking for?"

The voice was light, almost feminine.

Humility whirled again, accidentally grazing the prominence of her hip on the roughly hewn passage wall. The tawny skin was slightly broken, peeled to draw droplets of blood which spilled on the pure white of her gossamer gown.

"Jameel!" she exclaimed. "You, you startled me, skulking in the dark like that! Why did you douse the sconce?" She tried to keep her voice steady and her tone light. Her sensuous lips managed to smile through her mask of fear. As her confidence returned she raised her arms to place them about the huge man's neck, even though she knew that womanly wiles had no effect on the eunuch.

Jameel stepped aside, gesturing with a hand as huge as a dinner-plate. Peering into the darkness of a deep alcove, Humility gave a gasp of both terror and sympathy.

The white man, Jonas Fairweather, was shackled to the wall, his broad naked back continually wetted by a steady trickle of ice-cold water seeping from the rock.

"No …" the word was strangled in her throat, bursting forth as a barely audible croak.

Jameel laughed, the sound high-pitched and echoing through the maze of passages to return to them, multiplied eerily several times over.

The emir's prisoner was upside down. The pale broad chest heaved painfully. It was striped with trails of blood where a lash had struck many times. He was naked and seemed all the more vulnerable for the paleness of his skin, even though it was tanned from the African sun.

"No ..." murmured Humility again, for her eyes were drawn to his groin.

He was, despite his pain and discomfort, fully erect. She stepped closer, peering into the shadows of the alcove.

"He is ringed!" she gasped.

"To show the beauty of his penis," chuckled Jameel.

Jonas's blue eyes were closed. The fair lashes were thick upon his tanned cheeks. The wide lips were open, and his breathing was harsh and laboured as if in a pain-filled sleep.

How Humility longed to kiss those lips; to touch and caress the turgid erection, perhaps take it in her mouth and taste the seepage of semen which she saw shining there. How she longed to smooth the broad sweep of his chest, take each nipple, one by one, into her urgent little mouth. How she longed to give the poor man comfort. She licked her lips hungrily.

"Don't even think about it," grunted Jameel, as if he read her mind.

Humility whirled upon him. The huge eunuch never ceased to amaze her with his powers. It was as if his castration had given him some compensatory talents.

"I have prepared the white man for the emir's pleasure," added Jameel. The big dark face split into a grin. "Not yours, or any other woman's from the nest of vipers you call the harem."

Humility gasped and covered her mouth with a dainty hand. So her suspicions as to the emir's vile motives were correct after all! She stepped back to stand close to Jonas again, wanting to feel the hardness of his muscular body holding her close. Wanting to feel his lips upon her sex, his mouth drinking her sap. The erect penis, held so by the tight leather ring at its base, quivered as she brushed the velvet of her cheek against its turgid silkiness.

"Woman!" growled Jameel. "You'll have me executed!"

A huge dark hand shot out, grabbing Humility's slender shoulders and ripping her flimsy gown from neck to buttocks. The dank air struck chill on her punished skin and she shuddered. Tears filled the rich gold of her eyes, making them shimmer in the guttering light of the sconce. Why was the emir so intent on humiliating and hurting Jonas? Oh yes, she knew that her master was just as fond of young men as he was of young women, but she didn't really think he'd have the audacity to force his attentions upon a European; and a European who was his guest with quite a large force of compatriots.

"What is he going to do?" she asked, turning back to face Jameel.

Her gown slipped in fluttering shreds from her golden shoulders, baring the perfect mounds of her breasts, and the delicate swell of her belly with the jewel shimmering in the neat button. The white muslin fell about her feet.

"Isn't it obvious?" sneered Jameel, barely glancing at the puff of palomino curls at the apex of her thighs, or the gentle curves of her hips.

Of course it was obvious, Humility chided herself. The emir would taunt and tease Jonas until he tired of playing with the magnificent staff of pink flesh, and then ...

Humility shuddered, longing to touch Jonas's manhood, his scrotum, the full shadow between the muscular and splayed thighs.

"And don't think I'll allow you -" Jameel pulled her roughly to him, "you little strumpet, to touch the master's toy!"

The eunuch felt soft, like a warm satin cushion, holding her close, and she shuddered in his strong embrace. It was not the same strength as that which she'd felt in Jonas's arms; that was masculine, a beautifully safe feeling.

Jameel wore only a loin cloth about his broad hips. Humility could feel the thickness of his limp penis. He gave her a mirthless grin, which overtook his plump features. It made her quiver with renewed fear. The threat was plain.

"If the whim takes him ..." murmured Jameel close to her ear, his foul breath warm against her neck. She struggled in the big man's grasp, looking over her shoulder with wide and fearful eyes at the helpless nakedness of Jonas.

"No!" she screamed, throwing her lovely head back in a cry which was both denial and prayer. She could feel Jameel's plump limbs against her slender ones; could feel her sex brushing the uselessness of his organ hiding beneath the loin-cloth; felt the pain of his vice-like hands clasping her upper arms. She tried to struggle, shaking her body from side to side, making her lovely breasts shimmy against his wide chest. She threshed her slender calves against his, trying to hook him down.

"You're wasting your strength, woman!" exclaimed Jameel. "And you may need it when the master graces us with his presence - !"

"Ah, Humility."

The chocolate smooth tones of the emir were unmistakable. There in the shadows was the master, borne upon a cushioned litter set upon the shoulders of two of the largest slaves in the palace.

"Trying to gain satisfaction from Jameel, I see." A sardonic laugh echoed through the dank and dripping passages. "You are quite insatiable, my dear, and I do not know whether to be proud of you or disgusted."

56

Humility felt a flush suffuse her whole body. To accuse her of trying to tempt poor, mutilated Jameel was the worst humiliation of all.

"The very least you could have done was to slip into a dress before throwing yourself at my poor dear gaoler."

The emir made descending gestures with his dark hands and the two slaves gently lowered the litter to the uneven floor.

"Jameel tore my gown," she said meekly, her golden head lowered and her forehead resting against the eunuch's chest.

A snort of disbelief was the emir's reply to her statement, followed by a laugh. "The lies you girls tell to defend your doubtful honour!" He swung her round, pulling her from Jameel's grasp, making her stagger against him. He immediately thrust his fingers into the warm dampness of her sex, rubbing them back and forth.

"You are very wet, Humility," he purred. "Dripping, one might say." With an amused look in the hawklike eyes, he glanced behind her at Jameel. "Don't tell me that you've been stimulating my *favourite*." He placed special emphasis on this last word, and the very emphasis made Humility chill. "And what did you expect to do with her?"

The fingers rubbed harder, tweaking the rawness of her clitty and making darts of sensation spear to the furthest points of her body; making her breasts tender as they swelled, making her arch against her master.

"You cannot help yourself, can you Humility?" he sneered. "Man, eunuch, woman ... you care not. Isn't that so?"

Her face flamed and then paled, leaving two patches of colour on her tawny cheeks, but her wilful body urged against her master's caresses, despite the tears which tumbled down her sad features.

A tiny muscle twitched angrily in the emir's square jaw. The movement was just above the carefully sculpted beard, and it was a movement Humility had learned to fear, just as she feared the thinning of his lips.

Convulsive pleasure made her arch against his fingers, and this despite the floundering uncertainties in her mind. Her soft lips formed a perfect 'O' as she mewed at the overwhelming pleasure sweeping through her body.

"Oh, Humility," sighed her master. "How can you even think of leaving me when I am so generous with the sensuous enjoyment I give you?"

His knowing hand cupped the ripe fullness of her sex and she felt the soft flesh pulse against his fingers.

"Do you think," he continued, spacing his words in a frighteningly even way, "that I cannot be hurt?" With his free hand he lifted her lowered chin, forcing her to look into the unfathomable depths of the onyx eyes. His face was closed and cruel; guarding some terrifying secret.

Humility's eyes widened with alarm. She tore her gaze away and twisted to look at the white prisoner - her beloved Jonas.

"You are cruel, Humility!" hissed the emir. "To be so blatant in your desires for another!"

Tears filled her eyes; she knew what had to be done. With trembling hands she lifted the light silk of the emir's robe, exposing his urgent manhood. He grinned arrogantly, his mercurial black eyes sharpening with renewed interest. "Do not think that you can appease me with your caresses!" His voice was irascibly patient, staidly calm.

Humility cast a glance at Jonas, gasping at the pain - both physical and mental - she saw in his now open eyes.

"On your knees, bitch!"

It was Jameel who spat the order, pushing her shivering

shoulders downwards, pressing her face close to the heaviness of his master's scrotum. She felt the tight smoothness of the emir's erection against her cheek as she was forced to the dirt floor. The slave wrenched Humility's arms back and over her head, forcing her down to touch the filth of the floor with her forehead.

"Be careful, Jameel," warned the emir. "Do not allow her lips to brush the dust of the passage and thus sully my penis!" He ended the command with a chuckle.

"Leave her be," Jonas croaked hoarsely.

Humility, forced low before the emir, sobbed softly, wishing that Jonas had not spoken; he would only worsen the situation.

"But, young sir," purred the emir, "this entertainment is for your benefit. We wish only to give you pleasure, as is our duty as your host."

Through tears and the lustrous curtain of hair, Humility raised her eyes, pleading mutely with Jonas to be silent; not to anger the emir further.

"Do you not wish to see to the full ..." The emir paused, gesturing to Jameel to hold his robe at his waist to free his genitals of all encumbrance, "this lovely creature's talents?" He opened his dark lips and extruded his tongue, wagging it lewdly from side to side.

Knowing her duty Humility clutched her master's buttocks, gently drawing him closer, and heard him sigh pleasurably. "Such a knowing caress," he murmured. "She has perfected every nuance, young sir."

Humility choked back a sob as she grazed her lips over the tautness of the emir's scrotum, feeling the heaviness of the balls under the smooth skin. She had to admit that the feel of her tongue upon her master's manhood excited her. It made her own sex feel gloriously warm and heavy. She could feel her inner folds becoming increasingly swollen. She could feel her clitoris tingle. She could feel warm pearls of dew seep from between the folds to gather upon the neat curls of her plump outer lips.

"Does not the gentle pain which Jameel has afforded you increase the pleasure before your eyes?" The emir stood with his loins thrust forward and elegant dark hands upon his lithe hips. Humility knew he would be looking with great interest at the bloody lash marks across Jonas's chest and belly. He would be looking with even greater interest at the tortured turgidity of the white man's penis, the fullness of the balls, the sheen at the polished globe.

She heard the emir's breathing quicken as her tongue traced a path from the base of his cock to the moist pinnacle. Her soft lips took that mighty globe between them, and she heard Jonas groan loudly. The sound made her belly churn. She wanted to run to Jonas. She wanted to release his strained limbs from the manacles, to take the leather ring from his cock, and to impale herself upon it.

"Oh, yes, Humility," sneered the emir. "I know what wicked thoughts are going through your mind."

He thrust his organ deeper into the warm moistness of her mouth, filling it with his throbbing flesh. She could feel the slickness of its rounded tip butting her palate, but she would not give him the satisfaction of hearing her gag. She even managed to produce a mew of pleasure and was rewarded by a more vicious thrust.

"And when you have relieved me, Humility," taunted the emir, "do you know what I shall do then?"

Knowing that her master did not expect an answer she continued to ingest his cock into her throat, relaxing the latter as a sword swallower would at a circus side-show. His breathing became harsher, more shallow, more excited, more rapid. Humility knew she was bringing him to a swift climax.

"I shall ..." panted the emir. His hips pumped rapidly at the kneeling girl, bringing grunts of protest from Jonas. She could hear him tugging at the manacles, trying desperately to pull them from the rocky wall.

"I shall ... take your white lover's ..." the emir continued raggedly, "... cock ... into my mouth ..."

"No!" hissed Jonas.

Humility felt her master's organ pulse violently between her lips and in the warm depths of her mouth.

The emir laughed. It was a sharp sound, as cutting as a rapier. He threw back his head and pumped his loins. "And how do you propose to ... to stop me?" he managed breathlessly. "Ahhh ... Yesss!!" In a hot silky gush the measure of his excitement fountained into Humility's open throat. She swallowed it all, relishing the salty bitterness in spite of her misery. Her master continued to pump long after spilling the last drops into her.

The air in the cavern was suddenly warmer on Humility's skin. The odours were no longer dank and stale, but freshly musky; stimulating.

"Place her before him," whispered the emir to Jameel. "Legs fully straddled, her pouch available to him." It was said in a sneering, taunting manner. "We shall all enjoy each other."

The big eunuch dragged Humility to her feet, and she tried to ignore the pain which she saw in Jonas's blue eyes. The slave threw her down so that she lay before the captive, and positioned her as the emir wished.

Humility bowed her head as her soft sex was brought nearer and nearer her love's mouth. Jameel lifted her buttocks with a satin cushion, fashioned to spread her cleft and bring her secret place adjacent to the captive's lips. She felt her cheeks flush with humiliation, but could not prevent the anticipatory flutter of her opened folds.

The blue eyes looked into hers. There was tenderness there, and their gazes seemed to melt one into the other. That look helped to calm her.

"Have you ever experienced the joy of a man's mouth upon your cock, young sir?" The emir sat upon a short stool before Jonas, squatting over Humility. Looking up she saw that the stool was a mere ring of smooth wood which left her master's genitals dangling over her upturned face.

"No, damn you!" spat Jonas. "Nor do I wish to do so! I'll kill any man - !"

The emir sighed with mock impatience. "Strange how you Westerners have this prejudice against the wider experiences available to us in this marvellous world of ours."

Humility saw the emir above her lick his thin lips, and then lean forward to impale himself upon Jonas. The latter gave a long disbelieving sigh.

"Do not think only of yourself, young sir," said Jameel, giving Jonas an encouraging kick. "Service the woman with your mouth."

Humility quivered as soft lips kissed first one plump sex-lip and then the other. Her delight was even greater as a stiff tongue plunged swiftly and deeply into her, lapping at the seepage of creamy juices.

A handful of her hair was grabbed and pulled viciously as Jameel positioned her mouth beneath the master's thickly dangling manhood. She winced and moaned softly, but obediently began to caress the emir again with her lips and tongue.

"Do not be so eager, whore!" hissed Jameel, slapping her straddled thighs and the softness of her belly.

Humility realised that she had been pumping her hips

at Jonas, and she tensed herself, pulling back on her fervour. But it was so difficult. Jonas was so sensual in his caresses. She felt the touch of his tongue exploring high into her female entrance, the whip of it across her sensitive clitoris, and the lap of it sipping her juices. In an attempt to slow her urges she concentrated upon the emir. Having produced his excitement so copiously and so recently, she suspected it could be difficult to bring him to prompt rigidity.

She heard Jonas groan loudly and knew that, in spite of the prejudice about which the emir spoke, confusing waves of pleasure were washing over him. But she also knew the leather ring would delay his orgasm, giving him the most exquisite pain.

Despite Jameel's admonishment, Humility could not help herself. The thought of Jonas's suffering brought her to a rapid climax. Her soft sex fluttered beneath those caring lips. Juices seeped between them, spilling over her thighs and into the valley between her buttocks.

"The woman cannot control herself, young sir," grunted Jameel disapprovingly. Humility had a vague vision of the slave removing the torturing leather ring, and knew what the immediate consequences would be. She held her breath, and then felt the warm overflow of semen splash onto her belly and breasts as Jonas suddenly cursed vehemently and jerked against the rocky wall. The stirring flesh slipped from her mouth and slapped against her chin as her master fought to keep his face buried in poor Jonas's twisting groin, and she heard him swallow noisily.

Apart from heavy breathing from three sets of lungs, there was silence in the gloomy cell for long minutes. Eventually the emir's laughter again filled the cavern and he raised himself from the stool. "Get from my sight!" he snarled as his laughter faded. "I am now bored with the two of you!"

Humility looked up at his imperious figure; fear as naked in her eyes as she was herself. What was he planning now?

"Didn't you hear me?" he asked petulantly. He was stroking his swiftly swelling cock with thoughtful touches.

"But, Jonas ..." she began hesitantly.

"Jameel will release him," snapped the emir, "just as he will also be delighted to finish what you could not!"

Jumping to her feet and finding defiance came easily in anger, she stared at him, her petite hands resting tautly on the gentle curves of her hips. "That's not fair!" she said crossly. "You have always been more than happy with my caresses!"

"Until now." His eyes became black slits and his mouth a cruel line. "Now you bore me. Your allegiance is elsewhere and that does not suit me at all."

"But - !"

"You would be well advised to take your new friend and get out of my sight, before I decide to be less generous to you both!"

Humility wondered what was going to happen next. Surely he would not let her go so lightly. Her eyes darted to Jonas, now freed from his bonds and slumped wearily against the wet wall. She wondered what evil plans the emir had for him.

Realising it would be wise to leave this oppressive place while they still could, she guided Jonas by the arm. She looked back just once, and saw Jameel kneeling before his master, ignoring everything but the magnificence of his illustrious penis.

CHAPTER FIVE

Jonas stood on the bridge of the Don Cortez. His compelling blue eyes were focussed on the distant horizon. His firm features were set in an expression which told nothing of his dark thoughts.

A fresh shirt, cut full to accommodate his broad chest, was pressed to his muscular form by the fair winds. His long legs, clad in his best buckskins, were planted squarely apart. His feet were shod in polished top boots.

"How did you escape from that devil?" asked Harry Dawkins. The older man was at the wheel and wanted to chat companionably with the handsome first mate, but Jonas was too preoccupied with Humility.

The flight from the emir's palace had been a nightmare, only made bearable by Humility's closeness. The two of them were thrown from the palace by the huge guards.

"Aye," growled Jonas. "Devil is right. Evil incarnate!"

Harry turned expectantly from the wheel, his old face tanned by a hundred voyages such as this one and his grey eyes bright with interest. "The lads and me found him very hospitable," he remarked. "Wouldn't trust him though."

Jonas said nothing. New lines were etched about his eyes and mouth, muting his age and strength. They'd been given a horse, right enough, when they were pushed so ignominiously from the palace, but the journey down the tortuous path was slow and difficult.

"We never knew whether the ship would wait," he

finally said quietly.

"Cap'n Griggs values you, lad," explained Harry. "That's why he waited."

Jonas snorted his disbelief. "He wanted Humility," he said bitterly. "He'd heard of her beauty, and he knew she'd fetch a good price."

He saw Harry clutch his groin and grin in agreement. "The fancies always do." He eased his legs in his soiled canvas trousers to emphasise his point. "That hair, the tawny skin, and those limpid tortoiseshell eyes." He sighed longingly. "A beauty made to please men - and no mistake."

"So she shouldn't have been thrown in the hold!" Jonas had a possessive desperation in his voice. "Pray that she survives the voyage."

The handsome face closed and the tired blue eyes became blank as he remembered how Humility had been gloriously passive across the bare back of the horse. The emir had allowed her no clothes and Jonas thought she would be more comfortable lying belly-down in front of him.

His big hands clenched and unclenched, feeling again the silken smoothness of her body as he held it safe across the stumbling animal. He felt once more how her flesh trembled under his stroking fingers; how her shapely thighs seemed to open automatically to accommodate his touch.

"Schooled for years by that devil!" he mumbled bitterly to himself.

He remembered how, with one hand holding the rope which had served him as a crude rein, he could not but allow the other to delve softly between the shaking, but inviting, limbs. "So soft and silky," he sighed. "The folds so plump and parted."

66

Harry grinned at him afresh, but was quickly told to mind his business.

Jonas remembered how the sweet curve of Humility's hip fitted so perfectly into his crotch; how he could feel his cock rising eagerly for many hours in his breeches. His greatest desire was to stop in the heat of that arid wilderness and take the girl roughly on the dusty, stone-riddled roadside, but there wasn't time; they had to catch the ship.

The heat made his desire worse, of course. The sun beat down on his bare head, protected only by his thick fair hair. At last, he took his hand from the warm moistness of Humility's cleft and rested it lightly upon the full smoothness of her bottom.

Even now he remembered the way she looked up at him.

"There was fear in those lovely eyes," he whispered. "Fear. I saw it mirrored in them. It was as if she thought she had done something to displease me." He found himself biting his lower lip. "What a life that poor girl must have had with that devil!"

"Did you?" Harry drew Jonas from his reverie.

Jonas frowned, drawing his thick brows together. "Did I what, Harry?" Had he been speaking all his thoughts aloud?

"Have her?" asked Harry eagerly. He rubbed the full crotch of his canvas breeches again and shuffled his buckled shoes.

The handsome face closed again, the wide lips drawn to a fine line and the blue eyes fixed on the shimmering horizon.

He'd had to have her; couldn't help himself. They'd almost reached the town. Jonas could smell the sea and see the rigging of the Don Cortez. There was a stand of old olive trees, small and stunted. The colour of them was dun, almost like the soil on which they grew. There was shade from the fierce heat of the sun beneath them and Jonas jumped from the horse, pulling Humility down to stand beside him. Her delicate hands were quick to reach up and lie lightly on his broad shoulders, but she dropped them just as quickly, fearing she might anger him with her boldness.

"No, Humility," he murmured, his lips curving to a smile. "I want you to hold me; hold me close, as close as you like." He pulled her to him, almost roughly, making her gasp. "I need you!"

They'd sunk together to the dry, stony ground, their bodies scarcely noticing the sharp pebbles which dug into their flesh.

"We must be quick," he said urgently, fumbling with the buttons on his breeches.

He lay on top of her, pushing roughly into her. He shouldn't have been so rough, but his need was great; painful. She met his thrusts gladly. That was no tutored giving. Her lust was as great as his. He could feel her cunt clutching him, drawing him in, pampering his cock. He felt her shudder to a climax, the soft wetness pulsing against him. There was nothing he could do to prevent his own pleasure following hers.

"I'm going below," said Jonas suddenly.

Harry threw a hand on the younger man's broad shoulder. "D'ye think that's wise, Jonas?" he said, looking about him furtively. "Won't you be tempted to do something foolish?"

Jonas shrugged him away. "I can't live with myself if she's been shackled end to end like those other poor wretches."

The older man looked worried, new lines adding to the

weathering of the years. "You know what the Cap'n said," he warned. "She's not to be given any favours." He grinned, looking suddenly younger. "Neither must she give any, not to you or any other crew member."

Running a hand through his breeze-swept hair, Jonas clenched his jaw. "I've got to do something, Harry. I can't sleep for thinking of her in that hell-hole below."

Harry shook his head and clenched the wheel so hard that his gnarled knuckles showed white under the deep tan. He looked up, as if checking the fullness of the square sails, but truly seeking help for his young friend from the heavens.

Relenting, Jonas placed a comforting hand on Harry's shoulder. "I shan't do anything stupid, Harry, I promise you," he said softly.

"Aye, you see as you don't, young Jonas. I've got used to having you about the ship," he said kindly. "Don't want to have to supervise your keelhauling!"

Jonas gave a wry grin and shuddered, but said nothing. The voyage was going well, despite the hold-up as Griggs waited for Jonas. The wind was set fair. The ship sailed before it, and the sound of it in the rigging was a comfort to him. The men were in good spirits as they worked about the decks. Not too much longer, he thought, and they'd make landfall in the West Indies. Then, he'd make a bid for Humility and take her to his grandfather's plantation.

He smelt the slave deck long before he reached it. There was an odour about imprisoned humanity which was unmistakable; foetid to the point of bringing bile to the throat. Jonas shuddered at thinking of Humility chained in that stinking pit.

At the entrance to the slave deck there was a lantern hung on a hook, but unlit. It swayed with every dip into a trough of the waves and rolled heavily. The movement of the ship seemed more violent down here in the bowels of the vessel. Jonas planted his feet firmly, steadying himself as he took his tinderbox from his breeches to light the lantern.

Holding his breath he opened the low hatchway. The smell hit him like a warm humid curtain, and he was forced to swallow hard to contain his retching.

"Humility," he called softly. He heard a chorus of groans in answer. Dark bodies formed a naked carpet stretching away in the shadows of the hold. "Humility!" he called again, louder this time.

There were upwards of two hundred human beings chained down here. They lay side by side, like fish in a salt barrel. There was no room to move, not even to escape their own excreta.

The smell was much worse as he went further into the hold, stooping because of the low headroom in the narrow deck.

A hand weakly clutched his booted ankle and he looked down. A tall Negro, perhaps darkly handsome before he was captured, looked up at him. Sores broke his ebony skin, oozing thick yellow pus. "Water!" he croaked weakly. "For pity's sake ... water!"

Was this how he'd find Humility - dying from some disgusting disease? Sores ... Fear suddenly gripped him; was smallpox raging through the Don Cortez? If it was the whole ship's company might perish, himself and Humility included! Or were the sores a sign of the scurvy? He vowed to arrange for vinegar to be added to the slaves' drinking water.

"Humility!" he tried again.

For some moments only groans and cries for help greeted him from the shadows.

"Jonas," came a small voice. It seemed to issue from

the bows; that part of the ship which took the brunt of the waves.

Stumbling in his haste to reach her, tripping over chains which held the slaves, tripping over limbs but bringing scarcely a sound of protest from the weak captives.

"Oh, Humility!" Jonas knelt in the swill of bilge-water, tainted with excrement. He held the lantern high, looking down at the lovely face, dreading what he might see. But she was as beautiful as ever. Perhaps more so, he thought, smoothing back stray curls from the tawny forehead. The tortoiseshell eyes looked larger in a face which seemed smaller from the poor diet which she'd received.

A heavy wrist chain clattered as she lifted her hands in a weak greeting. She stroked hot fingers down his cheek, as if seeking reassurance that it was really him.

"You have a fever," he murmured, stroking her forehead again, and a chilled blackness filled his mind with fears for her safety. Placing one arm about her slender shoulders he lifted her upper body, holding it to him. He felt the heat of her breasts, the wonderful soft shape of them brushing against his chest, and he could not help but add his own groans to those around him.

"It's nothing," she murmured, but she was limp and heavy in his arms. There was no strength in her.

The glorious fall of hair was lank and coated with filth; all colour gone. She tried to ease her legs and he heard her whimper pitifully. He gasped with horror as he moved the lantern; her shapely ankles were caught with rigid leg bolts.

"Oh Humility, I'd no idea it was so disgusting down here," he exclaimed. "I'll have you out of here in a trice!"

"And me!" came a cry which seemed to echo over and over throughout the deck.

A bitterly cold despair seeped into the anguished

loneliness which overtook his body. He definitely knew now what he'd subconsciously known since he took his ticket as first mate on the Don Cortez; the slave trade was not for him.

"Hold me, Jonas," Humility pleaded desperately. "Hold me tight. Hurt me!"

It was as though she needed the further pain to prove that she was still alive. He heard her breathe deep soul-drenching drafts, and he cradled her in his arms.

"Harder," she urged. "I can't believe it's really you unless you hold me harder."

It was then that his passion overtook him and his embrace became an act of raw possession. Forgetting the presence of the other slaves, he clutched Humility's chained body to him, one hand twisting the ripe fullness of her breasts until she murmured with ecstatic pain. He grasped the tangled wet length of her hair, forcing her head back and making the smooth length of her throat available and vulnerable to him. Such was his passion that he bared his even white teeth and bit the offered length until he tasted blood.

"Yes!" she encouraged, and the whisper was rasping; urgent. "Now I know it's really you; that I've survived this awful place."

Jonas scarcely heard her, scarcely heard the clink of her shackles as he held her roughly. His cock was hard and long in his breeches and a pain in his belly told of urgent hunger. He tore at the buckskin, releasing his thrusting manhood. He felt it brush the softness of Humility's cheek.

"Yesss ..." she sighed again. "Let me taste you, Jonas."

In the dark dankness of the slave-holds, uncaring of the other wretched occupants, Jonas thrust his hungry erection between Humility's lips. He heard the awful clink of her

72

fetters. He reached over her, grasping the firm mounds of her breasts, felt the buds of her nipples harden and engorge under his touch. He was overeager, he knew that, and perhaps he hurt her dear mouth. He thought he heard her sob, but maybe that was caused by her own eagerness.

He felt the slickness of his naked tip butt the very rear of her palate. He felt his thickness stretch the margins of her mouth, but she sucked gratefully, loving the feel of his taking.

He wondered if his aggression was fair to her in her imprisoned state, and then his passion drove all thoughts of her needs from his mind. There would be time enough to care once he'd relieved the ache in his groin.

Humility's lips cosseted his length, petting it at each drive into her. Jonas felt his cock pulse, felt a massive drawing sensation in his groin, and knew that he couldn't hold back for much longer. The tip of her tongue dipped into the slick salty pit of his pore. He thrust harder, more furiously, grunting his passion.

"Now, my darling, now!" he groaned. "Are you ready to take it?" Vaguely, in some far distance as if through a thick fog, he heard the sound of Humility's fetters as she reached up to place gentle hands on his crouching legs. Her touch was more than he could bear and, throwing his head back in a cry of triumph, he let go his fountain of issue, spilling it gratefully into her open lips.

"Whore!" A growl of hatred came through the stinking darkness.

Sinking from his peak of pleasure and panting hard from his passion, Jonas peered into the shadows, looking for the speaker. He lifted the flickering lantern. He looked down into Humility's pale features, and saw the dew of tears glistening on the smooth cheeks. "What does he mean, Humility?"

"Oh Jonas, the Captain …" her voice was broken by a fearful sob. "He means the Captain."

"Griggs?" He spat the name viciously. "Griggs has been here?"

"Many times," said another unseen voice.

"He forced me," sobbed Humility. "What could I do, chained like this?"

In the light of the lantern Humility's hands were lifted, looking so small and frail in the heavy manacles, with the rusty chain swinging only inches from the glorious flesh of her breasts.

"I understand," comforted Jonas, leaning over her, wiping away the spill of semen which gleamed white at the corner of her soft lips. "Did he lie on you? Did he ravish you?"

Humility closed her eyes, tears pearling the thickness of her lashes, and sobs choking in her throat.

"I see that he did," said Jonas sadly, leaning further over her prone body to touch the lovely pouch of her sex between thighs parted by the rigid leg bolt. He felt her quiver at his touch; passion mixed with misery.

"Does the leg bolt cause you pain, Humility?" he asked. The wonderful softness of her sex mound felt like a tiny pillow under his hand. It was lightly dusted with the palomino curls, wet at the very apex of her thighs with her own sap.

"My legs ache," she murmured, "from being forced in one position for so long."

"And from entertaining the Captain," said a neighbouring slave spitefully.

"I couldn't stop him!" Humility sobbed. "Truly, Jonas, believe me!" The tortoiseshell eyes were wide as they begged him to trust her words.

Jonas allowed a finger to dip between the inviting

softness of her sex and stroke the arching erectness of her clitoris. He felt it nudge against the pad of his finger, and it told of her urgency.

The ankle bolt was a rod of iron, rigid and thick, attached to cuffs locked about Humility's slender ankles. In the depressing gloom cast by the lantern Jonas could see cuts where the iron had chafed the flesh, and could see dried traces of blood running down her limbs. Her legs were held apart by the bolt and could not be closed. Any movement, no matter how slight, would cause excruciating pain. This Humility must have felt when Griggs came to her.

Jonas withdrew the intruding finger, but she gave a soft moan of loss.

"No Humility, it will cause you terrible pain if I lie with you." Even as he said it he felt an urgent quickening in his loins, despite the short time since her earlier attentions to his needs.

"I don't care," she protested. "I want it!"

"The whore can't get enough!" accused the same rasping voice from the darkness.

Looking up at the low beams above, Jonas saw the threatening coiled length of the bo'sun's bull-whip. Viciously he pulled it free from the hook.

"One more word ..!" he threatened.

"It's true!" answered the voice. "She can't get enough! Pain or not!"

It was necessary to snake the long whip in a transverse direction in the low-ceilinged deck. Jonas heard it crack lightly, finding flesh in the darkness, and heard a groan of pain.

"Whore!" hissed the voice, more subdued this time.

The whip cracked again. Jonas had now discerned the direction of the spitting accusations, and a great howl went up as the whip found its mark.

"There'll be more if I hear another word from you," he promised into the shadows. "It'll be the worse for you!"

Kneeling still beside Humility, Jonas stroked her lank hair from her face. He gently kissed her forehead. All the horror of the slave-hold seemed to fade into insignificance; the darkness, the sounds of the creaking hull, the cloying smell of decay and the suffered pain.

"Are you sure, my darling?" he whispered softly.

"My life will be complete," Humility murmured, her voice barely audible, "if you lie atop of me."

The very plea was enough to set his groin on fire. He felt his penis jerk and stiffen. "But the leg irons -"

"Oh, Jonas, please!" she sobbed. "I am willing to bear the pain just to feel you close ... inside me!"

Gently he lowered himself onto her, taking care not to inflict the same pain which Griggs had surely given her. He heard her sigh, perhaps with pain, but such was his renewed excitement that he could not contain it. He slipped his thickness between the soft and welcoming folds, felt the smoothness of his globe nudge at her entrance.

"Oh, Jonas," she panted, "don't stop! Don't hesitate! Fuck me!"

On Humility's lips the crude word sounded like the invitation of an angel; no cruder than the kiss of such a one's lips.

He sank into her, lying still for a long moment, taking care not to put added stress upon her fetters. They listened to the creak of the hull, the sound of the wind in the rigging, and were quite oblivious to the cruder sounds of imprisoned humanity.

Drawing upwards Jonas positioned himself to thrust into her again. He felt her draw an inward breath, and knew she was eager to feel him thoroughly inside her. He plunged downwards, sinking into her irresistible softness, feeling the slickness of her dew. He felt his balls draw up and knew that, in spite of her terrible pain, she was urging him to a climax. She was eager to feel the full strength of his passion.

A moan of ecstasy sighed through her lips at the very moment that Jonas spilled his sap into her. It fountained into her helpless, chained body. "I'll have you released," he grunted. "I'll get you out of this hell-hole!" He was breathless from his passion and his exertions. "I'll buy you when the ship reaches port ... see if I don't!"

"I am not worthy," she whispered sadly. "Do not waste your money on such as me."

Moving slowly, so as not to cause her further pain, he rose to his feet. "I'll ask Captain Griggs for the key immediately," he said, ignoring her pleas. "I should have done it weeks ago ... it's just that, I thought I'd make it worse for you."

"He won't give it to you," Humility warned him. "I know he won't."

A cruel laugh bellowed out from the inky shadows. "'Course he won't!" rasped one of the other prisoners. "Why should he - when she gives him his fun on such a reg'lar basis?"

The crack of the bullwhip rent the foetid air. "One more word from any of you and I'll have you flayed!" Jonas warned. "Same applies if you insult this girl by anything you say!" The whip traversed the deck once more, snaking across the rows of sweating prone bodies. "Anything, mark you!"

Jonas breathed a sigh of relief as he again drew a draft of fresh clean air out on the upper-deck. He had to lean over the ship's rail to clear his head of the cloying smell from down below. Retching would have been easy, but he suspected that if he allowed himself that luxury his stomach would never stop giving up its contents. He breathed deeply again, and then turned on his heel to present himself before Captain Griggs.

"One of the female slaves," he said abruptly as soon as the master of the Don Cortez allowed him access to his small cabin.

Griggs was a large man with meaty features, dominated by a bulbous nose which spoke of too much rum. His dark eyes were small, sunken in the mass of flesh. Drops of moisture clung to his damp forehead, and a full lower lip constantly shimmered with an excess of saliva.

A shudder of disgust ran through Jonas as he thought of this gross body taking his pleasure from Humility's chained and naked form. Why had he never noticed before how repulsive Griggs might be to a girl like Humility?

"Which one?" asked the Captain, scarcely bothering to look up from his charts.

"The mulatto ... the fancy." Jonas had to choose his words carefully; try not to show how deeply he felt about the girl.

"There's more than one," said Griggs looking up, his beady eyes glittering with lust and his full lower lip becoming even more moist. "Be more specific man."

"The palomino," said Jonas cautiously.

Griggs frowned and adjusted his breeches about his belly and crotch. "What about her?" Now there was something covert about his expression. "Not thinking of bidding for her yourself, are you?" He gave a cunning, foxy smile. "When we reach Cap Renaud?"

He moved about his chart table and began to prod Jonas with a stiff finger. "That'n'll bring a pretty sum when we've cleaned her up ... And that reminds me." He jutted his several chins pugnaciously at Jonas. "Get those decks swabbed down. Get the cargo up on deck for an hour a day until we make landfall. Don't want 'em looking peaky at the auction, now do we?" He chuckled hugely as though he'd made a great joke.

Jonas remained where he was, his long muscular legs planted squarely apart, his big hands clenched hard at his back.

"What're you waiting for?" Griggs rapped out the question.

"A favour, sir," replied Jonas evenly.

Griggs frowned again and cocked his head to one side. He looked wary. "And that is?"

"The palomino," said Jonas, trying to keep his voice steady. "If I pay you twenty thousand reales now, can I take the girl to my cabin? Can I own her?" The money was all he had in the world, and goodness only knew how he'd manage the plantation without it.

Griggs gaped and then laughed, his great body shaking with mirth. "So that's it!" he scoffed. "Can't control that randy cock of yours, eh?!"

"Can you?" The snipe was out before Jonas could stop it and he was glaring furiously at Griggs, his hands itching to shake the disgusting lump of lard by the throat.

"Get out!!" roared the Captain. "The whore'll take her chance on the block with the rest of 'em!! Get out!!"

CHAPTER SIX

"Humility?"

Vicomte de Salace stared at the girl who'd been placed before him. His eyes, pale brown and feline, narrowed as they lingered upon her nakedness.

Humility found his gaze intimate and searching, and she felt her cheeks flush.

He turned to the huge man standing beside him. "A strange name for a slave," he said. "Would you not agree, Henri?"

Oh, Jonas, sighed Humility within her mind. This man looks so cruel. He will use me uncaringly, I know. How will I ever survive without you? Without your love?

I know, she thought, that these men will desire me and use me as you did, and there will be nothing I can do to prevent myself from enjoying their taking. But my love will still be for you.

She glanced with lowered eyes at the servant. Dressed in a splendid livery of shimmering satin, the man called Henri smiled, his dark eyes both openly amused and lustful as they lingered on her perfectly shaped breasts.

The Vicomte was tall and slender and dressed in the very height of fashion, even in the heat of Haiti. His dark tail-coat was a perfect fit over a plain shirt of finest lawn. A muslin cravat was tied in intricate folds over a collar so high that his slim neck was stretched to the limit. The haute couture made her more aware of her unclothed vulnerability.

She lowered her thick lashes once more, hiding her own eyes which so easily filled with tears since Jonas had been taken from her. Would he ever find her and be free to hold her close in his strong embrace again; to hold each trembling breast in his big palms or cup the fullness of her mound?

"A delightful name," Salace murmured thoughtfully, deciding that he liked it after all. "And so very suitable for a slave, particularly for a slave who's to be used as I intend."

80

Humility shuddered. The Vicomte had paid a high price for her at the auction in Cap Renaud. A very high price indeed. Jonas bid up, making the final figure greater than anything which had been paid before for any slave on Haiti, fancy or no.

She remembered the venomous look the Vicomte had given Jonas. Revenge. Bloody revenge.

A hand, slender and pale as alabaster, reached out to touch her, but did not quite make contact with her golden skin. The contrast between his pale French delicacy and her tawny hue was marked. Even more, the contrast between Jonas's strength and the Vicomte's slender weakness was distinctive. She flinched involuntarily.

Her defensive reaction seemed to amuse him. The thin lips curved in the ghost of a smile and the tip of his long patrician nose flared briefly but, just as quickly as it came, the cruel glint of humour faded.

Humility lifted her head and tried to remain proud and impassive. After all the training and experience with the emir she should be capable of taking each caress, each degradation, every small taunt, without resistance.

Her full soft lips felt dry with apprehension. What had happened to her? She wondered nervously that she could not take whatever befell her with fortitude and strength as she used to do before she met Jonas. Love, she decided, had made her soft and weak. The gentle curves of her slender body trembled. The high breasts pouted. She found her belly softening and her cunt becoming open and moist. Unwittingly, her shapely thighs parted. It was the sudden vision of Jonas, naked, his penis hard and erect and being caressed by the emir's girls-in-training which filled her mind. She shook her head, trying to rid herself of the scene.

"Expensive," murmured the Vicomte. "I trust you will be worth it, cherie!" He turned to Henri. "What say you, my friend?" Stretching his long neck to peer around her slender body the Vicomte looked at the spheres of her bottom, his quizzing glass held delicately in his long pale hand. Henri returned the gaze steadily and proudly, adjusting the starched muslin stock at his neck.

Humility, eyes lowered, surveyed the big slave's white silk stockings and below knee-length breeches. Highly polished black shoes embellished with silver buckles shod Henri's feet.

Humility hung her head lower, allowing the great mass of her palomino hair to hide the high and exotic cheekbones so perfectly set in the oval of her face. Tendrils of her hair stroked the taut erectness of her nipples, curling around the cafe au lait tips, brushing them at the slightest movement. A moistness between the perfection of her thighs made her quiver with need, and she dared not gaze upon slave or master for fear that they would perceive the wanton desire. No matter that they could not know that the desire was not for them, but for Jonas Fairweather.

"We shall make her worth it, milord," answered Henri with a broad and lustful smile, made darker by dark thoughts. "And then there is the question of revenge upon the man who made the price so high."

"Quite so!" agreed the Vicomte, lowering his quizzing glass.

Humility was suddenly chilled by that small phrase. It held the threat of dreadful and terrifying retribution upon Jonas.

The two men, slave and master, looked beyond the gracious veranda where they talked, to the shimmering sapphire blue of the Caribbean Sea washing the beach of silvery white sand. The sails of the ship were furled and it lay serene in the mid-day heat.

Humility shuddered again. The memory of the horror

in the slave decks was bad enough, but what the future held ...

She felt the heat of Henri's black eyes upon the slenderness of her waist, and the tiny swell of her belly softened. All concerns for the future were dispelled for the time being. It was as if his eyes caressed her like gentle fingers. There was a warmth in his gaze which spoke of tenderness, although nothing could replace Jonas's loving caresses in her memory.

The Vicomte's pale hand, the one which reached out and almost touched her moments before, trailed over the voluptuous curve of her buttocks. "Mulatto," he murmured, appraising her with his narrow eyes. The cool fingers spread the full hillocks of her bottom and invaded the heat of her most intimate crease, pressing open the tightness of her bud.

"No!" she cried, pulling away from the prying chill of the aristocratic fingers. Even as she shrank away she knew it was wrong. She was owned by this man, and owned at a high price. She had no right to behave thus; no matter that her love was for Jonas.

Henri held her, his large hands like fleshy vices. She could hear his breathing, harsh and quick, and feel the warmth of his breath close to her ear, disturbing the tendrils of her hair.

"Henri," snarled the Vicomte, looking at her crouching figure with disdain. "Deal with this disobedient whore. Take her away and make it plain that I own her and shall do as I please with her. But for now I am wearied of the sight of the wench." He waved his hands impatiently, his petulant features angry and hostile.

"If you please, milord ..." Humility pleaded gently, wanting to tell the aristocrat the truth about her background; how the emir's men had taken her from her

83

father's palace in the tiny mountain kingdom in North Africa; how the emir's women had petted her until she was grown, and then trained her to please and pamper the monarch who was her master.

Henri gripped her upper arms, shaking her roughly and pulling her to him. It was impossible to prevent the tingle which shot through her tutored body on feeling the silken touch of his livery.

At his groin there was a distinct bulge which brushed the plumpness of her mound. His lips parted to display straight white teeth. The smile was startling against the darkness of his face. Olive-black eyes glinted at her, conveying some message which Humility could not discern from their murky depths.

The Vicomte looked on, cynical amusement in the pale brown eyes and the wide thin lips curving in the same cruel smile.

"Do what you wish with her, Henri," ordered Charles de Salace. "The punishment quarters have been empty for far too long. Perhaps Madame le Chat will bring her to heel."

A sob began in her throat; a sob which she tried to hold back. Surely he wouldn't scar her after paying so dearly to possess her?

Madame le Chat! Humility shuddered. It took little knowledge of French to translate the evil implement - the cat o' nine tails! She could already feel the cut of the nails fixed to each leather lash biting into her dark skin; could feel the warm trickle of blood where they broke through.

It took no second bidding for the huge Henri to throw her over his shoulder. Humility coloured fiercely, only too aware that her bottom was on full view to the Vicomte.

"Will you view the treatment, milord?" asked Henri, his deep voice betraying his excitement.

Humility felt his strong hand cupping the lower curves of her buttocks. The mere touch of those fingers sent a warming shiver through her. Her bud, so easily aroused, jerked between the trembling leaves of her urgent sex and the flush on her tawny face increased. If only she was not so receptive!

"Perhaps," said the Vicomte airily, gazing not at Humility, but beyond her to the lush vegetation of the plantation garden.

The chair scraped as he rose to his feet and she heard the creak of the veranda-boards as his highly polished boots walked around her. She was very aware of the fullness of her breasts against Henri's satin livery. The pouting mounds became fuller. She felt her dark nipples tauten and tingle beautifully. She knew, through some deep seated instinct, that Salace would touch her intimately again at any moment. She quivered in apprehension.

Oh, how correct she was in her apprehensions! "Open her legs, Henri," he ordered casually.

The soft flesh of her inner thighs trembled lightly and she could feel her labia swell gently, pouting out in invitation. The Vicomte chuckled.

"It seems this dusky mademoiselle is not so modest as she would have us believe," he said, and Humility felt the whisper of his breath upon her sex.

Henri stood perfectly still and impassive, and yet she could feel his excitement growing. There was a tension in his broad shoulders and she could hear the subtle change in his breathing.

"Splay one leg across your shoulder, Henri," husked the Vicomte. "Let us have her fully open."

Humility was aware of the soft whisper of the tropical breeze across the trembling hillocks of her buttocks. It invaded the deep crease between the perfect globes and made the light dusting of palomino curls flutter.

Henri grasped a slender calf and eased her easily open. Humility could only gasp as her legs were parted, baring the moist folds of her sex. Revealed as she was she felt hopeless, and dreadfully abandoned by Jonas. Not that her love could help that abandonment; he'd tried his best to buy her at the auction.

"Hm," murmured the Vicomte. "Something has excited the wench. Look, Henri ..."

It was the thoughts of Jonas in the heat of the marketplace at Cap Renaud, watching her naked on the small dais, her hands on her head for all to examine; those thoughts had caused the excitement.

Once more Humility felt the heat of the slave's breath as he turned his head to gaze into her most intimate parts.

"Saturated," said Henri.

"Indeed," agreed the Vicomte, and she heard the lilt of excitement in his cold voice.

"I shall investigate, milord," said the big slave, and Humility could not help the light shudder which made her belly quiver at the thought of his thick fingers sliding between her folds. It was not a shudder of distaste, but rather one of longing - despite her thoughts of Jonas.

"Yes," mouthed the Vicomte, the word a sibilant whisper which was a caress to her ears.

The pads of two fingers circled over the erect tip of her clitty. Unbidden tears filled Humility's tortoiseshell eyes, for she felt excitement that she knew always preceded her reaching a pleasure peak. She felt her bud become more heated, more sensitive with every slow circle.

"Enter her," rasped the Vicomte.

The fingers, slippery now with her juices, sank slowly between her quivering inner lips. Humiliation consumed her as her wet passage pampered the invading digits. She heard Henri chuckle, and felt him thrust more swiftly and firmly. She heard the sucking of her flesh and felt the burn of colour upon her cheeks.

"How eagerly she clutches," remarked the Vicomte. "An exceedingly willing creature."

Humility felt the coolness of Salace's thumb smoothing around the puffiness of her outer lips, and felt it slither around the silk of the dew which wetted her downy curls. It felt quite different from the thickness of Henri's fingers, which plunged so rhythmically in and out of her entrance.

"Now why, do you suppose," questioned the Vicomte, "did she pretend such coyness?" The chill of his slender thumb drifted upwards to the fullness of her buttocks. It hovered at the peak of the deep valley, pressing hard upon the sensitive tip of her tail.

Because I am trained, she longed to answer. I am trained to be coy, to be modest, to be anything my master requires. But she did not reveal these secrets to the two men.

She knew that, at any moment, the bony digit would slide deeper to find her most intimate entrance. She knew that then she would be quite unable to hide her passion, which was rising swiftly and making her belly soften and become as molten liquid against Henri's broad shoulder. She bit her lower lip, trying to hold back further tears, but at the same time the most wonderful quivers fluttered through her sensitive flesh.

The Vicomte, his thumb still hovering around the hotness of Humility's bottom crease, peered around Henri's big frame. Softly, he lifted the tumbled tresses of her hair, lifting the curls to peer into the tear-glazed loveliness of her eyes. The touch of his slim hand was almost affectionate, and yet there was a sinister threat underlying the gentleness.

"There is something very special about this girl," said

the Vicomte. "This is no ordinary slave, Henri. Perhaps, she is after all, worth every penny I paid."

"Perhaps, milord," agreed the big man, his fingers still plunging into Humility's slippery depths. "She has a pleasant musk, sir," he added, sniffing the silk of the naked buttock lying close to his cheek.

The Vicomte pressed harder, deeper, and Humility's breathing quickened. With all of her body she bore upon both probes. She felt her clitty slip from its tiny hood, the sensitive tip grating softly upon the covering skin.

"One does not pay for musk alone, Henri," commented the Vicomte with a light chuckle. "One pays for willingness. Yes, willingness is most valuable." The aristocrat became more excited and enthusiastic. "See how she quivers, Henri!"

Henri drew a deep breath before speaking. "Very receptive," he agreed hoarsely, his fingers slipping easily into Humility's pulsing, silky passage.

In a daze of an emotion so close to passion that she could not bear to admit, Humility felt her tawny body glow with a slick of perspiration. She felt a trickle of it, warm and slow, gather at her waist to dampen Henri's splendid livery. A tiny stream ran down her backbone to moisten the Vicomte's thumb. If only she could reach her peak - but both men kept her hovering at the delicious brink.

Suddenly and surprisingly the thumb was removed, and she felt the sting of a slap upon her bottom. "The punishment quarters with her," announced the Vicomte in a bored tone.

The punishment quarters! Humility gasped. What had she now done to deserve punishment? Only moments before the Vicomte had remarked upon how willing she was. Henri's fingers were also withdrawn, and Humility heard the sucking of her own bereft flesh. She felt desperately cold. Her belly ached with emptiness.

"Perhaps a race around the perimeters of the estate will cool the hussy down," chuckled the Vicomte.

Humility felt the caress of Henri's hand at the lower curve of her bottom. It seemed to say: 'Do not be afraid, pauvre petite. I shall be gentle'. The hand stroked across the lower curve, pausing only momentarily at the pooling wetness between her puffy lips.

Helplessly, she felt herself swung along the veranda on Henri's big shoulder. His long strides jolted her already trembling body.

Through the swinging mist of her tumbled hair she peeped at the Vicomte. It was as if she was of no account. The cruel topaz eyes gazed out to sea, watching the slave ship ride at anchor.

Poor Jonas, she thought. Those topaz eyes spoke of the most dreadful punishment; the most painful revenge. Only then did Humility think about her own fate.

"What will happen to me, Henri?" Humility ventured to whisper, her voice shaken by the slave's sure strides.

She felt his big hand tighten its grip upon the smallness of her bottom, squeezing the tawny hillocks tightly together. "You will be the Vicomte's plaything until he tires of you, ma chere petite."

Humility shivered under Henri's grasp. "Does he quickly tire?" she asked, dreading the answer.

They had left the area immediately surrounding the mansion and had reached a lawn; green, soft and springy. Occasionally they passed through the shade of tall coconut palms bent by the fierce summer winds of the Indies. Humility was grateful for the brief respites from the blazing sun.

"Unfortunately, yes," said Henri, sounding genuinely

apologetic for his master's action. His hand stroked between the silkiness of her dangling thighs, allowing his fingers to trail up and down the spilled dew of her earlier excitement. "But it may be different with you, since he paid such a high price."

Humility sighed. "When he tires …" she said hesitantly, "… if he tires - what then?"

The slave's fingers surreptitiously prised open the velvety softness of her labia and slicked up and down her moist cleft. "Then you may be given to me …" The fingers worked in her hot flesh more quickly. "Pray that you are."

Another sigh whispered from Humility's parted lips, for his fingers were bringing her to the peak which was earlier denied her.

"But that is entirely upon the Vicomte's whim," Henri added slowly.

A great shudder ran through her slender frame, making her breasts mould against his broad satin-clad back. She could feel her cunney clutching upon his probing fingers, soaking them with her juices.

"If he denies you," she managed to gasp moments later, her voice a tremulous whisper, "what then?"

Henri bent to enter a low doorway, and Humility smelled the dank stale smell so clearly remembered from the Don Cortez. Sweat and spilled sex juices, together with other nameless odours which she would sooner deny, cloyed at her nostrils.

He set her upon her feet and held her close against his impressive frame. His large hands were surprisingly tender as they squeezed about her waist.

"Then, ma pauvre," Henri said regretfully, "you will be put to work in the fields."

"But the Vicomte paid such a high price for me," she protested. "The cane fields? Would he really do that after paying so dearly?

Henri shrugged. "He would do it if only for revenge against the man who bid against him."

Was now the time to tell Henri that she was a princess? Would it help to improve her fate? Probably not, she decided hastily; it could well make things much worse.

Henri slid his hands down the contours of her ribs, waist and the swell of her hips, admiring the shapeliness of her smooth flesh. The olive-black of his eyes was soft with sympathy as a finger wiped away a tear which spilled onto her cheek.

"Is there nothing you can do to save me, Henri?" she pleaded.

The great dark head shook sadly, the handsome face gleaming like polished ebony in the gloom of the primitive building.

She'd heard of the fate of those who worked in the fields from her companions in the holds of the Don Cortez. She would be, for sure, worked to death; scarred beyond recognition and aged far beyond her tender years. Tears glazed her eyes as she looked up at the huge fellow.

"For now, ma petite, enjoy today," he advised, putting a strong hand at her waist to draw her to him. Humility felt the coolness of the luxurious satin livery which clothed his body, and beneath it the heat of his growing need. The feel of it made her shudder deliciously.

Henri gave a low chuckle, recognising her urgency, and swept her up into the cradle of his arms. She felt the tension of his massive biceps bulging under the satin and wondered that the frail material could take the strain without ripping asunder.

"What are you going to do to me?" she asked. She could hardly raise her voice above a timid whisper.

Henri strode the length of the rough hut. It was

constructed of interwoven palm fronds and the roof was dried cane foliage. The floor was sandy earth, dry and soft under his feet. He took her to a place at the far end where four metal staves, taken from an old barrel, were driven into the floor. Gently he laid her down and turned her over until she lay upon her stomach. She felt the fine earth, warm from the heat of the day, soft as a mattress against her skin.

"The Vicomte requires you to be shackled," he said, kneeling beside her and firmly stretching her arms until the inner sides of her wrists felt the cold resistance of the staves. "All of his bed wenches are shackled on their first day ... no matter their price."

Humility passively opened her thighs, arching her bottom, assuming that Henri would also require her to be shackled at the ankle.

Seeing this movement, the lift of the milk chocolate hillocks, Henri laughed softly. "So eager, ma chere, but you can relax for the moment and lift those perfect globes later.

"Such shapely limbs!" he sighed when her wrists were firmly gripped in the rough metal of the manacles. They were cold and tight about her tiny bones; almost the size required for a child.

His hands explored the soft lines of her back, her waist, her hips. The big fingers lingering hotly at each gentle curve. "I am ordered to smack you, Humility," he said in a tone which she could almost believe was regret.

She breathed in quickly, feeling her face burn. She felt again the pain of metal tearing into her flesh as Madame le Chat flew through the gloomy warmth of the punishment quarters. "Not ... the cat?" she begged.

Henri let his fingers drift over the smooth and unblemished shoulders, and shook his head.

Even though she tried to remain passive her slender arms stiffened, causing the manacles to bite into the tender flesh. She arched her neck, looking up at the slave pleadingly. Their eyes met in the gloom, one pair wide and apprehensive, and the other smiling in a gentle, consoling manner.

"Non, ma chere. But it can be a very mild chastisement ..."

This man desired her - Humility thought with a sigh - as they all did. Did she unwittingly weave some magic spell upon men that they could not resist her? Or was she a witch? Had she become so through the tutoring received from the emir? Was her own wish for revenge so great that she called upon magical powers?

Henri's cock was suddenly swaying from the satin breeches. It was stiffly erect, dark and thick, shining with a gloss of issue. He knelt, holding the weapon lightly with finger and thumb, offering it to her moist lips. Humility knew what she must do.

"... Or it can be harsh!" he added hoarsely.

Humility pursed her soft lips, shaping them in readiness to kiss his penis. To her, after years of training in the emir's palace, the feel of a man's flesh sliding into her mouth was no punishment, but a delight. Would the taste of Henri be so different to Jonas, and all the others? She saw him gazing down at her with affection in his dark eyes. The cold pain of the manacles upon her dainty wrists was forgotten. The feel of the soft sand upon her breasts and the strain upon her shoulders were mere caresses as her lips stretched wide to close around the massive darkness of his globe.

Through the gloom of the dilapidated building floated Henri's sigh of pleasure. Her lips caressed his throbbing thickness as she slowly ingested the organ into her throat.

Despite the discomfort caused by the arching of her neck and the tight shackling of her arms, Humility felt an eagerness in her belly. It was a feeling not dissimilar to that which she had felt with Jonas. Her depths felt moist and molten. Her sex flesh felt hot and swollen as she wiped her tongue over the salty bitterness of Henri's cock.

"Yes, little one, yesss!" he hissed. His large hands moved under her tightly arched body to cup her breasts, thumbing the tautened teats which were so hot and painfully wrinkled. Perhaps he didn't know how firmly he grasped the full globes, lost in his own passion as he was.

Sucking the length deep into her willing throat Humility eagerly consumed the hot spurts of semen which came quick and strong. If only her hands were free, she thought, she would milk the fullness of his scrotum.

A long deep sigh signalled the ending of the big slave's pleasure. Humility heard the calming of his breathing and felt his hands comb roughly through the silken mass of her hair, pressing her sweet features to the muscular hardness of his flat belly. His cock, still partially erect, brushed damply against the velvety softness of her cheek.

"And now, ma petite ..." he said gazing down at her with luminous olive-black eyes. He seemed to look at her, thought Humility, with something like awe. But that could not be. She was worthless; high priced or not. It was long moments until he spoke again, and when he did his voice was low and hoarse as if he was afraid but did not know why. "... The punishment."

Humility raised her own pleading eyes. Her lips were soft and parted, still slicked with his spillage. Her tongue slid briefly along their fullness.

"It is for the best," he said, stroking her hair from the dampness of her forehead. "We are both slaves of the Vicomte, and must do his bidding." He moved slowly to her feet, gently pulling them open until they were spread almost to their limit. he seemed no longer afraid, his confidence back in full measure. "Good," he sighed.

She knew then that he was squatting between her open thighs, viewing the dewiness of her splayed sex. She was quite unable to prevent this wetting of her sex-lips. The melting feeling had come upon her as Henri's pleasure had spilled into her mouth.

"Yes, excellent."

She felt his thick fingers smooth over the wetted curls. It made her vulnerability increase; not being able to see what he intended to do next.

"Up on your knees, ma petite," he ordered.

Obediently, Humility shifted her limbs so that her legs were folded beneath her. She lifted her bottom high while her arms were still fastened tightly in the manacles. She knew her sex pouted at him, the hardness of her pleasure-pip glowing between the sheen of her folds.

The spanking began. Henri's big hand swiped across both buttocks, making the lifted and offered flesh quiver with the force of the blow. Humility bit her lip, trying not to make a sound of complaint. She even offered her rump higher. She heard him draw a deep breath as the next blow fell. It stung in greater measure than the first and yet her fluids ran more freely, making the palomino curls gloss luxuriantly.

"Henri," she whispered.

"Do you cry for mercy, ma petite?" he rasped.

Humility shook her head before pressing her cheek to the soft earth and offering her open sex so sweetly displayed between the glowing mounds. "Take me!" she sighed. "My need is unbearable!"

CHAPTER SEVEN

Humility awoke next morning further exposed. The gold-flecked tortoiseshell eyes flashed wide open, the dark lashes fluttering fearfully.

Questions tumbled through her mind. Where was she? Where was Henri? What did he intend doing to her? So much had happened since she and Jonas had left the emir's palace.

Her tawny skin felt peeled; her flesh laid bare and raw. Her breasts were taut under golden skin, the teats painfully erect and inflamed. Her slender hips were arched and tapered to long straight legs which were splayed to their limit.

With her arms stretched and fixed by iron manacles to the head of the heavy oak bed, she felt that her shoulders would be pulled from their sockets. Her sore wrists were butted hard against the polished, carved wood. The cruel tethering cut into her fine flesh as she tugged hopelessly at each bond.

She sighed softly; she remembered. The Vicomte de Salace was her master now, and proving to be a cruel one.

The beating given by Henri at the Vicomte's instruction had left her sore and bruised, but there was something else. An inner soreness. A swelling between her splayed thighs. She felt her cheeks colour quickly, burning with humiliation.

Questions again. Who claimed her secret loyalty? Jonas?

The Vicomte? Henri? She felt so confused.

Once more she tugged at her bonds, thrashing the wild mass of hair across the white linen of her pillow. Did the Vicomte imagine she would run? There was nowhere for her to run to. The island was a prison without bars. She fought back the tears which threatened again. To weep would have been easy, but she must accept that her use as the Vicomte's plaything would be her life from this time on. Until he tired of her.

An image of Jonas naked and lying on top of her, his gloriously erect penis thrusting between the plump lips of her sex, brought a delicious swirling sensation to her belly. Thoughts of Jonas and thoughts of her master enhanced her awareness of that part of her body between her spread thighs; that part which was made more vulnerable by the tethering of her ankles to the carved foot of the bed. It was slick with seminal fluid. It glossed the smooth skin of her thighs. It trickled down over her buttocks and seeped into the rumpled satin of the bed coverings. Her skin was slippery with the tropical heat.

A damp smell enveloped her; it was her own musk blended with the perfumes from the Vicomte's garden. Heat and fecundity, aromas of life and death, and life growing upon that which had decayed. Scents drifted from the garden; glorious flowers and sweet juicy fruit. The house was stirring and she could smell the tempting aroma of coffee. It made her realise her thirst.

Beside her on the massive bed the Vicomte stirred, moving against her. He placed a hand, long and slender, on the tiny swell of her belly, stroking the taut smoothness of her skin, made more polished by the heat.

Humility tensed, her long legs stretched tightly in the cruel tethering. Her sex prepared itself for his further invasion. The plump labia seemed to flutter, open and ready. She felt her clitoris arch and pout for him. All of this was the result of the years of training under the emir.

Morning light crept timidly to fall upon the Vicomte's body, shadowed by the interlaced branches beyond the window; branches of avocado and mango. Branches which dripped with the milky perfection of orchids hanging in eloquent sprays; beautiful saprophytes, gorgeous uninvited guests.

The Vicomte opened his eyes and looked at her, and she saw the topaz darken dangerously as he smiled. "And what shall we do this morning, my dear Humility?"

His voice dripped honey and his caresses were almost loving, but this only made her all the more wary. Her shoulders ached from the long night's tethering, and she tried to ease them as she answered. "Whatever pleases you, master," she said in a submissive tone she knew would gratify him.

"Hm," he murmured thoughtfully, "of course we shall do what pleases me." He didn't look at her, but stared up at the richness of the satin canopy draped above them. He moved his pale hand upon her belly and a shudder ran involuntarily through her flesh. It was a shudder of anticipation for the surfeit of pleasures which she knew would come quickly, one upon the other. "But," he continued slowly, cupping his long cool fingers upon her sex mound, "you naughty little slave ..." He laughed, amending his words: "You naughty, *expensive* little slave!" Humility flinched at the emphasis he placed on the word 'expensive'. Despite this his touch made her breasts rise in a further gesture of offer. "I have a plantation to run. I cannot always be here to service you."

Humility felt a crafty finger slither between her open labia, making her own juices join the many floods which her master had injected into her.

The Vicomte lay back with a sigh, throwing his pale arms above his head in an attitude of mock submission. "It would be so wonderful to be a slave like you, Humility." His voice was low, silver-toned and seductive, invading the lustrous hair which spilled about her ears. The voice was a caress and, at the same time, an instrument of torture, teasing her mind, holding an underlying threat towards Jonas. It was there, all the time. "It would be so wonderful to lie upon satin sheets," he continued to goad, "and do nothing all day but receive pleasure from a virile master."

The silvery words made Humility all too well aware of the threat that lay behind them.

A sudden movement heralded the Vicomte's leap from the soft nest of bed-sheets to straddle her hips. He thrust out his own loins, holding his thick erection in both hands. "See how you torture me, Humility! See how I awake with this huge monster spearing up from my belly! What am I to do with it, now that you've created it?"

The silver tone was gone. His voice boomed through the splendid master bedchamber. He shook the long length of turgid flesh with the skin stretched to transparency, shimmering in its fineness. The penis seemed unearthly, and Humility quivered in her bonds, longing for its intrusion into her well-prepared body.

"Have you any idea how much you cause me pain?"

She sensed his vexation, or the pretence of it. Annoyance seemed to shadow his face, but still she could not perceive whether it was real or pretend. The elegant fingers slid up and down the thickness of his cock and, with his free hand, he cupped the swollen balls, rolling them between his spread thighs.

"Perhaps you do not care?" He cocked his head to one side in a coquettish gesture, his long dark hair swirling over his naked shoulders.

Humility was horrified. The Vicomte was now her lover as well as her master. To say that she did not care was unfair! Of course she cared if she truly had caused him pain, no matter that he was cruel and was threatening revenge on the man she loved! It was her duty to make him happy and to delight in the pleasure she gave him.

The beautiful perfection of his penis glanced across the slickness at her entrance. Despite her confused feelings about this man, she gasped; a whispering intake of breath; a soft sigh of longing.

"You want it, Humility," he whispered. "Don't you?"

He leaned close until his pale features were close to hers, letting the words brush over her face like a caress.

With her slender throat occluded by unsaid words, Humility tried to nod.

"I want you to tell me," he urged, purring into her shell-like ear. "I want you to tell me loudly and clearly, using the crudest words you know." The purring gradually disintegrated into a dark rasp, grating through her consciousness.

Was this part of his revenge?

Leaning over her body, he nestled his taut scrotum between the folds of her sex, pressing them open. Humility was inflamed, burning in her need for him. Her sap flowed heavily, coating the fullness of his balls. All of this made her need greater, but she turned her head away, her tortoiseshell eyes closed and her mouth pursed.

"Naughty Humility," he goaded hoarsely. "To tease the Vicomte in this way." He brushed his lips across her velvet cheek. He nestled his balls further into the cup of her sex.

"Oh, master," she managed faintly. Her belly was soft. It seemed to swirl; to draw him in. Her labia delicately clutched the eager bundle of his genitals, but still she could not say the words he wished to hear. The helplessness of her tethering seemed to become more severe and her pains were almost unbearable.

"Tell me, Humility!" he hissed venomously.

His sudden anger frightened her. She instinctively arched her neck, exposing the unblemished flesh of her throat as an offering of appeasement. She felt the quickening of the pulse in her vessels. The blood was flowing swiftly through her body, making the skin flush and burn. Her heart pounded fiercely. Her breathing came quick and harsh.

The pale hands were clasped tightly upon her breasts, and yet she welcomed the pain of his grip; it enhanced the fluid sensation deep in her belly.

The Vicomte giggled insanely. His head was thrown back, like some great beast of prey about to strike for the kill. His pasty and hairless chest rose and fell with his excited breathing, and his penis was as hard as tempered steel against her belly.

"Fuck me," she managed to mumble at last. The words were a weak and tremulous whisper, but at least she'd obeyed his disconcerting demands.

Again he giggled, this time with the satisfaction of hearing her submission, and then he bent to suck a pulsing nipple between his lips. They chewed on the highly sensitive bud, gently rubbing back and forth and making her arch yet more. The teasing of the nipple went on for an interminable length of time.

And then the pain began.

"No!" she whimpered.

His teeth were like tiny blades nipping at the delicate flesh, but she didn't mean that he should stop the torment, rather that he should add to it by probing into her receptive body with his length of steel.

"'No', Humility?" he said coldly, lifting his head and tossing back his long hair. "You surely don't mean that, do you? I know you don't mean that. I know you wouldn't deny me - your master."

Drawing breath was becoming increasingly difficult for the poor girl. The Vicomte seemed to remain deathly cool, but the sultry air was surely increasing in temperature. It scorched her throat and lungs, and her arched breasts rose and fell in rapidly shallow movements.

"Fuck me," she pleaded. This time her voice was clear and crisp, cutting through the heavy air.

"Hm," he pondered cruelly, allowing his fingers to return to her breasts, merely lying there, the pads doing no more than grazing the swollen flesh. His eyes narrowed and his head tilted again to the side. "I wonder."

Humility's vision was blurred by tears. There was nothing she could do to hold them back as she moaned: "I want you!"

"I want? You sound like a spoilt child, Humility. Nicely brought up girls say: 'May I have', or 'I should like'. They do not say: 'I want'."

He shook his head and tutted in mock disappointment at her unladylike choice of words. His boyish buttocks slid tantalisingly back and forth between her thighs. His thick and elegant penis teased the downy curls which covered her mound.

Humility looked up at him, her expression one of deep misery and sorrow. How could she convey to him that her need was deeply felt, that at that moment she truly wanted him? Was not the play-acting simply because he'd paid an enormous price for her? Her tortoiseshell eyes glistened afresh with tears which spilled like liquid diamonds down her smooth and flushed cheeks.

"Well, Humility?" he teased, prodding the tenderness

of her breast with a sharply manicured nail. "Still no reply? Still no words of love for your master?"

A pearl of semen, heavy and warm, dripped from his polished globe. His hands rested lightly on his hips, and his penis jutted straight up from the darkness of his groin. Even in the muted light of the bedroom Humility could see the pulsing of the gracious length. The zenith of his pleasure was close.

Her soft lips slowly parted. "I love you," she whispered sensuously. "Please master, make love to me. I need you."

"Oh, Humility!" He allowed his chest to sink down and brush the peaks of her excited nipples. "I believe you! You truly love me! No one has ever told me such a thing before!"

A gentle smile, made all the sweeter by the dew of tears in her eyes, lit her face as his mouth came down to meet hers. Humility wanted to guide his erection into herself, but she was helpless. The very helplessness made his taking of her all the sweeter. No matter that he'd bought and owned her, he needed love, just like any other human being. He needed to be loved for himself, not for what he represented.

The silky globe prised her willing entrance open. A sigh of glorious pleasure whispered from her lips, the warm sweet breath fluttering tenderly across his face. He entered her further, and she moaned deeply as she felt him opening and filling her to the hilt. His entry into her body seemed to enhance the helplessness of her bondage, and increase the beauty of his surprisingly gentle plundering.

The Vicomte lay still, joined to his expensive plaything by his supreme desire for her. Humility could do nothing else but lie beneath him. The only muscles she was able to move were those of her slick passage. With these she pampered him, cosseting his length, petting every centimetre.

With her spirit soaring on a cloud of pleasure, Humility rose above her slavery to the Vicomte. Jonas was not forgotten, but of necessity for her own sanity, she had to place him at the very back of her mind. Even the Vicomte's taunts and the little tortures, she told herself, were surely signs of his love for her. Jonas now had to be a vaguely remembered dream. How could he be anything else? All she had ever known in the whole of her life was slavery. He, Jonas, with his loving tenderness and sincere caring, must have been a dream.

"Yes, Humility," whispered the Vicomte in a low but perfectly composed voice. "You allow me to fuck you very well."

Allow?

Her breath was suddenly sucked from her body once more as he sank into her again.

Allow? What choice had she but to allow him to invade her with his penis? An involuntary clutch of her silky channel made him gasp.

"Merde!" he exclaimed, and his long cool fingers slapped lightly at her arching breast. "You hurry me Humility, with your pampering!" He looked down at her angrily, his dark eyes full of fire which was both anger and passion. "I do not like to be hurried when I fuck. Always at my pace, Humility. Always at my pace."

The slap caused no pain, but merely served to enhance what his penis was doing. The long length of flesh pulsed inside her, buffeting the very entrance to her womb. How could his tenderness also be so cruel?

He began to thrust into her more aggressively, clutching her aching shoulders with those cool fingers. She felt the grate of his crisp pubic curls on her puff of soft ones. In her passion she tried to grasp the iron manacles, but the tightness of them made it impossible and her fingers clawed at thin air. In the chains she was helpless, and could only lie and allow him to plunge into her as though he would tear her flesh asunder. She heard his breathing ragged and shallow; heard his animal grunts, culminating in a wonderful cry of release.

Humility felt happy for him as he showered her insides with the silky flood of semen, although her own pleasure still swirled, unsatisfied, within the yearning softness of her belly.

"Glorious." The single word was panted into the tumbled mass of her hair. His breathing slowed and his sweaty chest pressed down upon her sensitive breasts.

"What say you, ma petite?" he asked some minutes later, looking down at her and pressing her shoulders into the soft bed. His penis was still buried within, slicked with his own silk and hers. It remained as erect as a lesser man's might be at the beginning of a plunder. Humility felt it pulse, and attempted to echo this with movements of her own. There was little she could do or say to reach her own satisfaction. She was powerless.

"Nothing?" He giggled that same bizarre giggle, suddenly rolling from her and striding to the far side of the chamber. He slid into a luxurious satin robe, stitched with gold and silver thread. She sighed as his penis was hidden from her. He turned, frowning, and peered at her inquisitively. "Your pleasure did not come?" he asked.

Humility turned her head away, closing her eyes, swallowing her sadness. She felt him sit upon the edge of the large bed, felt his fingers pry open the tenderness of her labia.

"I see it did not." The heel of his hand pressed into her still tingling sex, massaging the slickness. "I shall arrange for Henri to relieve you."

"Pleeease …!" The desperate plea was uttered before it could be suppressed.

With both hands he spread her labia, looking within the flushed depths. "You beg so hard for Henri?" he said dryly. "I could be forgiven for thinking that you desire him far more than me!"

"It's not that."

"Then what?" He slipped two fingers into her aching channel. The movement was swift and fierce and Humility tried with all her might, despite her bonds, to rise up to meet his thrusts.

"Unfasten the shackles and I shall pleasure myself!" She knew she sounded shamelessly frantic, her voice weak and shaking.

"So that's it!" The Vicomte was enjoying the joke hugely. His features were lifted sardonically in little quirky tilts of his eyes and lips. "You desire neither of us. Neither of us can satisfy you. You would rather please yourself!"

With light fingers he parted his robe, allowing Humility to see his penis, its hardness fully renewed. She lapped her tongue about her pink lips and shook her head. "I wish only to please you, master," she sighed desperately.

"And yourself, it would seem." The black gown fluttered in the breeze which sighed into the room from the scented garden, making an elegant frame about the statuesque flesh which thrust towards her. Humility's gaze was fixed to the turgid stem, still glossed with his earlier issue.

"How you inflame me!" he growled. "You're an impertinent minx, taking me away from my duties on the plantation!"

She could not discern whether his unpredictable mood swings were real or pretend.

"And now you invite me to impale your mouth, to cosset my cock with your ever-active tongue!" He shook his head, causing the dark fall of hair to sway about his neck and shoulders. "Well, Humility, you shall have your wish!"

He sprang upon the bed and straddled her breasts, squatting down to position his buttocks on her delightful cushions of flesh. He butted the globe of his penis at her parted lips, letting her taste the richness of her own musk and his.

A pale hand was held above her eyes. Something sparkled between the fingers. Something drifted down from them to touch her lips and the tip of his penis.

"Moonstone powder," he whispered menacingly. "The elixir of life, as used by the followers of Baron Samedi."

Humility shuddered. What was moonstone powder? And who was this sinister sounding Baron Samedi?

The Vicomte's swollen globe was brushed across her lips. Forcing the unsettling questions to the back of her mind she arched her neck to it, sipping greedily at the richness of its issue.

"Naughty Humility," teased the Vicomte, drawing his penis away, but sprinkling the moonstone powder upon the peaks of her breasts. A minute drop of his semen was added to the sparkling substance. She saw him quiver, and then he began tearing feverishly at the black robe as though it burned his skin. His dark his eyes gleamed with undiluted lust. His cruel lips parted and curled into a satanic smile. Humility felt a warm tingle upon her breasts where the moonstone powder dusted them. The tingle swiftly spiralled into a glorious sensation which spread throughout her body. She began to cry out, but her cry was quickly silenced by the Vicomte's cock, which plunged into her throat with one downward thrust.

It felt huge. The taste was luscious. It pulsed fiercely, the taut skin beating against the tension of her open lips and the roof of her mouth.

Her sex seemed to rise up; seemed to be quite separate from her tethered body. The sensations emanating from it were indescribably lovely, encompassing her whole body, enfolding it, caressing it. The Vicomte's penis was her jerking clitoris, and vice versa. They were one.

Somehow everything had changed. The scents of the garden seemed more fragrant. The sun beyond the velvet-curtained window seemed brighter and warmer. She was bound, and yet she felt free as the Vicomte spilled his copious seed into her, and her own pleasure sent her floating beyond the confines of the island.

Perhaps it was seconds later, perhaps hours, when the Vicomte lifted himself from her helpless body.

"I shall send Henri to clean you," he said, his voice bitterly cold and exact as though their coupling had never been.

When she spoke she could taste the intimacy of his body, made all the more delicious by the magic of the moonstone powder. "Could I bathe myself?" she asked meekly, longing to perform that personal task.

"I wouldn't dream of allowing it, ma chere," he said. "You are a guest in my house." He turned to her, smiling as he falsely bestowed privilege upon her.

"How can I be a guest and an owned thing at one and the same time?" Humility's voice was unwittingly sharp, for the night had been long and her intimate needs grew by the minute.

With a caustic leer he swept from the room, leaving her still helplessly bound. She glared at the closed door reproachfully; he wished her to love him and yet he had no love to give in return. A sob, imprisoned by her clamped lips, choked her throat. How bleak her future seemed! What pain would torture her body until the Vicomte tired of her!

Her misery numbed her exhausted limbs, and numbed her exhausted mind. Staring at the luxury of the satin draperies which canopied the big bed, she was only vaguely aware of the door quietly opening.

Slowly, with eyes dulled of their lustre, she turned her head in the direction of the softly creaking hinges. In the shadows she saw someone hovering.

"Ma petite," Henri's deep voice purred across the void between them.

In the half-light of the heavily curtained room she saw the huge slave, dressed only in a loosely draped loincloth. He held a bowl with steaming contents, and over one thickly muscled arm hung two or three towels.

"The Vicomte has requested that I cleanse you." He walked towards her with long silent strides on big bare feet.

She mumbled her embarrassment at her present condition, and watched him looming over her at the foot of the messy bed; watched his dark hands place the porcelain bowl between her trembling limbs. She saw the olive eyes widen as the slave saw the copious issue spilling from her sex.

"My master has used you well, ma pauvre," he exclaimed. He leaned over and pressed the swollen labia, spreading them further apart.

"But ..." Humility ached with need; ached with the terrible hunger in her sex. "But ..." she tried again. She allowed her eyes to close dreamily and licked her softly parted lips, trying to ease their dryness.

After swirling one of the white towels in the warm and fragrant water, Henri squeezed out the excess. The tinkling sound of the crystal-clear liquid made Humility aware of her other need.

With broad dark lips parted and curved in a friendly smile, Henri raised an arched brow. "But what, ma petite?"

The warm cloth on the sticky inner sides of her straddled thighs was beautifully soothing, but it was a caress, heightening the awful urgency in her pussy. Humility arched, and then bore down - anything to tempt Henri's touch to her aching sex.

"Oui, ma petite," murmured the slave. "My master warned me of your hunger, your needs. He warned me that you might try to tempt me into your embrace."

This last made Humility's cheeks burn with anguish. She closed her eyes. She had to shut the big slave out of her vision; his vigour and evident masculinity under the loosely draped loincloth. It made it all seem so much worse; her hunger, her natural needs, her urgency.

A broad thumb brushed over the naked tip of her clitoris. She thrust against it, almost without thinking.

"Oui, ma pauvre ..." The hypnotic rubbing increased, while the warm cloth washed away the evidence of the Vicomte's lust. "You must be satisfied. Your urges need to be appeased. I understand."

Humility's breathing became harsher and quicker. Her mounting desires could not be denied for very much longer, for she would surely go mad. She had again reached the point of no return.

Suddenly, and without warning, something warm and insistent was forced into her clutching channel. Trembling with conflicting sensations and emotions she opened her eyes wide, and watched aghast as Henri pushed a twisted length of towel into her.

"No ... release me," she panted desperately. "Please don't ... please release me." She tugged at the manacles at her wrists, bruising the golden skin. She tried to pull her ankles free of the shackles. She had to escape this shame - but her disloyal body stiffened for breathless seconds, and then shuddered uncontrollably from the strength of the climax which swamped her.

"You look so beautiful, Humility," murmured Henri. "You look so vulnerable and helpless." He knelt beside her, stroking the arch of her armpit and tickling the tiny bulge of muscle which lay there. His other hand strayed to the quivering mound of her pubis and tugged the soft length of cloth out.

She sighed with repletion and looked up at him dreamily.

"So vulnerable and helpless," he repeated quietly.

A great staff of flesh raised his loincloth, and she stared at it with limpid eyes.

"Yes, ma petite," he sighed, tugging at the loose covering to bare his manhood. "Perhaps you would now like to oblige me."

CHAPTER EIGHT

The girl stared beyond Jonas to some point in the corner of the room. Her eyes were wide and fearful. He towered over her, the periwinkle blue eyes glinting savagely.

"Look at me, girl!" he rasped.

She was extremely pretty and had a look of Humility, although her skin was darker and her hair raven, quite unlike his love's sun-kissed tresses.

Humility! Would he ever see her again? A small smile curved his lips as he remembered how he had bid up at the auction when the price went higher than his purse could afford, knowing that the aristocrat, Salace, was determined to have her whatever the price.

111

Jonas thrust his long legs wide apart. He was tense. Every muscle in his body bulged, twitching under the torn shirt and the grubby buckskins which clad his lower body.

"And is there no one but you to look after my interests here?"

Standing tall and angry, he was a daunting figure. His deep voice was quiet, but held an undertone of deep-felt vexation.

The drawing-room was gloomy, the storm shutters still closed. Cobwebs festooned the high ceiling and the once glittering crystal of the hanging candelabra. The fine cobwebs swayed in the warm air like ancient draperies rotted by the tropical heat.

Shaking her head nervously, the girl took a step away from the big white man. Her small toffee-coloured fingers twisted in her frayed skirts. Her soft lips trembled and her mahogany eyes looked anywhere but at him, despite his demand that she do just that.

Jonas sighed. If he expected to be met by an eager household of laughing servants he was sadly disappointed. The house was ill-kempt, the few pieces of furniture there were all but destroyed, the curtains torn and hanging in shreds at the long elegant windows. He dared not think of the state of the plantation.

"What's your name, girl?" he asked, his voice softening with his expression.

For the first time she looked at him, her dark eyes looking directly into his blue ones. "Clea, masta," she said in a servile tone.

"My name is Jonas Fairweather," he told her, allowing another slight smile to take away some of the harshness of his troubled expression. "But don't call me masta. I don't like it." It made him think of Humility. It made him think of the emir and the despicable way he had treated her - and him. He shook that disgusting memory from his mind. He paused, looking at Clea, the seconds dragging out in the lonely silence. "The word demeans you," he explained further, remembering what he had been saying.

The girl shrugged and knotted her fingers more securely in the worn cloth of her skirts. She lowered her head again, looking down at a thick dust-ball being blown about the dull bare boards.

Jonas felt a stirring in his groin as his eyes flickered over the fullness of her ripe figure. He could see the swell of a breast spilling over the simple neckline of the homespun gown. The worn cloth was all but translucent and he saw the curve of her waist, the arch of her hips. He could already feel the smoothness of her buttocks fitting very nicely into his big hands.

"Clea what?" he asked kindly, taking a step towards her, wanting to take away some of her fear of him.

She shrugged again. It irritated him, that shrug.

"You must have another name!" His irritation made him snap again and she cowered further away. He saw the sway of her breasts as she moved, and the lovely sight increased his arousal.

"I was born a slave, masta. Slaves don't get given no other name. I'se Clea." She looked up at him with those mahogany eyes, challenging him to disagree.

There was a pride about her and a lightness about her toffee-coloured skin which spoke of a high born background. Like Humility - so much like Humility. Her facial bones were delicately carved and there was an attractive flush of anger on the cheekbones. Her dark hair shimmered and swayed around her silky shoulders.

In other ways she was the very opposite of Humility, Jonas mused, allowing the brilliance of his blue eyes to glance over the lusciousness of the girl's figure. This one had a rebellious streak, whereas Humility was pliant and passive. His cock ached at the memory of her, and he adjusted its thickness in the buckskins, easing his legs to accommodate it.

Humility. He let the name linger on his tongue and let his lips form the word. He saw her as he had last seen her; naked and shackled in that hell-hole of the slave decks on the Don Cortez. And later; proud and displayed on the small platform at the auction. His fingers itched at the thought of feeling her flesh, and his arms ached to have her gathered in them.

"Humility," he sighed without knowing that he said the name.

Clea's head snapped up and her hair shone black as a starless night. Her mahogany eyes glinted in the gloomy room. She looked wary, like an animal cornered by a superior beast of prey. "What you mean, sah?" Her voice was soft and silky, but still unsure.

Jonas looked at her, puzzled.

"Humility?" said Clea, her smooth cinnamon forehead creased in fine lines. "I ain't no Humility!"

He laughed, striding over to her, suddenly coming to his senses. This time she didn't move away from him.

"Humility was a girl I knew," he explained.

Clea let him take her in his muscular arms, seeming to sense his need. "Knew?" she questioned. "She dead?"

His embrace was rough, almost violent. He knew he was causing her pain by the strength of his big hands around the curve of her waist, exploring the hollows of her back. She wore nothing under the flimsy gown, he could feel that.

It was impossible to hold back the groan of need as his fingers touched the satin smoothness of her skin. His cock throbbed between her thighs as he pushed them apart.

"I ain't your Humility," she reminded him, but she made no move to resist his advances.

"I know," murmured Jonas, his breath coming fast and shallow, his nostrils flaring as he savoured her musk. "You're Clea. My slave."

This seemed to please her, because she relaxed in his embrace; no longer tense or unyielding. Jonas heard her sigh.

"Where did everybody go?" Jonas asked absently, letting a hand slip the loose neckline from her shoulders. "The other slaves? Why is the plantation deserted?"

Clea said nothing for a moment, letting his fingers graze roughly over the bud of a large dark nipple. A barely perceptible shudder ran through her as the nub sprang swiftly to hard erection.

"Go?" She sounded vague and dreamy as Jonas brushed his lips against hers. "Salace. The neighbouring plantation. They all go there."

Desire overcame Jonas's curiosity. His lips claimed hers hungrily and she returned his kiss in the same manner. She gave herself freely to the passion of his kiss, moulding the soft curves of her body against him, grinding against the iron-hard ridge of manhood in his buckskins.

Jonas groaned softly, closing the bright blue eyes and arching back the thick cords of his neck. Her limbs were trembling against him and she nestled her head into the hollow of his broad chest. For the moment Humility was just a vague shadow in his memory, muted by the passion aroused in him by this new girl.

"Is there a bed left in this rat-hole?" he asked huskily, the words muffled in the blue-black fall of her hair.

Her answer was a musical murmur; a sweet nothing which meant everything. Jonas swept her up easily in the huge cradle of his arms. He strode from the drawing-room into the spacious hallway, his eyes darting through the shuttered gloom to the wide sweeping staircase which curved upwards to the elegant gallery.

Clea seemed weightless in his arms as he took the stairs, two at a time. She clung to him, returning his passion with a fire which inflamed him yet more.

Pointing to a door which stood slightly ajar, Clea directed him to a bedchamber.

"Through there," she said, her musical voice husky from her own need.

Using his shoulder Jonas pushed open the door and entered the room. His needs were too pressing to notice the crisp whiteness of the bedlinen, the freshness of the lace which canopied the huge bed, or the exotic posy on the nightstand which filled the room with its scent.

Only four long strides took him across the room to lay her upon the stretch of crisp linen.

"Remove your gown." he said roughly. With fingers which were none too steady he unbuttoned his shirt, gazing down at Clea as he did so.

With agonising slowness she drew off the flimsy gown. Excitement added shine to the mahogany eyes, and polish to the rose of her cheeks. Her sculptured legs were parted, and Jonas could see the blue-black curls of her sex dewed with her longing.

"Ain't had no man in a long while," she offered. Her soft lips pouted and parted invitingly, and she cupped her heavy breasts with dark fingers. "No, sah. Not in a long while."

Jonas frowned angrily. "What are you?" he rasped. He rubbed his crotch, feeling the heat and hardness of his penis. The ache was still there but his mind drifted away from Clea's boldness, settling instead on Humility's gentle compliance.

The smooth dark arms drifted upwards, lifting the firm breasts. The curvaceous hips seemed to sway across the swathe of white linen.

Jonas threw himself upon her, growling his fury, grasping the slender wrists with one huge hand. "I said what are you?!" he reminded her, his tanned face close to hers. With booted feet he viciously kicked her ankles apart.

A slight mew of pain reached his ears, but when he looked at her the soft lips were curved in a taunting smile.

"Don't you want me, masta?" she purred, letting the very tip of her pink tongue circle her mouth.

"Damn you!" he growled. "Don't call me masta!"

With one hand he fumbled at his waist to release his straining cock. The other hand still held her wrists tightly, digging into the delicate flesh and grating the fine bones.

"You're hurting me!" she whispered, but beneath the complaint her tone betrayed her excitement. Her breathing was rapid, catching in her long slender throat.

Jonas could feel the moist heat of her as he shucked his breeches over his slim hips. He could feel the tremor of her sex flesh, the erect hardness of her clitoris, and it inflamed him all the more.

Despite the open windows of the room, his exertions made him hot. He felt sweat beading on his forehead and chest, and their bodies slid together sensually. The vastly bloated globe of his cock nudged at her entrance. There was little resistance as he forced her open. He felt her swollen folds embrace him, fluttering invitingly.

With a groan he thrust hard and deep to the very limits of her womb. He felt the fine curls of her mound grate against his fair pubis, and he felt his balls slap heavily against her spread buttocks.

All too soon it was over. His semen fountained into her. His body jolted with the pleasure-waves, shaking against her as he held the sharp promontories of her hip bones.

Somehow he felt used; as though she had seduced him, rather than the opposite.

"What are you?" he asked again, heaving his heavy body from her softly accommodating one.

Pulling his breeches to a kind of order he walked to the open window, his back towards her, not wanting to see the confident expression he knew she wore.

"I was old masta's whore," she said calmly. "I was his bed wench."

Fury suffused the tanned and handsome features as he turned to face her. "Will you stop demeaning yourself?!"

"Why should I?" she spat back. "That's what I was. That's what I was born to be. Old masta bred me to be his whore."

The sinuous body curled into a tight ball on the white crumpled linen, and Jonas heard the girl sobbing softly. The sobbing, the angry words, and their demeaning nature, all combined to infuriate Jonas, and he moved quickly back across the room towards her. She looked up at him with tear-dewed eyes, but beyond the tears there was triumph. It startled Jonas and he halted for a split second.

"Yes!" she urged. "I needs a beating, masta! I needs it *so* bad!"

Jonas wished he had a belt, something leather and whippy, something which would make the gleaming hillocks of buttock-flesh smart and sting. He looked around wildly, frantic in his search.

"Here, masta! Under the bed!" Clea gestured beneath the lace valance.

His manhood, so recently satisfied, reacted sharply to the voluptuous body on the bed; the curve of a breast from beneath the snugly crouched body, the arch of a hip, the fullness of the bottom, the darkness of the cleft between the buttocks.

Following her eyes Jonas saw a black and shiny handle peeping from beneath the white lace, and he stooped to retrieve it. He heard Clea's hiccuping sobs change to rapid, excited breathing as he grasped the smooth black leather handle and stroked the black strands which followed it; long supple snakes of fine leather, so soft that they felt as smooth as human skin in Jonas's fingers.

"Yes, masta!" Clea urged eagerly again. She whimpered, arching her bottom high in the air, offering her flesh for chastisement. "It been a long time since I been punished, and I needs it so bad!"

Even offering herself for punishment Clea contrasted sharply with Humility. The pert, full buttocks were posed in such a manner as to bestow a favour upon him. She had made certain that he would see the swollen labia. Her thighs were spread and her cunney-mouth was pursed sweetly, still glossed with his semen.

"Please, masta!" she begged.

"Stop it!" he growled. "Don't use that word to me again on pain of punishment."

The whip flicked the offered hillocks and Clea gave a little mew which Jonas was sure was one of delight rather than pain. He saw a supple strand curl into the soft open sex, and saw the leather darken with her moisture.

"Give that lash to me," she begged. "Give my flesh the lashing it deserves. Old masta told me you'd be severe." The words were poured out in little husky whispers, muffled by the crisp bedlinen.

Jonas raised the whip. He was bemused. Had his grandfather discussed his likes and dislikes with this slave? It certainly appeared so. The long lashes fanned out, curling as though they were alive, wrapping themselves about the girl's bottom and hips. Her golden flesh seemed to reach out and draw up as the strands were lifted.

The crack of the whip on her flesh was loud in the soft femininity of the bedchamber. It seemed an intrusion. Jonas felt he didn't belong there.

Clea's musk seemed stronger; rich and heady as she writhed, glorying in her punishment.

"Oh, yes, mas ...!" She bit back the word he hated, but spread her thighs wider as dark weals rose on the golden skin. Trembling fingers touched her opening. "Just here!" she begged. "I really needs it just here!"

Jonas was dazed. The arm holding the whip rose and fell with clockwork regularity. His manhood arched thick and long in his breeches. The muscular breadth of his chest was shiny with the sweat of exertion.

He could see Clea's sex, so full and vulnerable and gloriously ripe, like a fruit ready to be plucked. He could see the dark, hard erection of her clitoris, like a nut kernel. "Beautiful!" he panted as he raised the whip once more.

"Yes," she agreed huskily. "Beautiful! You much better at the punishment than old masta. You strong ... you whip me good! Don't never stop! I always ready for you!" Her shining eyes turned on him, peeping beneath the tumbled fall of blue-black hair. The soft lips were parted, showing the white of sharp, even teeth.

Restraint was torture to Jonas. He threw down the whip, grunting angrily and tearing at his breeches. His cock rose up majestically from his groin. With no small struggle he shrugged out of his top boots and let his buckskins fall down his muscled legs.

Clea grinned at him over her golden shoulder, seeming not at all perturbed by the glow of her punished bottom.

"You ready now!" she encouraged happily. "You very ready to service Clea, and she wet for you!"

It irritated him, her patois. It didn't seem natural, as

though it was spoken to create a servile effect. Maybe, he mused as he climbed onto the canopied bed, it had pleased his grandfather.

Jonas flung himself upon her, rutting her roughly. "Will you always do as you're told?" he grunted into her hair.

"Always," she said obediently, arching back against him.

He could feel the heat of her buttocks from the whipping. Each stripe burned his toned belly. He gripped her hips, pulling her onto him, grinding against her.

Her sex sucked him in. It was as tutored as Humility's, even though the two girls were so very different. He tried to push Humility's image to the back of his mind, but they became merged. Humility and Clea. He could love them both. The thought fired his passion and he grasped Clea's hips even more viciously, making her whimper softly, but she met each thrust with feminine expertise.

Jonas could not hold back a groan. Pleasure spiralled from deep within, surging upwards and taking him, body and soul, with it. Somewhere far away he heard Clea call softly. The sound grew in volume, rising to a scream, and he knew she had risen with him.

He felt Clea's sex clutch his, petting it with pampering convulsions. He couldn't hold back any longer. The release was greater than his first, filling his body with sensations such as he'd never known before. Had Humility inspired such intense pleasure? He couldn't remember.

"It was good, wasn't it, masta?" she purred, sinking from her crouched position and curling into a tight ball.

Jonas rolled onto his back, and stared without seeing at the ceiling of the huge bed. "Hm!" he grunted, having not the strength to complain at her servility.

Now his physical needs were satisfied there were the problems of the plantation to consider. The Don Cortez had already unloaded its holds and all the slaves were spoken for.

"Where's Salace?" he asked at last.

"He your neighbour," said Clea. "He a Vicomte. French or some such."

"I know that," said Jonas. He grinned. "Oh yes, I know that."

A dark hand glided over his belly, not stopping until it reached the slippery warmth of his flaccid penis. Jonas frowned, trying not to react to her knowing caresses. She stroked the fullness of his ball sac, rolling the still firm little nodules gently in the fine skin.

"I'll go and see him." It had to be done. He had to face up to his adversary at some time. It might as well be sooner as later.

He felt Clea tense against his chest and her hands were stilled around the base of his penis.

"No, masta!" She sounded anxious, as though she was hiding something. "Vicomte Salace he very bad man. Very wicked!"

Jonas laughed, driving his hands into the shining midnight tresses to pull back her head and look deep into the dark eyes. "The Vicomte and I have met." He paused, grinning again. "We met in the marketplace at Cap Renaud." He remembered the venomous look the Vicomte had given him at the end of the auction. It spelled revenge. Jonas laughed out loud. "But do you think I cannot look after myself? Do you think I need to be protected from such men?"

"No, sah. You very vigorous man ..." She lowered her head a little to taste the blend of his and her juices which glossed the freshly reviving penis.

He sighed, closing his eyes as he marvelled at his own virility in her presence. "Not that vigorous, Clea," he said with a hoarse chuckle.

Her warm and agile tongue snaked around the fast growing thickness of him, savouring it as he used to savour a toffee-apple in his younger years at country fairs in England.

"Oh, yes, sah," she said firmly. "You very vigorous, but Salace ..."

Jonas looked at her nestled in a ball against him, her long legs curled lithely, one tawny arm thrown across his waist. "What are you trying to tell me, Clea?" he prompted tenderly.

She didn't answer at once; her tongue was otherwise engaged. He felt her lips suckle the beads of juices from his globe, drinking them down hungrily. Her tongue grazed lightly over and around the little frill on the underside of the erection. Her fingers slid lightly and tenderly up and down the thickening shaft. Jonas groaned, throwing his head back against the white lacy pillows.

"Salace has a pact with the devil!" she whispered at last, raising her eyes and looking with genuine fear into his.

"What nonsense is this?" Jonas chuckled uncertainly. He tousled the blue-black hair which spilled across his thighs. "You slaves are so steeped in superstition."

Clea sat bolt upright, her expression affronted. "Ain't no superstition. I was born with a caul over me, and dat gives me special powers." She glared, challenging him to contradict her. "I seen Baron Samedi and Papa Zaca!" she announced triumphantly.

Jonas used his thumb and fingers to try to relieve some of the ache in his penis. Tutting crossly Clea slapped his hand away and replaced her soft lips about his thickness. He groaned with tired pleasure and sank back into the pillows.

"Who are they?" he murmured, his voice a mere whisper as he gave himself up to Clea's wonderful pampering.

The satin-smooth lips drew upwards on his stem. Clea lapped her tongue across them, savouring his musk. "Dey voodoo gods, and dey possess folks when dey comes to earth." As the girl explained all this her patois became more pronounced. Her voice dropped to a sinister whisper. "The Baron, he specially powerful!"

Jonas folded her into his arms, holding her soft cheek and the swirl of her hair against his chest, revelling in its scent.

"Poor Clea," he soothed, almost to himself. "To believe such nonsense."

"Ain't no nonsense. You'll see."

"And these gods," he said, taking her gentle hands and placing them again on his cock, "they live here, on Haiti?"

Clea nodded vigorously, causing her hair to sweep lightly across his genitals. "Sure dey do! Dey can't cross water. Ev'ybody know dat!"

The clever lips were again on his cock, now that she'd told the story of Salace's supernatural henchmen. Jonas gave himself up to the pleasure, pumping his hips to thrust himself deeper into her throat.

"Tomorrow," he promised himself aloud, "I'm going to see for myself whether Salace is in league with the devil." He groaned as wave after wave of sensation washed over him.

Were the voodoo gods the reason he'd lost his slaves? He shook his head and allowed himself a wry smile. He was getting as bad as the girl; believing in such nonsense. He relaxed into the yielding bed and wallowed in the wonderful sensation of his balls emptying at last, the issue drawing upwards and erupting into Clea's willing throat.

Later, Jonas wasn't quite sure how much later, but the sun was making a fast descent in the tropical sky, the girl made him coffee. It was just the way he liked it; hot and strong, fragrant and dark, and sweetened with rough sugar crystals distilled from the cane in the plantation's own boiling house.

He sat in the big stone kitchen at a plain deal table, scrubbed white by dark hands in the days when his grandfather ruled the Sans Soucie estate. He sipped the strong liquid gratefully, looking at Clea over the rim of his mug.

"Why did you stay when Salace made it so dangerous?" he asked at last.

Clea sat in a high-backed rocking-chair, looking at him with those warm mahogany eyes. "Old masta too ill to move and needed looking after. I hid in the room upstairs ... his room. Hid under his bed and used his whip to protect him and me."

Jonas smiled at her gratefully.

"Field hands went first," she told him. "Papa Zaca made 'em go." She nodded, remembering, her eyes glazed with the terror of those days, then they cleared and looked straight at him. "Papa Zaca, he god of de fields."

There was the patois again, Jonas thought irritably, setting down his mug rather more noisily than was necessary. It was as if the mere mention of the voodoo gods cast a spell on the girl; making her more vulnerable to the mumbo jumbo. And that was what it was, Jonas was sure.

Clea looked at him, her face thoughtful. The dark red lips were parted, moving hesitantly as though she had something to say, but didn't know quite how it would be received.

He ran his fingers through his hair and his blue eyes

became troubled, sensing something in the girl. "What is it, Clea?" he said, taking her hand in his.

Looking into the lengthening shadows in the cool vastness of the kitchen, she remained silent, worried.

"Oh, masta - !"

"Clea!" he snapped, reprimanding her for again addressing him thus.

The fall of midnight-black hair curtained the delicate oval of her face as she bowed her head. "It'd be better if you left dis place ... Jonas." It was the first time she'd called him by name and it sounded wonderful. He reached over the table and stroked the perfection of her features with an exploratory finger, wanting to take her in his arms yet again and feel the convulsions of her pleasure.

"It bad place. Papa Zaca ..." the mahogany eyes were wide, the soft lips suddenly thin and pale. "Bad things gonna happen here!"

Jonas chuckled uncertainly. "The voodoo gods? The Baron?"

Jerking her face away from his caresses she looked at him with blazing eyes and jumped to her feet. "Don't scoff!" Her silky voice rose to a tone verging on a scream. "It bad luck!"

She was frantic.

"I'll protect you from the gods," he promised rashly, striding towards her and folding her tensed body in his arms.

Relaxing just a little and clinging to him with trembling limbs, she murmured into the broadness of his chest. "T'ain't just de gods. Dey bad enough, but dere's worse."

Jonas gathered up the thin material of her gown and cupped the heat of her sex in his hand, pushing a finger into the welcoming softness of her cleft. Only vaguely did her words intrude into his consciousness. He loved the way her receptive curves moulded against him and her whole body swayed as he petted her clitoris. Now she was more than ever like Humility.

"Dat Henri, de body slave of Salace," she breathed nervously. "Seems he loves some girl who recently come to de Salace place. Seems he crazy for her - do anything." Lowering her to the stone floor Jonas pushed up her gown, baring her thighs and the soft swells of her mound and belly. Her knees were raised and open. He could see the pinky-brown folds of her sex, inviting and gaping. Her buttocks, too, were open, still striped with scarlet weals.

"Dis girl," murmured Clea, "she de Vicomte's wench. Dere going to be trouble. I feel it ... here." She pointed to her sex and widened her eyes fearfully.

"Sssh .." urged Jonas. He knelt between the smooth thighs, smelling the richness of her musk and marvelling at the velvety folds that quivered before his eyes.

"You gotta know!" Clea continued urgently. "Salace will sacrifice de girl. Sacrifice her to Baron Samedi." She paled and bit her lip. "And if he ain't satisfied with dat he'll come for me too. I know!"

"Sacrifice?" repeated Jonas vaguely. He smoothed the love sap over the midnight curls of Clea's mound, spreading the labia outwards and making the little erection of her clitoris rise up.

"In a few days ..." panted Clea as Jonas lapped between her sex folds, "Henri swears he gonna ... kill all white men ... on Haiti. He ... he means it. He say they causing ... all the death and misery. You gotta escape!"

Jonas pondered briefly what Clea was saying. Could the girl with whom this Henri was apparently in love be Humility? Was she going to be the catalyst of an uprising?

He shook the thoughts away, concentrating instead on Clea's loveliness.

CHAPTER NINE

"But when you've finished with her, milord," Humility heard as she glided through the hall to the rear of the elegant mansion, "what then?"

It was Henri who spoke. Henri who was wise; wiser than the master. And who could be cruel at the same time as being kind.

The slave sounded eagerly anxious. Humility could almost feel his urgency driving into her, could almost feel his thickness opening her out. His huge manhood was like a drug which tempted her every day. The big man had a power in him which drew her.

Humility shuddered. The heat of the day was oppressive even in the cool shade of the mansion, but a chill made her quiver uncontrollably. She remained as still as the stone statue which supported the fountain in the centre of the hallway.

"Who knows?" The unemotional voice of the Vicomte hurt as surely as if he'd taken a whip to her. Did what they'd experienced together in the last few weeks mean nothing to him at all? He, the giver of pain, and she the receiver? "What do you suggest, Henri?"

In their separate ways both men gave her a feeling of security, a feeling of belonging, although neither displayed tenderness as Jonas had. She bit her lip, for the umpteenth time trying to drive thoughts of Jonas away. He had gone. She was merely torturing herself by thinking of him.

"Is the day close?" asked Henri dispassionately.

"When I tire of her?"

Humility felt her breasts grow heavy and full for the touch of the Vicomte's cruel hands. She had become used to his taunts, the strong fingers prodding and kneading her delicate flesh. Her belly rippled, softening with the thought of the magic moonstone powder he sprinkled upon her breasts and open sex to make her more receptive. Was she to be denied all of this after all the agony she had so willingly suffered to reach this stage?

"I must admit," said the Vicomte, "the novelty of punishing a woman who is all but white is beginning to pall. Despite her undeniable beauty the novelty of flooding her with my juices is on the wane also. What of it?"

The Vicomte was, noticed Humility, sounding bored. He sighed deeply, and she imagined him adjusting his perfectly white breeches about his beautiful manhood. She bit her lip again. What had she done wrong? Had she not been accommodating? Had she not opened her body to her master just as he wished?

Henri cleared his throat. Humility heard his footsteps approaching the partially open door. He saw her. He did not fully close the door, but allowed her to hear his plans.

"Baron Samedi is hungry for sacrifice, milord," said Henri, and Humility heard that eagerness return to his voice.

She heard the Vicomte's cruel giggle echoing through the elegant rooms. "True, Henri, my old friend," he said thoughtfully. "Very true."

Humility couldn't suppress the gasp of horror which whispered over her moist lips. Was Henri truly suggesting that she be sacrificed to the voodoo god of death? Or was there some other plan in his sharp mind? She had thought that perhaps he might love her. Perhaps protect her. Perhaps take her for his wife. She hung her head, unsure

129

of her own desires. If such a thing should happen it would be quite a tumble from her former life as a princess, but at least she would be a wife and mother, secure on the plantation.

The Vicomte laughed again; a thin laugh which intruded into her thoughts. She visualised his expression; saw his thin lips stretched tight across his even white teeth. "It's a possibility, Henri ... It's a possibility."

Humility hung her head unhappily. She was dressed in a high-waisted gown of lavender silk and gossamer muslin, and she smoothed the fine cloth, feeling the luxury of its texture. Was all this to be taken from her? After all she'd been through in her young life, was it now going to end so horribly on this forsaken island?

Jewels were pierced into her tender places, hanging heavily beneath her gown, tapping her skin as she moved, forever reminding her that she belonged to the Vicomte totally.

"Baron Samedi," she murmured fearfully, slowly sinking to the stone bench beside the fountain. The cool water tinkled musically behind her. The sound was refreshing, but she didn't hear it.

Baron Samedi, the much feared god of death. She'd already heard the legends of his evil ways from some of the other slaves who'd dared to speak of them. She tried to take in the consequences of what she'd just heard. She was to be sacrificed to Baron Samedi!

The tortoiseshell eyes closed. She saw herself quite naked, trussed to an altar, awaiting the god of death.

A sound made her lift her head. The heavy door was open and Henri was smiling down at her. His dark features showed no cruelty, but rather something else. Sympathy? Love? Humility gasped and touched her fingertips to her parted lips in realisation. Her time with the Vicomte was truly over. Lust, she realised, was what she saw in Henri's face. But it was even more than that. He had demonstrated his lust on that very first day in the slave quarters when he'd taken her in her shackles. This was more.

He took her gently by the elbow, leading her away from the salon where the Vicomte was taking his morning coffee.

"Henri ..." she ventured, looking up into his darkly unfathomable features.

"Sssh," he whispered. "Say nothing until we're well away from the house."

A thrill of uncertainty ran through her, settling in the whirlpool of sensuality which life on the Vicomte's plantation had created in her belly. It caressed the nakedness of her clitty which peeped so coyly from her sex folds.

Henri guided her through the elegant entrance hall and out into the richly scented garden which graced the front of the plantation house.

"Where are we going?" Her voice was low, full of entreaty. Her dainty slippers were darkened by the dew of the morning in the short grass. Her gown, too, was heavy at the hem, pulling the silk and muslin down to drag about her ankles.

"The dew," she whispered, looking up at Henri with apprehensive eyes. "It's spoiling my gown."

A triumphant laugh ripped from Henri's dark throat. "It matters not, ma petite!" he told her, but his huge arm was suddenly about her waist, lifting her from her feet so that she dangled like a puppet from his crooked limb.

The fine material of her gown was taut about her breasts, the soft cloth caressing the tenderness of her jewelled nipples. She wore white silk stockings held about her thighs by jewelled garters, and Henri gathered up the gossamer of the gown to lift it high over her bottom. If he revealed her buttocks with the intention of humiliating her, it did not succeed; her life with both the emir and the Vicomte shielded her from any such emotion.

She hung securely over Henri's strong limb like a rag doll, feeling the whisper of the warm air between her buttocks and over the moistness of her plump labia. The big slave, having bared the perfection of these parts, made no attempt to invade them, and in a sense this more than anything was a humiliation.

They left the splendour of the garden and entered a rutted lane, fringed on either side with mango trees. She felt the stagnant heat close around them. She felt the caress of stray sunrays fiercely penetrating the branches to strike the bared cheeks of her bottom.

The lane was quiet, the field slaves having begun their work before the first rosy light of dawn. Humility relaxed in the loop of Henri's arm, her eyes closing, lulled by the measured tread of his richly slippered feet.

"You heard my conversation with the Vicomte?" Henri asked after a little while.

"I did."

"Do you know of Baron Samedi?"

Humility quivered, shuddering her half-naked body against the big slave.

"I've been told he's the god of death," she murmured. Her voice was low, almost inaudible, as she hardly dared speak of her knowledge. Blood pounded in her temples and her breasts felt taut and full against Henri's strong body. The flesh was tender and sensually painful as the jewels pressed into them. Her nipples throbbed.

"Correct," said Henri sadly. "But pay no heed to what I suggested. Do you think I would allow you to be sacrificed to Baron Samedi, when I desire you more than life itself?"

"Then why did you suggest such a thing ..?" Humility's voice trailed away. She realised her life was once again changing, and again she had no control over its course. First she was taken from her father's palace by the emir. Then the emir threw her from his home in a fit of jealous rage because of Jonas, and as a slave she was sold to the Vicomte. Was her life now to end in painful and lonely sacrifice?

"To sow the seed Humility. He is an emissary of the devil himself, but I am sure that my desire for you will overcome the powers of evil!"

Humility was totally bewildered by what Henri was saying. Was he sincerely concerned for her safety, or were other motivations uppermost in his thoughts?

They came to a little clearing, shadowed by the overhanging branches of the lush jungle. Humility heard sounds of the richly hued birds and the growls and shrieks of other animals. They made her tremble nervously.

Henri soothed her with gentle strokes. "I am going to fight for you, ma pauvre," he comforted. "I am going to kill all the white men on the island." He gently laid her on the fallen foliage which formed the carpet on the floor of the clearing. She smelled the scent of decayed life; cloying and rancid in the heat.

"No," she sighed. "You can't do that." What if Jonas was still on the island? Tears sprang quickly to her luminous eyes.

Henri savagely clasped her breasts as he lay upon her, tearing at the jewels inserted in her nipples, making her cry out at the sharp pain. "What loyalty have you for the white men who rule us?" he whispered hoarsely against her cheek.

"My body is partly of them," she murmured. "I am as loyal to them as to those of black skin." The pain in her breasts lessened as his embrace became more tender. He hauled up the gossamer of her skirts.

Looking into Henri's fervent olive-black eyes she knew it would be politic to remain silent about Jonas. There was hatred there; terrible hatred. He wanted revenge for all the injustices he'd seen in his lifetime on the island.

"It is our time now, ma petite," he rasped.

She could feel his passion bulging solidly between her parted thighs. He clasped her slim wrists and threw them over her head while his free hand fumbled with the buttons of his breeches.

Humility made no attempt to stop him for his passion was contagious, and what he was doing, he was doing out of desire. Could she dare to hope for love?

"The Vicomte ..." panted Henri, now tearing at the bodice of her gown, "... must die, and with him, the devil!"

"But this can't be true - surely you are devoted to the Vicomte?"

"No longer!"

There was an impassioned fervour in Henri's voice, realised Humility. It made her both afraid and excited. She felt her sex peel open. She felt sure that if she did not submit to his needs she could well die with his enemies.

"You and I will rule this island!" he promised.

Was such a thing possible? Surely not.

She felt his dark thickness enter her and rose up to meet his thrusts, arching her body, offering herself as best she could although her wrists were still firmly held.

"But we are both slaves," Humility managed breathlessly. His taking was rough, forceful, and she welcomed it. She felt him pulse within her and felt her clitty twitch against him. Her lithe body writhed under him, not for any need to escape, but rather to urge him to his climax.

"Believe me, Humility," he panted hoarsely, his lips moving hungrily against her elegant neck, "we shall not be slaves for very much longer."

The grip on her wrists became tighter as his passion grew. The grasp placed a terrible tension upon her shoulders and upon her bared and upthrust breasts. The pain and the discomfort made her feel very small and very vulnerable. His penis seemed to thicken enormously, opening her out further as it was bathed with her fluids.

"What are you going to do, Henri?" Her words were no more than a panted whisper into the hollow of his shoulder.

The big man said nothing. The slow strokes of his cock into her willing entrance were measured and even, as if he wanted to extend their pleasure interminably. She could feel the heavy firmness of his balls caressing the parted cleft of her bottom. She could feel her own pleasure rising to a peak. Surely Henri could not hold out for very much longer. Humility could no longer deny herself satisfaction. She tucked her head against the solid chest and mewed her ecstasy.

This was the signal for Henri. He growled his need and began to plunge into her rapidly, viciously. Humility bravely accepted his thrusts; accepted his masterful taking and welcomed the flood of his semen as he released it into her. She cried out her joy, a cry which pierced the unusually eerie silence which now draped over the dense jungle.

"The Vicomte has planned an entertainment," Henri revealed to her much later as they lay side by side, enjoying the aftermath of their love-making.

Humility lay on the leaf and moss covered ground. Her breasts were still bared by his roughness, but she felt pleasantly drowsy. "Entertainment?" His words seemed scarcely relevant.

"A race," continued Henri, leaning over to caress the tawny swells of those naked breasts and the jewels which pierced their peaks. "Through Cap Renaud. He holds it whenever he acquires new slaves." His big dark face looked down into hers.

She returned his gaze pensively. She was curious, but fearful at the same time.

"What has that to do with me?" she asked cautiously. The tortoiseshell eyes widened with trepidation as she waited for his reply.

"You will be in that race, Humility," he imparted. "The bastard Vicomte will seek to taunt and humiliate you in front of his pathetic friends, ma pauvre." He smoothed a capable hand up and down the silky insides of her thighs, glancing lightly over the puffy wetness of her sex.

Humility quivered, wondering what new torments were held in store for her - what new humiliations.

"But we shall use the race for our own purposes, ma chere," he continued. "After the race ..." He left the words hanging in the air, like some terrible weapon to be used for revenge.

"What is it Henri?" stammered Humility, not really wanting to hear the answer. "What are you planning?"

His caresses became more intimate as his intensity increased. He smiled, but there was now no warmth in the smile. "In the chaos that'll exist after the race ... my people will revolt!"

CHAPTER TEN

The sun was high and beat down upon Humility, but she

held her head erect and proud, looking to neither left nor right. Her palomino hair was piled atop her head in the fashion of the ladies of Marie Antoinette's court.

"Nothing shall hide that luscious body of yours," Henri had said as he prepared her for the big day. "It shall be open to all viewers at Cap Renaud. The more diversion we can create, the better."

Humility said nothing, as she had been taught by Henri. She must not protest or demur at anything her masters required of her. She was now certain this was all for the best; nothing could be allowed to interfere with Henri's plans.

"The Vicomte would say that you should feel very honoured," continued Henri, "to be included in this race." He gave her a wry smile, as if to say that they knew better.

"But my hands ..." ventured the girl, and then nibbled her lower lip nervously as she realised she had transgressed.

"Are tied," agreed Henri. "It makes you look so much more vulnerable - as does this." He slapped her lightly across each breast as a reminder of the consequences for misdemeanours such as talking out of turn in front of the Vicomte and his friends.

Humility parted her soft, red lips and moistened them with the tip of her tongue as the sting of the slap made her nipples spring tautly and painfully to erection. Immediately her belly softened and she arched it outwards, silently begging for some kind of fulfilment.

"Oh, sweet girl," whispered Henri, taking Humility's hands and placing them firmly at the back of her piled hair to thrust her breasts out in the gesture of total subservience. "Would that I could please you once more." He grinned and stroked the bundle of his massive manhood in his satin breeches. "But as we both know, our lives are

137

destined for far greater things from now on."

Later that same day the post chaise, decorated with the Vicomte's coat of arms, was driven by Henri along the rough road leading to Cap Renaud. Neither slave spoke. They were each lost in their own thoughts of each other and their terrifying position in Henri's scheme of things.

Humility's breasts, held high despite the weight of the Vicomte's jewels, glowed. The tawny skin was a perfect foil for the shimmer of diamonds and rubies which dripped like tears of both water and blood from her nipples. She was a showpiece, she knew, simply another jewel to be admired by his sick friends.

Each gem was displayed in a cascade of sparkling fire, joined across her ribs by a simple gold chain. The rough road, full of ruts and boulders, caused the little carriage to jolt the jewels against Humility's skin. Any other girl would have groaned or murmured words of complaint about the pain, but Humility remained silent and stoic.

"Not far now," said Henri, giving the sweating horses a flick with his whip.

Humility turned her elegantly dressed head in his direction. "How can I race if I have no whip?" she asked meekly.

She heard Henri's breath quicken despite the noise of the trotting horses. She was aware of his dark eyes upon her and his allowance of his gaze to drift down to her open thighs.

"The horses will be changed," he told her, but his tone was guarded, as though he was hiding something from her. "Racing horses which can gallop along the straight road at Cap Renaud." He gave her a sly glance and then turned away quickly. Humility wondered at the odd look.

The race would be dangerous, she knew that. The post

chaise could overturn or collide with another competitor. Her lower lip quivered with apprehension.

Henri sighed and, surprisingly, she felt the carriage slow and then stop on the verge by the side of the road. He tied the supple leather of the reins to the whip which he placed into the little slot beside the driver's seat. The horses snorted and quivered, sending foamy sweat to spray and splash the dust around their hooves. Their smell was strong, blending with the odour of damp, heated vegetation. Humility lifted her nose, flaring her nostrils, breathing the scents of the island. Unwittingly, she closed her slender thighs, hiding her sex.

"Oh, no, my precious," Henri opened her knees, spreading her thighs to their fullest extent. "You must always be open when on display in the town."

Humility held her head proudly, her tortoiseshell eyes heavy as she caught the scent of her own musk drifting from between her splayed thighs to join the other jungle scents. Her hands ached as they remained obediently on her head, but the pain merely added to those other feelings which came from deep within. Her limbs felt lethargic. A heated sensation pervaded her body, issuing from her open sex. It was as if the sap of the jungle mingled with hers; sweet and headily sensual.

A tickle, light as the flutter of a butterfly's wing, made Humility flinch and brought her swiftly from her reverie. Daring to lower her eyes, she saw that Henri was lightly drawing the lash of the whip across her swollen nether-lips. he did it again and again until the soft leather was dark with her juices. He lifted the strand of leather to his nose, sniffing her musk and smiling knowingly.

"Delicious," he murmured, and he opened his lips to suck her taste, drinking the tiny droplets with relish. "Your love sap will give me strength for what I plan - for what I must do."

The satin breeches were suddenly open and his great dark length gleamed in the dappled light seeping through the canopy of tangled branches overhead. The silky globe was almost black with its inner flush and its natural pigment. It made the pearl of seeping semen seem all the more pure and perfect.

Humility's spillage was copious, and her inflamed clitoris peeped proudly from her swollen folds. Her breasts smarted as the nipples became more painfully clamped by the jewels at each passing moment of excitement. Again she felt the slender strand of leather between the silkiness of her parted thighs. It was damp with her juices, warm and supple. Henri somehow fashioned it in a tiny knot and looped it around her aching bud.

Leaning back on the plush seat he thoughtfully admired his handiwork, while stroking his hand slowly up and down his own length. He smiled at her, his eyes ablaze with passion. His splendour rose up stiffly from his loins.

Breathing fast, each breath in tune with the pleasure spasms which tore through her, Humility tried to speak. "The race ..." Her voice seemed over-loud in the humid silence of the trees, and the words seemed strange on her dry tongue. "The race ..." she attempted again.

Henri pulled at the whip, causing greater tension upon the loop about her tormented bud. The soft words died in her throat, throttled by her own passion and the heat of the roadside vegetation.

"Oui, ma petite?" he prompted, his voice deeply timbred, issuing from low in his broad chest. "What is it you wish to know of the race?"

"The race ..." she tried again. "Who else will be in the race?"

Henri gently tugged at the supple loop of leather, making

140

Humility mew softly. With his other hand he massaged the great column of flesh towering from the satin of his breeches even more determinedly. "The Vicomte and some of his special friends will be there," he answered huskily. His dark eyes gleamed and his broad lips curved.

The darkness of his large scrotum seemed to suddenly vibrate and draw upwards, shuddering on the richness of the satin breeches. A fountain of semen immediately sprayed from the smooth globe, splashing Humility's breasts with warm, silky pearls. She felt her clitoris swell in the loop of leather and she moaned softly, arching her long neck as spasms racked her graceful body.

"Good!" complimented Henri. "I know the Vicomte will enjoy seeing you well used!" The dark eyes glittered and the mouth curled into a slightly manic smile. "It will spark his anger and give me the excuse I need for my plan!"

Humility looked at Henri in horror; she hadn't seen him in such a mood before. He frightened her. Her jewelled breasts dripped with the blatant evidence of his passion, but she'd had no idea this was merely a part of his overall plan against the Vicomte.

The loop of leather slipped from her subsiding clitty, but the servant let it lie, teasingly, at her entrance, collecting the trickles of her pleasure.

Henri fastened his breeches, brushing imaginary specks of dust from his livery with the backs of his long dark fingers. He turned to her, his eyes ablaze. The whip flicked lightly upon the rump of one of the horses. The animal snickered, turning to eye its passengers with an expression of disdain. Humility, her tawny flesh flushed from her own ardour, drew herself high on the narrow bench of the carriage. The two horses began to move, lifting their graceful legs from the rutted dust of the road.

"You and the Vicomte -" she began.

"Cap Renaud is ahead, ma petite," interrupted Henri. "I advise you to keep close council. From now on, and particularly in front of the Vicomte and his people, I must treat you according to my station. You will understand."

The warning made Humility shudder with apprehension. The pearly drops of Henri's issue cooled on her skin, which felt unreasonably hot. In the looming shadow of the town she felt terribly exposed.

She looked at the buildings, white in the noon sunshine, the stucco looking like glossy icing sugar. Heat shimmered above the cluster of buildings, giving it the look of a mirage on the edge of the sea. The ocean itself was a brilliant ultra marine stretching to the pale horizon.

"The Vicomte ..." she ventured, "will he truly have fresh horses for my carriage?" She threw an anxious sideways glance at Henri.

The huge slave ignored her question, obviously not wanting to answer. He stared straight ahead at the busy town, urging the sweating horses forward into the bustle.

The road became more crowded. Servant women with baskets and bundles upon their heads stared at Humility. She hung her head, not wishing to meet their eyes as they stared enviously at the richness of the jewels swaying from her breasts. Even worse, she knew they also stared at the flushed pink of her open sex. Her thighs trembled with tension and she tried to close them, but was stopped by a warning look from Henri.

He drove on at a measured pace, smiling at acquaintances and blowing kisses to girls who called out bawdy greetings. A young man, handsome and richly dressed, placed a staying hand upon the carriage door. At first this young swain was dumbstruck, his sensual lips parted and his eyes glazed with wonder at Humility's beauty and subservience. She felt her skin glow more than ever beneath the heat of the sun, and the embarrassment at her subjection to the searching scrutiny.

"Is this beauty for Madame's house?" he asked, allowing his lust-filled eyes to rest upon the lusciousness of Humility's narrow waist and the swell of her hips. "If she is, may I be the first to visit her there?"

A great bellow of laughter burst from Henri. "Certainement, monsieur!" he said, looking down at the eager young man.

Humility was horrified at the servant's statement. Trained though she was by the emir, and trained as a girl to be used by men, she had no wish to return to that existence.

With the tip of the whip Henri tapped the young man's knuckles which grasped the carriage door so tightly. "You may inspect the quality," she heard him say. "Touch the heaviness of her breasts, the gentle slope of her belly, and ..." he grinned, looking meaningfully between her thighs, "perhaps even delve into her pretty cunt, Monsieur Marcel, but then we must be on our way for the race."

Inspect?

Marcel's eyes glinted with interest. "Aha!" he exclaimed, reaching out to cup one of Humility's trembling breasts. "Is she the one?"

Wondering just what he could possibly mean, her eyes widened with alarm and stared at him questioningly. She was aware of the sudden tautening of the jewelled clips biting into the tenderness of her nipples, and the experimental lifting and weighing of her breasts. She was suddenly conscious of her body as never before.

Henri nodded. "She is the one."

Marcel noticed the drying issue in her cleavage and smiled wryly. "It will be a good race," he said. He lifted the jewelled pendants upon her breasts, and stroked the fullness of each lower slope. His fingers were cool and he had a sensual touch; light and considerate.

Humility could not help but tremble. She felt herself warming to this young man's attentions. There was an uninvited moistening between her folds; a naughty quiver of her clitoris.

"Such long and elegant legs," complimented Marcel, lowering his caresses to the smooth dip of Humility's waist. "Strong too. I may yet place a small wager on her."

Long and strong legs? Her forehead creased inquisitively. What had the length and strength of her legs to do with a race run by horses?

The caressing fingers stroked the inner sides of her thighs, making her close her eyes and arch her slender back. She could not prevent the offering even though she knew it thrust her sex even closer to the young man's probing. Despite herself she felt it soften and open for him.

"Oh yes!" he chuckled enthusiastically. "It will be a fine race - a very fine race!"

Henri clicked his tongue at the horses. "Indeed, monsieur," he said politely, "but now we must go to the livery stables to prepare, and to meet Monsieur le Vicomte."

Marcel kissed his fingertips, glossed with Humility's juices, and blew a light kiss in her direction. "I wish our beautiful participant all good luck and enjoyment," he said, his voice low and seductive.

A shudder, slight and barely perceptible to the onlookers, ran through Humility's body. The race was not all it appeared, of that she was sure.

The carriage rumbled forward and Humility ventured a backward glance at Marcel. He was grinning arrogantly after her as he stood in the middle of the road with his long legs astride. He waved, and lewdly brushed his fingers to his lips again.

Ladies dressed in the very height of fashion stared in disgust as the carriage rolled past. They hid their shocked faces behind fans and spat cruel remarks in the direction of Humility.

"Sit straight!" hissed Henri. "Legs open wide and breasts high! You know what's required of you!"

Tears filled the tortoiseshell eyes, and Humility touched her pretty lips nervously with the very tip of her tongue. There was a sea of faces passing about the carriage, and curious eyes which scrutinised her with intent and disdain. The focus of most attention, she noted with an unhappy swallow, were her spread thighs and what they framed. At least, she tried to console herself, the faces were anonymous. She drew back her shoulders and lifted her head proudly, but tear-filled eyes betrayed her. Stray curls escaped the lustrous height of her hair as she looked far into the distance, trying to ignore the vile sniggers and accusatory stares.

"Humility?!"

The voice was strong and achingly familiar. Oh, how cruel her imagination!

"Humility!"

The voice again, soaring above the aimless chatter of the busy port.

"Jonas?" she whispered in disbelief. All the love she felt for that man, from the very first time she'd seen him in Dakar, came flooding back.

A gang of young men, who had until then been intent upon the other ladies parading about the town, turned their full attention to her. Their eyes locked upon every aspect of her vulnerable beauty. They cupped their groins crudely, growled their lust, and circled the carriage, forcing it to slow further.

Humility gazed longingly over their heads; it *was* Jonas! He was there, alone! Slender hands clasped upon her head, she smiled at him sadly. He was so close, and yet seemed so far away. Her quivering breasts were held high as she yearned for him across the void. The sight of him made her ache with breathless yearning.

She was suddenly brought back to her fearful predicament by a number of grubby hands snatching at her. She twisted away from them.

"Alors, young monsieur's!" shouted Henri.

Jonas could not reach her through the crowds. A sob caught in her throat as she longed to feel his safe arms about her.

"Mademoiselle Humility belongs to the Vicomte!" Henri warned. "She is brought to Cap Renaud for the race, which I'm sure you will all enjoy! Leave her be!"

The men drooled hungrily at her jewelled nakedness. Several already had their cocks in their hands, and were lewdly caressing the thick lengths.

"She's too proud!" growled one, a rough looking character with sparse stubble on his chin.

"Too beautiful!" panted another. He reached into the carriage to touch the flawless skin, but Henri swiped his clawing hand with the whip. With a curse and a grimace the fellow snatched back his injured knuckles, but viciously threw the contents of his other hand. Humility mouthed a silent plea to Jonas as spoiled fruit splattered over her breasts, spilling like entrails down her quivering belly and over her mound.

"Good shot, Davy! Haughty bitch!" sneered another young fellow.

"Get her!" The cries were of both fury and lust. The carriage was rocked and shaken dangerously from side to side.

"Get your hands off her, and off the carriage!" shouted
Henri over the din. "Do not force me to get down from
here and take the whip to each and every one of you!"

There was little doubt he could and would.

Eventually he managed to drive them a little distance to
comparative safety, where they sat in shaken silence,
catching their breath.

"Mad young bastards!" hissed Henri.

With a slight lift of her head Humility's eyes met Jonas's
across the square, and his look gave her renewed strength.
"Can we go to the stable now?" she requested sadly.

Henri grunted, clicked his tongue, and urged the horses
forward again through the streets.

"You are keen to start the race, ma petite?" he eventually
asked.

The sweet aroma of the fruit on her naked body mingled
with her own musk and made her head ache. The pulp
dripped in the stifling heat, spilling into her intimate
crevices; over the slopes of her breasts, marring the sparkle
of the jewels, and seeping between the curls of her mound.
"I wish to bathe my skin," she explained, trying to hide
the sobs which threatened, and trying desperately to ignore
the continuing jeers of the gorgeously dressed women and
the rowdy gangs along the route.

"If the Vicomte pleases," Henri pointed out.

"But why should he not allow it?"

Without responding further Henri turned the carriage
into a cobbled yard filled with grooms busy about their
tasks and, directly in front of them, stood a gleaming little
barouche.

"Only one carriage?" Humility asked suspiciously. "No
others? A race with only one carriage?"

Henri remained silent. The young grooms grinned at

147

each other, making her blush self-consciously. But this blush was not for her nakedness; she was far more ashamed of the filth smearing her body in the face of the immaculate young grooms.

"Ah, Humility!"

The Vicomte strode elegantly across the yard towards them. He smiled broadly, but a perfectly etched eyebrow arched at the sight of her condition. "I see that Henri has prepared you for the race!" The caustic smile became a full-blown laugh and the Vicomte threw back his head, making his thick hair sway from side to side on the yellow silk of his coat.

"But I need to bathe," gasped Humility.

"Non, Non," demurred the Vicomte. "You look quite gorgeous au naturelle!" He leaned into the carriage, took a smear of mango from her mound, and looked at her lazily before tasting it. "Perhaps a little over-ripe," he said slowly, "but gorgeous nonetheless." He turned to Henri. "Would you not agree, my friend?"

"She is gorgeous," agreed Henri, leaping from the carriage.

Looking from one to the other Humility felt fresh tears fill her eyes. "But may I wash, milord?" She could feel the sticky smears drying on the naked curves of her body; the despoilment. "I cannot ride in this state."

"Ride?" exclaimed the Vicomte, looking at Henri in mock perplexity. "Have you not yet told the young wench?"

Henri shrugged. "I thought I would leave that to you, milord."

There was a tense friction between the two men that had not been previously noticeable as the Vicomte turned to Humility. His eyes gleamed with ill-suppressed excitement. "You shall run before me, ma petite. I do not wish that your so beautiful figure be spoilt by indolence and laxity."

Humility caught her breath. Her hands, clasped so obediently upon her head for so long, suddenly fell to lie between her splayed thighs.

The Vicomte appeared to ignore this misdemeanour. "Yes, you will run very fast with those long legs lifted high," he explained. "And I shall follow in this barouche with my little whip lightly flicking those splendid thighs and buttocks." He ignored her gasp and the quickening of breath - but he couldn't ignore the swiftly raised breasts and the consequent tinkle of jewels.

Humility already felt the sharp pains she would have to endure. Her body flushed at the prospect of the impending humiliation.

"The higher you lift your legs, the lighter will be my little flicks." The Vicomte's long fingers probed her sex and made her sit very straight and still, waiting for his further invasion.

He drew in his breath in surprise. "How very wet you are, Humility. How very soft, and warm, and wet." His voice lowered and he spoke with a touch of menace. "Now what can you have been thinking about?" His eyes narrowed at Henri. He'd noticed the dried semen on her breasts immediately, but had placed the knowledge aside for use when he considered the time to be right. "My little plaything is somewhat aroused. Were there many happenings along the way?"

"A few, milord," Henri replied without looking at Humility. "Young Marcel -"

"Ah, young Marcel!" repeated the Vicomte, sliding his middle finger into his statuesque plaything. His eyes searched hers and she was forced to look away. "A most lascivious young man. And did you enjoy his attentions,

Humility?"

To her dismay Humility's sex clutched the Vicomte's finger hungrily as she closed her eyes sadly and shook her head. She was thinking of Jonas reaching out to her in the marketplace, and remembering the despair on his face when he found he was unable to reach her.

CHAPTER ELEVEN

The start of the race, and Humility trembled on the dusty road which stretched ahead of her. It was white and rutted, and shimmered with heat all the way to the azure sea.

She tried desperately to ignore the expensively dressed ladies and gentlemen who lined the route. The richness of their attire made her so much more conscious of her own humiliating condition. Under the blazing sun flies and insects were attracted to the sugary stickiness of the dried fruit, and they tickled unbearably as they crawled over her nakedness. With her wrists tied together at the back of her neck she was powerless to wave the tiny beasts away. Their interminable buzzing sounded loud in her ears, but above it she could hear the musical voices of the graceful ladies and the arrogant gentlemen.

"A superb little filly!" It was the Vicomte, sitting in the dainty barouche. He looked so splendid in his yellow silk coat, a long whip poised majestically in one hand whilst the reins were fed loosely through the fingers of the other. "The breasts!" he sighed sensually to the admiring audience, but so clearly for Humility's benefit. "Notice how full, but so gloriously high and firm they are. They deserve every jewel I've so generously bestowed upon them!" He blew Humility a kiss, before leaning down to brush the flawless cheek of a fair lady who looked up adoringly into his eyes.

"Turn around, Humility," he suddenly ordered. "Show these dear ladies and gentlemen your sweet buttocks."

Humility closed her eyes against the shame and turned slowly.

"Oh hurry, young lady," he chided. "We're all anxious to begin the race." He fluttered his fingers impatiently, giving the spectators an ingratiating smile. "Just show the good ladies and gentlemen the wonderfully voluptuous curves of your backside, and then we can be off!"

Dust swirled up from the road before a sudden gust of warm breeze. Tiny pieces of grit pricked Humility's flesh like a thousand vicious needles. The Vicomte's friends gathered around the barouche murmured discontentedly.

"You see, Humility," exclaimed the Vicomte. "You're causing these good people discomfort by your slowness. Turn around immediately!"

Head held high and hands clasped tightly at her neck, Humility turned, clenching her buttocks to tauten the cheeks and to display them to best advantage.

"Doesn't she look lovely?" said the Vicomte admiringly. "The tiny waist curving out to those glorious hips and backwards to those tilted cheeks."

"A glorious creature!" sighed one gentlemen. "Glorious, despite the darkness of her skin!"

"Golden!" demurred the Vicomte. "In some lights - at dusk for example, she positively glows." He looked fondly at Humility. "And look at her hair ... soft glints of blonde among the dark brown." He looked at the apex of her thighs and smiled. "I like it especially at her pussy."

"But she's wearing boots for the race!" complained a chubby and heavily rouged lady from beneath the mouth-wateringly cool shade of a ridiculously large-rimmed hat.

"Don't you think you're spoiling her?"

"And spoiling our fun?" added a spiteful-looking young lady in a slightly less large hat. "We like to see their peasant faces full of pain!"

The Vicomte considered their comments for a moment, gesturing to Henri to spin Humility round. He then inspected her from the toes of the polished boots up to her gloriously coiffured hair.

At last, having made his decision, he spoke to his assembled friends. "No, the boots will remain. I wish to keep her value, perhaps for breeding purposes. Her babies will fetch a high price at auction. I do not wish her sweet feet and legs to be cut whilst running along this rough road."

This announcement, more than anything else, brought livid scarlet patches to Humility's cheeks. That the Vicomte could even think of using her in such a way! She swallowed hard, fighting back the tears which threatened to spill over her lashes and down her cheeks. Perhaps Henri was right! Perhaps the Vicomte did deserve to die in the planned revolt!

At a signal from the Vicomte, Henri picked up a side-drum and rolled a tattoo which brought the gathered throng to silence. The loud retort snatched Humility from her alien thoughts of revenge and made her stomach churn with fresh trepidation.

"At the fire of the cannon!" announced the Vicomte, standing tall in the barouche with his arms raised, "Humility shall run all the way to the sea! For, as you must all have noticed, she is covered in filth of one kind or another!"

The spectators murmured and nodded their agreement as though they were listening to a parliamentary speech.

"Filthy girl!" shouted one anonymous gentlemen. "I'd

teach you a good …" the voice fell silent and floated away on the sea breeze as the owner realised he was in danger of embarrassing himself in front of the masses. There were a few awkward coughs.

Humility shuffled her booted feet. The warmth of her own strange pleasure rippled low in her belly, and her clitoris pouted and tensed. The boots made her more aware of her vulnerable degradation. They were so neat and clean. They were so highly polished, clinging snugly about her ankles and calves, although loose about her thighs. The slightest movement caused the soft leather to caress the tenderness of her sex, and increased the uninvited feelings of relish. Humility bowed her head and nibbled her lip, hoping that the fine ladies and gentlemen would not notice the juices on the high cuffs of her boots.

"Are we ready, Henri?!" shouted the Vicomte, sitting forward eagerly on the seat of the barouche.

Henri nodded.

An expectant hush descended.

Raising her head and squinting a little in the bright sunshine, Humility saw, way up ahead along the road, a soldier from the tiny garrison touch the fuse of a cannon with a lighted taper. She felt her limbs begin to tremble in anticipation as she watched the smoke of the burning fuse.

The noise of the explosion startled her.

As she lifted a leg to take her very first step she heard a cry of glee from the Vicomte. It made her tremble all the more, for she now wanted so much to run the race well; to run fast and to look graceful; to beat the Vicomte!

"Higher, Humility!" His voice was full of enjoyment. But then why should he not be delighting in what he was witnessing? He owned her. He could do with her whatever he chose; use her for good or ill. She lifted her head proudly, trying to do her best. She stretched her neck, flared her nostrils, and breathed in as much of the tropical air as she could. Her breasts heaved upwards and her muscled belly curved as she sucked it in.

The whip flicked her buttocks and seemed to scoop them up as it cracked against the flesh. The race was on, and Humility's long legs sped along the dusty road, sending up clouds of dust which encrusted upon the splashes of fruit pulp. She heard the noise of the barouche wheels, and heard the sound of the trotting horse. After only a few yards she was breathing heavily, much to the delight of the cheering crowds lining the road. Some yelled for the Vicomte, crying that he should crack the whip harder and flay her tawny skin. Others cheered encouragement to Humility herself.

"Run, Humility! Run!"

Was that Henri's voice urging her on? With the blood pounding in her ears it was hard to discern. Sweat coated her golden skin and dripped from the tip of her nose.

"Beautiful, Humility!" That was the Vicomte, she was sure.

It was becoming increasingly difficult to lift her legs, clad as they were in the thigh-high, strength sapping boots. She tried so hard to be graceful. She tried again to lift her long limbs higher, but as she did so her knees brushed her breasts and caused the hanging pendants to sway heavily back and forth.

The reward for her pains was a harder flick of the thong of leather which cracked across the upper slopes of her buttocks. Although the blow stung she did not resent it. It was accompanied by words from the Vicomte; words which were sensual and caressed her ears just as surely as the whip caressed her buttocks.

"Let the ladies and gentlemen see your unique beauty, Humility! Show yourself with pride!"

His breathing was heavy too, and when she ventured a glance over her shoulder she saw his topaz eyes gleaming with wild excitement.

The whip flashed from side to side, urging her on, catching her buttocks with engaging flicks which stung her as she ran faster and faster. It was bizarre; Humility felt calm, almost happy. She was actually enjoying the exercise of the race. Her breasts were held high, as was her head. Her knees were brought up at every step.

"Exquisite, ma cherie!" urged the Vicomte. "Quite exquisite!"

Higher still went Humility's long legs, and her buttocks seemed to pout with pride as the little lashes of the whip found their mark. The more the people cheered, the faster and more gracefully she ran.

The Vicomte's voice was fading now as Humility gained ground and acquired her second breath. She could see the enticing sea and the diamonds which always seemed to dance upon it. She could smell the fresh salt on the breeze. The sailing ships anchored out in the bay rode the small waves with ease and looked quite beautiful, framed as they were by the coconut palms which fringed the view.

It was all so lovely. Even though she was a slave, she suddenly felt peaceful and happy. But then, for how long? What of Henri's plans?

She at last reached the sea and fell to her knees, her full breasts heaving as she panted and gulped for air. She barely noticed the pain of the clips holding the heavy jewels. Her golden skin was glossed with sweat. Drops of salty moisture ran into her mouth, and trickled down her neck and between her cleavage.

Eventually Henri was by her side, smiling his admiration. "You did well!" he panted. "The Vicomte is pleased with your performance!" He bent to whisper in her ear, looking round furtively as he did so: "Not long now, cherie, and we shall both be free."

Humility shuddered at the significance of these words. They troubled her greatly.

"You lifted your legs high," continued Henri in his normal voice. "The Vicomte admires that. Other girls who've previously taken part in the race have stumbled as they tried to escape the whip." He grunted and shook his head. "That is not possible. It is the whip that gives the greatest fun."

"I know," she said shyly. She peeped at him, her sensual mouth open a little as she darted her tongue across her scarlet lips. Her buttocks glowed with the sting of the lash.

Henri lifted her in his arms and placed her upon a hillock of coarse grass. He removed her boots. The freedom felt delicious and she stretched her legs and wriggled her toes. The big slave was gentle as he untied her cramped arms, allowing her to lower them and ease her stiff muscles.

"Where is the Vicomte?"

"He is over there, with his friends." They both looked over their shoulders at the Vicomte, who stood by the barouche where the road swept alongside the beach. He was beaming proudly and receiving the congratulations of the privileged members of the crowd who'd been invited to assemble at the starting line, and now milled around their hero at the finishing line.

"Run!" Henri suddenly slapped one of Humility's thighs. "Run to the sea and bathe. You've done well, and you now deserve the freedom!"

Humility needed no second invitation. She rose and sped eagerly across the white beach, the fine sand feeling soft and warm between her toes. Her exhaustion was forgotten. Her slender arms were thrown back behind her body like the resting wings of a bird. Her hair had fallen loose from the intricate coils and trailed like a golden shimmer down her back.

"Beautiful!" she heard as she plunged into the clear blue water. She turned to see Henri watching her avidly as he bared his huge body to the sun.

Others were now gathering on the shore, their richly coloured garments enhanced by the deep blue of the sea and the paler blue of the sky. All eyes were on Humility.

She arched fluently out of the warm water like a shimmering mermaid reaching for the cloudless sky. As she ducked again beneath the surface she felt Henri splashing beside her. His strong arms clasped her thighs and his urgent lips grazed her labia.

"Now my servants will delight you all with a display of their sexual talents." The Vicomte stood with his friends, smiling at the two splashing bodies in the water. But the smile was tight and his eyes were dangerously dark with envy.

Humility's face burned, despite the wonderfully refreshing water. She grasped Henri's shoulders and struggled in his persistent hold. "Put me down," she whispered, whilst glancing timidly at the watching Vicomte in the distance. "I'm afraid."

"But this is our chance!" rasped Henri excitedly. "Don't you see?!" He carried her through the water to the white beach, laying her down at the very edge of the softly lapping waves. He held her gently in his arms, allowing his lips to brush her taut nipples, one by one, arousing a melting sweetness in her. His sturdy legs enfolded hers, but despite the wonder of the embrace she was still fearful of the Vicomte, the wind buffeting his long hair and his hand shading his menacing eyes.

"Is she clean?!" her master's voice cut across the sand. It sounded cold and cruel, whereas, such a short time ago, it had been warm and encouraging. The chill of it made her shudder against Henri's nakedness.

"Oui, milord!" shouted the huge servant, lifting her in the cradle of his arms.

"Then bring her to me!"

Humility tensed. There was a terrible tension between the two men which even reached across the distance between them. It was a terrifyingly dangerous hatred.

Droplets of water sparkled and fell from her body like diamonds as Henri set her on her feet. Her nipples were erect and her breasts lifted. The jewels trembled and shook against her dusky skin.

"You are mine!" hissed the Vicomte, dragging her to him, leaving Henri very naked and very vulnerable. Humility looked to the big slave for some guidance, and her gaze was drawn to his hugely erect penis. She understood all too clearly. The Vicomte was envious of his slave, and Henri was using the friction between the two of them to start the uprising.

"Lie down - on your belly!" The orders were barely audible; her owner was so angry he could hardly spit out the words.

The crowd of onlookers were drifting away, embarrassed by the obvious envy shown between master and slave. Humility lowered herself to the white sand, her arms outstretched before her and her long legs open.

"Lift your bottom!" The Vicomte growled the command without taking his glaring eyes from Henri, and Humility became increasingly conscious of the glow remaining there; the little stripes of heat criss-crossing each perfect cheek. She was aware, too, of the silky wetness between her labia increasing as she arched her back.

"Shameless!" hissed the Vicomte to no one in particular. Envy dripped from his tongue. "You see how shameless she is?!"

The white shore was almost deserted now. A few stragglers stood hesitantly watching the bizarre tableau. Some stayed to admire Humility's beauty; her subjection, the obediently lifted and chastised buttocks. Some had their eyes firmly fixed on Henri's naked magnificence, at the darkness of the erect shaft which gleamed with the sheen of sea water and his own issue. Others could only gloat at the undisciplined display of envy by the Vicomte.

With a total disregard for his own dignity the aristocrat tore at his breeches and fell upon Humility. Henri turned away, unwilling to witness this performance which he knew was born out of spoilt jealousy, and intended to demonstrate just how worthless their existence was considered by the Vicomte and his entourage.

"Where the hell do you think you're going?!" spat the Vicomte.

"I thought -"

"You are not in my service to think! You will stay and watch until I say otherwise!"

His taking of Humility was intentionally rough and uncaring, but the lovely slave girl accepted him bravely. As the Vicomte plunged into her helpless body he fixed his stare on Henri; challenging him to react - to defend her. But the slave returned his stare passively, the only signs of his seething rage and hatred being his clenched fists and his clenched jaw.

CHAPTER TWELVE

"You do not have to go through with this, ma pauvre," said Henri anxiously. "You are so young and so very beautiful. You have your whole life ahead of you."

"If the Vicomte says I must be punished for my wantonness, then I must be punished. And surely it is the distraction you're looking for?"

"Yes ... but nobody has ever survived at the hands of Baron Samedi. Let me kill the Vicomte now and spare you from this nightmare -"

"No Henri," she touched a finger to his lips and answered softly. "You cannot risk yourself. Your followers need you."

Humility stood naked and very still as the big slave dressed her mane of tawny hair in high coils. Her tortoiseshell eyes stared straight ahead, beyond the open window of her room to the lush garden. The exotic plants were tinged blood-scarlet by the setting sun.

After the race Henri had returned Humility to the Salace plantation. She was bruised and sore from the vile way the Vicomte had plundered her on the beach. It was then that Henri had decided once and for all to precipitate his revolution.

"Perhaps it will not be so bad, Henri," she murmured bravely. "Perhaps Baron Samedi will be merciful." She looked at him with wide and limpid eyes.

Placing a last pin in her hair, Henri said bitterly: "I do not think Baron Samedi is ever merciful, ma petite." He stroked the perfection of her breasts, enjoying the silkiness of her skin, and allowing his fingers to linger on the dark brown buds of her nipples. Humility bit her lower lip as she enjoyed the painfully teasing caresses.

"What does he look like?" she managed bravely. Her voice was stilted and thick from the intimate caresses. The huge slave slid a hand over the tight swell of her belly, and then sideways to the curve of her hip, making her quiver with delight.

Henri shrugged and she saw his satin livery swell at the join of his trunk-like thighs. "No one is sure. There are some who say he's a monster - half goat and half man. And then there are others who say he's old - as old as the hills themselves." The slave allowed his hands to fall wearily from her body as he turned away and looked out upon the stillness of the tropical garden. He paused, his smooth dark features creasing into a frown. "But I suspect that he is truly someone we both already know well."

A nervous little laugh escaped Humility. "We both know well? What do you mean, we both know well? I don't understand, Henri!"

"It is said that the god of death inhabits the body of anyone who is willing," Henri said, his voice betraying both his anger and his fear.

Humility shuddered violently. The sun was nearly set, and it would soon be time for the carriage to take her to the clearing in the dense dark forest where she would meet the god of death, if such a one truly existed.

Picking up a china pot from a dainty rosewood side-table, Henri turned again to face her. His dark eyes glistened in the fading light. Pain was etched in merciless lines on his features. "Don't be fooled if that devil seems to be the kindest of gods," he warned. "His kisses may be the most sensual you have ever experienced, but ..." he paused, apparently lost for words.

"But what, Henri?" A frown creased the smooth skin of Humility's forehead and she tipped her pretty head to one side, perplexed and anxious.

A groan, a deep-throated groan of agony, rose up from Henri's lungs. "Oh, ma petite!" he said hoarsely. "I would give anything to offer myself as a sacrifice in your place!"

A sweet smell reached Humility's nostrils and her wide eyes darted to the little china pot held in Henri's big hand. She remembered the moonstone powder which the Vicomte had used upon her so effectively. She remembered the unbelievably ecstatic sensations it had brought upon her body; upon the perfection of her breasts and amid the folds of her sex. Even in her mouth she had tasted paradise at the sprinkling of the bright dust. However, although she yearned to experience such glorious pleasure again, she knew that too much would take her to realms of pleasure from which she could never return.

"What's that? What do you have in the pot?"

"Molasses," Henri replied.

"Oh," Humility sighed with relief, "is that all? And why do we need molasses?"

"To feed the ants, ma petite," answered Henri sorrowfully. He dipped a large forefinger into the pot and brought it out dripping with dark syrup. He stroked it across the upper swell of Humility's breasts. A barely perceptible quiver made the lovely hillocks of soft flesh shimmer under his attention. The merest touch of Henri's gentle but strong finger made her sex pout and swell, and caused her whole body to glow with the tenderness she felt for him.

"I can bare the nips of a few ants," she said with more courage than she actually felt, her lovely soft lips flickering a little in the sweetest smiles.

"Oh, ma petite," sighed Henri again, drooling the thick sweetness around each nipple and watching the stickiness trickle in golden trails down the curves of her body. "You do not know the pain those tiny jaws can inflict ... Pray that I am able to reach you before you are tortured too far!"

Standing very still she tried to prevent more quivers of fear as he caressed the substance over and into every lovely hillock and crevice. She felt him smear the sticky syrup deeply into her bottom crease, paying special attention to the wrinkled tightness of her little rosehole.

Each of the tawny curls on her mound were smoothed and coated with the thick molasses. Humility was surprised that he didn't invade her sex with the treacle, but she didn't allow any hint of that surprise to show; Henri knew what he was doing.

The busy forefinger dipped into the pot again and was withdrawn more thickly covered than before. "Red soldier ants," he continued, his voice stifled and unnatural, "scorpions, black widow spiders, and ..." he paused again, tilting the pot to pour more of its contents into his palm.

Humility stood as still as the trees beyond the window in the calm of the balmy evening. The gentle movements of Henri's conscientious hand was soothing, although the heat of the evening was becoming unbearably oppressive under the layer of molasses. "And what, Henri?" she prompted, although she wasn't sure she wanted to hear any more.

"Snakes, ma pauvre. Poisonous snakes. They are all devoted servants of Baron Samedi."

A knife with a long silver blade and a thick, richly carved ivory handle somehow appeared in Henri's other hand. Humility watched with fascination as the blade flashed, reflecting shafts of silver and red light from the setting sun. She was slightly bemused as he held the weapon by the razor-sharp blade and presented the handle for her inspection. The carvings were ancient, smoothed by hundreds of years of use, but the figures were still quite clear. Humility's eyes widened yet more at the disconcerting scenes which became clearer as she studied them.

A huge serpent coiled itself around two helpless figures, both bound close together upon a stake. "The Garden of Eden," she murmured fearfully, lifting her eyes to meet the olive-black of Henri's.

"Indeed, ma petite," confirmed Henri, holding the knife even closer to her. "And the snake?"

Humility tried to focus upon the ivory carvings. She gasped at what she saw. "The tail of the snake protrudes from Eve's fleshpot!" she stammered hoarsely. Her own sex seemed to blossom. It became moist with her love-dew and swelled with a desperate yearning. It ached, as it always did when she was aroused.

"And it's head, Humility?" he pursued. "Where is the serpent's head?"

Humility's hips instinctively arched forward. "The serpent …" She shuddered and panted breathlessly.

"Yes Humility?"

"The serpent is …"

"Yes, what about the serpent?"

"It's swallowing Adam's penis!" She felt a thickness within her, as though she had become the serpent. Sensations spiralled around her, making her soar ever upwards to an exquisite orgasm. "Ooohhh …" she sighed. "Oh, Henri, I cannot bear this pleasure. Have you sprinkled me with moonstone powder already? Make it stop! Please make it stop!" The empty aching became worse. Her sex felt, for all the world, like her belly when it was hungry. The emptiness grew for a moment, making her gaze questioningly at Henri, then it subsided, but only a little, like a wave rolling gently upon a sandy beach. Then it began again. The sensations grew, gathering strength, making her crave fulfilment.

"Does the knife possess magic powers?" she gasped at last, her breath coming fast and shallow.

"Oui," he whispered, "there are some who say so." He began to coat the ivory handle with molasses, looking with sorrowful eyes upon Humility's angelic beauty. "They say it possesses black magic which comes from Satan himself." His jaw was set, angry that Humility should have to suffer so for the sake of the revolutionaries, but then the evil on the island had to be - and would be - overthrown. "Salace!" he suddenly hissed venomously.

Humility, still in the throes of delicious pleasure, felt her smooth limbs quiver. Her legs began to shake and weaken, and yet she splayed them further. She thrust them wide, bent at the knees, and arched her pelvis. There was little she could do it seemed, to prevent herself from offering herself for sacrifice to the talisman.

"The knife, Henri!" she groaned. The tortoiseshell eyes reflected her inner-turmoil as she pleaded for the handle of the knife to be inserted into her offered sex. She massaged her swollen labia, opening them to bare the gleaming inner lips.

"The knife." She spoke with more dignity now. Despite her confusion she was calmer; resigned to her fate. The training at the emir's palace stood her in good stead. She could take the continuing pleasure of orgasm over and over again.

The big slave looked at the flushed folds of Humility's sex, and then down at the dripping ivory handle. The shimmering stickiness clung in heavy beads to his dark hands. "Not yet," he whispered pensively.

Laying the knife down he picked up a piece of lint and hurriedly wiped his hands.

"Oh, Henri," murmured Humility. "What are you doing? Please, you know what I need!" Shockwaves of pleasure made her slender body shake. Her breasts were uncomfortably tender and overfull, as though the fine skin would burst.

Henri looked grim as he shucked out of his luxurious livery, throwing satin garments carelessly to the floor until he was naked. His magnificent penis rose majestically from the darkness of his thickly curled pubic bush, and pulsed eagerly against his flat belly. It gleamed in the fading light. With a voice croaking emotionally he proclaimed his love for the poor girl. "It is my fault that you are to be tortured." He smeared himself with the molasses as he spoke. "I shall go to Baron Samedi's altar myself. I shall do whatever must be done to save you from that!"

"No!" Humility threw herself at the man. "You cannot! I will not allow it, you have far more important tasks ahead of you! You must lead your men! They need you! They are lost without you!"

His musk blending with the sweetness of the molasses was heavy in the air.

Suddenly his feverish lips were hard upon hers, searching and setting her soul aflame. He crushed her to him and their bodies slid and squelched, slick with syrup and sweat.

"You?" he snapped as their kiss ended. His sardonic smile was cruel and tender at one and the same time. "Who are you to say what I can or cannot do?"

His confusing plethora of moods bewildered her further, but she lowered her eyes and answered submissively as she knew she should, "No one - I am no one."

She could feel his thickness throbbing against her belly, long and powerful, its globe already coated with silky issue.

"But you are a very special no one," he sighed, lifting and cradling her in his arms.

She closed her eyes and felt him bend to explore the length of her body with his mouth, licking at the forest of curls on her mound and delving into the crevice of her sex. The kisses were slow and dreamy, and Humility could do nothing but give herself up to them.

"But , mmm …" she murmured weakly as he laid her gently on the bed. "But, Baron Samedi …"

"He must wait."

Humility felt him throw her slender arms above her head. His superior strength meant she was utterly trapped. His heavy body lay upon hers and a shovel-like hand gripped her wrists like a vice.

"But," her whisper was barely audible through her awe and trepidation, "he is a voodoo god!" The passions aroused in her by the magical knife were replaced by even greater ones. She felt her sex convulsing between her spread thighs, grasping at Henri's flesh. She felt her clitoris swelling and burning. Juice seeped warmly from her folds to dew the silk of her inner thighs with pearls of excess.

Henri growled, probing at her entrance with his turgid globe. "And there are some who say he is nothing more than a mortal man … an evil man." He was breathing heavily, the breath rasping hoarsely in his throat as he butted her opening.

"A mortal man?" whispered Humility in disbelief. Henri entered her, making her sigh blissfully and causing her body to lift his weight in her eagerness to take all of his length.

"Possessed by the god," he grunted, stressing each word

with a slow thrust of his hips. "Samedi … possessed by Samedi."

His words barely registered in Humility's spiralling mind. The passion seared her. She burned as in a fever. Her head spun. The room in which she lay was no longer real. Henri thrust himself into her, his thick penis opening and invading.

"Possessed?" The word drifted dreamily from her moist lips. The only real sensations were those arising from her sex. "How?" she managed. The big slave seemed to be consuming her with his ardour. She felt his sweat dripping from his broad forehead, dampening her lashes and her carefully dressed hair. He moved his mouth over hers, devouring its softness, stilling the questions which still hovered there. Humility felt the pulse of his manhood and knew his summit was close. With a swift and practised petting she allowed her sex folds to cosset his length. She heard him groan appreciatively and felt his stroke quicken. Pleasure engulfed her. Little else had any meaning. The soft night perfumes drifting in from the garden; the evening breeze; the musky odour of Henri's body - all blended to make her passion that much more memorable.

"Oh, Henri!" she sighed as she felt a great fountain of semen wash inside her. It came not once but many times. "What will happen to us now?"

A grunt was his only reply as he shuddered on top of her. In their pleasure-throes the young lovers were unaware of ought else. They did not hear the slight creak of the hinges as Humility's bedroom door eased open. Neither did they see movement in the deep shadows of the moonlit room. If they heard a soft footfall of expensively clad feet they were not aware of it until it was too late.

"So, my good and faithful servant!"

Sheer terror gripped Humility at the sound of the Vicomte's voice. She stiffened, her tortoiseshell eyes wide with the shock of the unexpected intrusion. He was there, in the doorway, his menacing topaz eyes glinting evilly. He held a three branched silver candelabrum above his head, uncaring that the wax dripped hot onto his fingers.

Behind him stood two of the other house slaves, huge and ebony black, wearing breeches and white full-sleeved shirts. They each held folded ropes and grinned broadly, and with evident relish, at the two on the bed.

Humility had known since she arrived at the Salace plantation that Henri's position with the Vicomte was much envied by the other house slaves. Instinctively she clung for protection to the man who embraced her. Her pulse thudded in her temples. "No!" she cried. She could feel Henri's manhood, still thick and throbbing, immersed within her own warmth. Her body ached at the thought of what the Vicomte might do to his slave.

The cruel eyes taunted her, looking more wild in the light of the flickering candles than she'd ever noticed before. With a disdainful wave the Vicomte dismissed her as of no account. "Who are you," he sneered, "to speak words of protest to me?"

And who are you, cried Humility's fearful mind. Are you a devil, or are you a man?

He was exquisitely dressed as always, but there were dark shadows under the eyes as though he'd slept little, and his long dark hair was unkempt, hanging in greasy tendrils. "How dare my newest little whore presume to rule my household?" His words were carefully chosen and honed by the mouth of a master. They stung Humility, lashing her like the thongs of a whip. How could the Vicomte ever have proclaimed a love for her if he truly thought of her in such a manner?

"Take this man away!" he ordered. "And then continue to prepare this whore for the good Baron." A bitter smile curled the thin lips. He was clearly enjoying the prospect of inflicting suffering upon them both.

Henri didn't struggle as he was hauled roughly away from Humility. She reached for him as he slipped from her grasp. He smiled at her, but his smile lacked conviction. He swore words of revenge and brave promises. "A curse on you, Salace!" he spat angrily as the two men dragged him towards the open door. "You thrust the girl upon me when you tired of her, and now that - !"

"When did I ever say I was wearied of her?!"

"The evening of the race!"

"Get out! Get out of my sight!"

Naked and held firmly by strong hands Henri was taken from the bedchamber. Icy fear twisted around Humility's heart as she was left alone with the Vicomte. With eyes wide in the darkened room she looked up at him, waiting to hear what terrible fate now awaited her. She wondered what despicable punishments he would devise.

"And so, Humility," he approached the bed, shaking his head like a disappointed parent. "Again you spurn me for my body servant." The elegant candelabrum was waved slowly over the glistening length of her body. It paused only momentarily at the upthrust hillocks of her breasts and the glossy curls at her mound.

"Again, milord?"

"On the beach - it was clear then that you desired to be with him more than with me. Highly embarrassing, young lady, to be belittled by two slaves. And in front of my friends, too. That sort of behaviour will just not do."

"As you said milord, I am not worthy of you. I am nothing but a whore - a plaything for your pleasure, if and when you choose." Perhaps this admission would appease him.

The swansdown mattress dipped as he sat beside her, and she stiffened with apprehension at his closeness. The laugh which whispered from his aristocratic throat was low and sinister. "Come, come, Humility, what nonsense are you trying to convey?"

In a complete daze of fear she watched him place the candelabrum on the night-table, watched his hand hover over her trembling breasts, watched a finger flit around the taut peak of a nipple. "Molasses?" he questioned, but she knew instinctively that he required no answer. The manicured fingertip made its way to thin lips which bore a satanic smile. A slender tongue snaked out and licked at the digit. Humility shuddered; the tongue reminded her of the serpent etched so artistically upon the ivory hilt of the dagger. "Such sweetness. And it's all been wasted upon that heathen slave of mine." The finger drifted down to her tensed belly, which rose and fell slowly with her shallow breathing. Humility winced, waiting for the next touch - but it never came.

"Wasted," the Vicomte repeated sadly.

He glanced about the room and saw the knife discarded by Henri earlier. "Mara!" he shouted suddenly.

A pretty, ebony-skinned girl with fiery red lights in her hair and dressed in a plain white dress, belted tightly at her narrow waist, walked timidly into the room. She cast cautious glances at Humility's nakedness.

"You see, Humility," said the Vicomte, "how very obedient and humble is Mara? How quickly she responded to my command? That is what I expected from you." He sighed, his disappointment clear. "If only you had lived up to my expectations, Humility. If only ..."

He bent from the waist and Humility watched him lean

closer and closer until his thin lips covered hers and she experienced the passionate, but cruel, ravishment of her mouth.

"If only," he repeated as their lips parted. He turned to Mara, who stood so meekly awaiting her master's bidding. "I must leave now, there is a task of great importance to be done. You know what you must do to prepare this wicked girl for Baron Samedi?"

"Oui, milord," the servant replied. Her voice trembled and she seemed unable to look at Humility. "She must be smeared in molasses to attract the ants and scorpions, and the knife must be driven into her until she feels the pulse of the serpent."

The Vicomte smiled sadistically. "Quite. And mind you do your duties well, otherwise it'll be you visiting the Baron next!" Mara trembled visibly. "I'll not be long," said the Vicomte arrogantly as he looked down at Humility one last time before leaving the oppressive atmosphere of the bedchamber.

The two girls did nothing but look at each other for some time. Mara toyed awkwardly with the front of her skirt, before eventually breaking the difficult silence by shyly asking Humility to stand. "And we must hurry," she added, "they say the wrath of the Baron is terrible if he is kept waiting."

Feeling hot and uncomfortably sticky, Humility rose from the bed. "Can you bring water so that I may wash? Henri –"

"I know what Henri did." The shy voice became sharp and brittle. "And there is no time for you to wash."

Humility stood quite still, shocked by the sudden change in the girl's shy demeanour. There was a new hardness in the brown eyes, a pursing of the wide lips. There was cruelty, too, in the smearing of fresh molasses upon her

172

skin. The pinches and prods, thought Humility, could not be entirely by chance.

"And now the knife," said Mara, smearing syrup upon the ivory figures on the carved hilt. Humility shuddered with increased apprehension. "Open yourself," urged Mara. "Quickly!"

With trembling fingers Humility did as she was told. Her labia were swollen and quivering, slippery with Henri's juices and her own. Mara sank to her knees before her. The knife hilt seemed to grow larger and darker under the coating of molasses. It seemed to pulse, the end becoming thicker and more bulbous. Humility was sure she could see the sinewy body of the serpent trail slowly up the hilt. It was twisting and undulating as it grew larger and climbed higher about the embracing figures. She was going mad! Her eyes closed. Her lips parted as she waited for its disgusting touch. They peeled opened to form a perfect O. She held her breath.

"Yes!" sighed Mara from below. "Oh, yes! I shall kiss your little bud. I shall close my lips about it as I plunge the knife. It will drive you quite mad with ecstasy, and the Vicomte shall never lie with you again!"

Humility groaned, but could not close her lovely thighs or release the hold upon her labia. She felt the promised lips, soft and adoring, pursed around her bud, abrading it with gentle strokes. She felt herself begin to shake uncontrollably as the tip of the hilt eased her entrance further open in readiness for her total violation.

Pausing in her attentions to Humility's sensitive flesh, Mara looked up, her lips and chin slick with juices. "Feel the serpent's movements, Humility," she hissed. "Feel how it moves within you ... Can you feel it?"

Humility held her breath again and nodded hypnotically, and then the ivory hilt pushed slowly and inexorably up into her receptive warmth. "Yesss ..." she murmured dreamily. "I can feel it. I can feel it moving within me." Her hips swayed lazily, and her pubic curls brushed the kneeling girl's face.

Rising to her feet, Mara kissed Humility with an intimacy which left her feeling even more weak, more excited, and more confused. "The carriage will collect you in a moment," she whispered into Humility's hair. "You will be bound by your wrists to the roof, and your ankles will be shackled to the floor."

"But the knife?" gasped Humility. Her eyes sparkled with tears in the flickering candlelight.

"You must hold it within yourself, with your legs open so that your lovely thighs are unharmed by the sharp blade."

Silky juices flowed from Humility's sex at every pulse of the magic serpent. "I cannot hold it!" she sobbed, and tears brimmed on her dark lashes.

Mara shook her. "You must! Do you wish to displease the Vicomte even more than you have already?" Her dark eyes flashed. "And even worse, do you wish to displease Baron Samedi?"

It was impossible to hold back the moan which was part pleasure and part fearful apprehension. Humility trembled, knowing another orgasm was close, and more juices would make the ivory hilt even more slippery. With a tremendous amount of effort and concentration she gripped the weapon.

Mara appeared to recognise what was happening, for she gave a nod of satisfaction. "Good, you are ready now." She led Humility to the door. "I shall take you down to the carriage."

CHAPTER THIRTEEN

Charles de Salace shuddered through a cataclysmic orgasm, but he took no great satisfaction from it. His mind, it seemed, was not part of his body. His head ached intolerably. Somehow nothing seemed in focus.

"Get out of here! Get out at once!" he growled, pulling his cock from the shuddering girl. Nothing could please him now - nothing.

The girl cowered, her ebony body curled upon the silk expanse of his bed.

Only a few hours ago he would have enjoyed her immensely. The pert roundness of her young breasts would have delighted him. The dark aureoles of her nipples would have been teased unmercifully by his thin lips and sharp white teeth. The nubile suppleness of her limbs would have wrapped gracefully about his waist, abrading her mound of soft curls delightfully against his groin.

"Oh, monsieur - " she began, looking up at him with uncertain eyes.

"Didn't you hear me?!" he growled, easing himself from the bed and stooping to pick up from the floor the satin robe he'd earlier discarded.

A long thin blade of wood, smooth and whippy, was suddenly in the girl's hands as she knelt upon the rumpled bedcovers. "Perhaps, master," she began hesitantly, "the paddle on my bottom would make me more enjoyable for you."

The Vicomte's eyes, until then so dull and listless,

brightened a little. He allowed the robe to hang open on his pale body. He felt his penis throb slightly, but then the girl's raven body became, in his mind, superimposed by Humility's. He staggered a little at the image. How could this be? Panic made him clutch at a nightstand. It wobbled and he almost lost his balance. His head throbbed and he used trembling fingers to rub at his temples. "Merde!" he spat. His eyes narrowed viciously and he snatched the paddle from where it lay across the girl's open palms. "Are you using that voodoo on me, Mara?! You witch!"

She cowered away and lifted her hands protectively. "Non, monsieur! Mara doesn't know any voodoo!"

There was a presence in the room. Something was taunting him; something which hid in the shadows, sniggering behind clawed hands. The Vicomte shuddered, peering over his satin-clad shoulder with eyes wide with terror. "You are!" he hissed. A little spittle dribbled from the corner of his mouth. He snatched her fragile wrists, pulled her from the bed, and threw her across the richly carpeted room. Vaguely, Salace heard her sobbing, whimpering, and begging for mercy.

Only a short time ago he would not have dreamed of paddling one of his girls himself. That was one of Henri's tasks, but the big body slave was no longer part of the Salace household.

A terrible loneliness enveloped the Vicomte. He grieved for the loss of his friend and confidante. He grieved for the loss of Humility; the gloriously beautiful submissive purchased from the Don Cortez. His gaunt features creased into a dark frown. The Don Cortez! The appearance of that damned slave ship in the harbour was the beginning of all his troubles! His crazed mind went back to the auction and the Englishman who'd bid against him. "A pox on him!" he cursed. He lifted his head and sniffed the air like a beast trying to detect the scent of its prey. There was a faint smell of smoke. He grinned. At least his remaining servants still obeyed his orders.

Mara smelt the smoke too, and she frowned curiously.

"Where is Humility?" the Vicomte murmured, but the question was asked of no one in particular. "And where is that devil, Henri? How dare they leave me, and leave together?"

Mara looked up at him, her expression both fearful and bemused. Had her master lost his mind? He had sent Henri away, and he had condemned Humility to punishment by Baron Samedi. Could he not remember?

Again he saw Humility's sweet features overlaying Mara's ebony visage. Her buttocks, so full and dark and smooth, were lifted invitingly. Her shapely thighs were open wide. Her ripe little sex seemed to hang heavy and so juicy between the smooth limbs. It begged for attention.

Mara sensed what he was thinking. "I deserve it, monsieur," she gasped. "I surely do. I know I'll be a better bed-wench for a good beating."

The pleading whine angered Salace. Humility never whined. She gave herself freely and submissively, but she never whined. He raised his arm. The paddle handle was smooth in his fingers. It caressed his palm. He gripped it more firmly and brought it down on the plump hillocks of dark flesh. Mara gave a little mew as the flat blade struck her, but her bottom rose higher, inviting more. It opened further, making the wet folds more available.

He felt his cock thicken, rising out of the parted satin of his robe. He wondered why he had not taken this task before, instead of allowing Henri to have all the fun.

"How does that feel, Mara?" he grunted. "Tell me what you feel." His eyes glinted cruelly. The delicately carved aristocratic features seemed to be more sharply etched, the skin tightly stretched over the bones. The features flushed, and the teeth looked whiter, sharper.

The girl pretended to sob, her head buried in her hands. "It burns, monsieur," she told him breathlessly. "It burns like a fire, and it makes me so wet!"

The paddle fell again. The blow was lower, stroking the wet folds on the upward swing, and Mara expelled little hissing noises. "My cunney, monsieur," she purred. "The paddle touched my cunney - flicked it. That burns too. It burns nice."

He missed Henri. As he beat Mara he knew he'd been wrong to send him away. He, Salace, had actively encouraged a liaison between Humility and his body slave. It was pure envy that made him order punishment. He missed the big man. He'd been a good friend, as well as a good slave.

There were noises in the scented garden below the window. Night noises. Animals, he assured himself. But what if they were not? What if there truly was a revolt beginning, as was the rumour going around the island? He needed Henri! Damn the man! Where was he when he needed him?!

Mara's musk was strong. It filled the room as her excitement grew. The ebony buttocks were aglow now from the beating, and pearly strings of sap dribbled from her open folds. "Monsieur!" she gasped.

"I have no mercy, ma cherie," grunted Salace.

It was true. He felt as though his mind had been taken from him; that it had been replaced by something evil - something he did not understand. He shook his head, trying to clear it. "I have no mercy," he repeated, and his voice sounded flat and unfamiliar to his own ears.

"Non, monsieur," Mara panted fearfully. She saw him look at her with blank expressionless eyes which made her shudder. "I do not want mercy. I want ..." What could she say to appease him?

With a final blow from the flat blade of the paddle, Salace tore at the luxurious robe and threw himself upon the kneeling girl, stabbing wildly at the cleft between her buttocks. "I must punish you, Mara!" His voice was hard and ruthless. He felt the thickened globe of his penis nudge at the tightness of her rear entrance. If he entered, he sensed she could grip him tightly, perhaps painfully.

"Oui, monsieur, punishment is what I needs. I knows it. I surely do. I knows it!"

For some reason the girl continued to irritate him immeasurably, although she never had before now. Something deep inside him wanted to tear into her dark little rear, splitting her asunder; wanted to hear her scream and beg for mercy; wanted to watch her head rolling from side to side and her little fists helplessly pounding the floor; wanted to see her perspiring back dip under the discomfort of having her rear passage filled by his relentless cock. A wolfish sneer darkened his pale damp face as he quickly pondered a number of perverse methods he could employ with which to enjoy her to the full. He drew away from her, although the renewal of his need was greater than ever. "Stop whining, cherie." He sat back on his heels, eyeing the smooth dark hillocks of trembling flesh, flushed under the ebony blackness. "I do not enjoy you when you whine."

Mara folded her arms over her head and sobbed quietly. "Pardon, monsieur." She parted her thighs further and raised the punished buttocks, offering herself for his use.

Using the ball of his thumb Salace opened her rear entrance, testing its elasticity. He heard her gasp a sharp intake of breath, and he felt the sphincter clutch his probing digit. He shook his head and withdrew the inquisitive thumb. "You are not yet ready for that, Mara. You would choke my poor cock. You would strangle it with your tightness."

"No, sah," she denied, keen to please her master. "I promise you. I ready - very ready. The paddling made me wet. Look, sah." With two fingers she scooped the silky lusciousness of her own lubrication and smeared it liberally about the tightly wrinkled rosebud of her anus.

Salace watched her, his eyes fixed with pleasure and interest, the tight sneer softening. He saw the bud pulse against the fumbling fingers. It excited him. His breathing became quicker and harsher. His loins felt heavy and warm. His balls were tight and hard.

The noises in the garden grew gradually louder. Animals snuffled and grunted, sounding unearthly in the still night air. The smell of burning grew stronger. The sounds and smell served only to increase his fervour, and to increase the growing feeling that he was no longer human; not of this earth.

He threw himself upon her again, feeling the silk of her dew about the tight opening. He thrust gently and felt the place open like a rose coming into bloom. He felt her butt against him, bearing backwards eagerly. There was no whining now, only soft murmurings of sheer enjoyment. The sensation about his thrusting cock was almost unbearable in its beauty. There was, indeed, a tightness, but it was a caress - a pulsing, warm caress. He felt the heat of the paddled hillocks burn into the tight drum of his belly. He dug his fingers into them, seeking purchase, pulling her further onto him. His head was thrown back in triumph. The smooth pale chest rose up as he sucked in humid air. The muscles in his stomach and thighs tensed as his rigid loins thrust into the writhing girl.

"Oh, sahhh ..." she panted deliriously. "You fuck me

so *good*. I coming so hard, but my cunney -"

Salace moved a hand from one hip and slipped it over Mara's soft lips, stifling her words. "Sssh," he hissed. "Later, ma petite. Much later!"

The gagging hand slid down then and grasped the dark smoothness of a swaying breast, tweaking the nipple to painful erection. The hand slid further to the taut plain of the girl's belly, feeling its soft pliancy under the hardness of his pummelling fingers. They drove into the tight curls of her bush, separating the plumpness of her labia. Salace felt her jerk with pleasure as he touched the jutting pip of her clitoris. He closed his eyes, thrusting into her viciously, seeing in his mind's eye the velvety little bud. In his imagination he saw it peeping from the silk of its hood, moving under the rhythmic teasing of his fingers. A surge began in the very base of his groin. The silky warmth of his issue was forced into her. He felt it gush. Just as the sweet waves of pleasure washed over him, so his semen fountained thickly into her darkness.

All the strength drained from Salace. Now that he'd taken his pleasure he wanted nothing more than for Mara to leave his presence immediately. And yet, if she did, he knew there would be nothing left but loneliness. Where was Henri? What was there on the island for the big slave if he no longer lived and worked in the luxury of the Salace estate? Where could he have gone?

And Humility. Where was she? Were the two of them together again, laughing at his misery? "Humility!" he groaned. "Je regret!" His head began to ache again. The blood roared through his temples. He could hear and feel it surging through vessels swollen beyond all imaginings. He pulled away from Mara, searching distractedly for his robe. Not so very long ago Henri would be on hand to help him dress. Now there was no one.

"You fucked me so good, sah," exclaimed Mara, looking up at him with huge dark eyes. Her soft lips were curved in a tenuous smile.

Salace said nothing. He glared down at the girl, but he saw only Humility's beauty and beyond her, Henri, proud and reproachful.

Mara crawled to him. Her fingers grasped his thighs and stroked the pale skin. "How can I serve you now, sah?" she pleaded, trying not to whine, but her voice thin and quivering.

"What is it to me how you value my fucking?" he said contemptuously, without hearing her last offer. "It matters not to me whether you enjoy it or not. You mean nothing." He shook his leg to loosen her grasp. "What is it to me?" he repeated sadly. He could think only of Humility's breathtaking loveliness; how she pleased him, seemingly without trying. Mara could never do that, nor any of the other girls on his plantation.

"There is something I must do," he said suddenly.

Mara, still on her knees at his feet, lifted her hands in supplication. "Let me dress you, monsieur. Allow me to fasten each button with my lips so that the roughness of my fingers does not spoil your fine clothes."

He sighed with exasperation as he strode to the velvet covered bench over which he'd earlier flung his clothes. "Just get from my sight, Mara!" he growled. "There may still be time to find Humility and make peace with her." He struggled into his breeches, cursing as he almost stumbled.

"Let me help you!" pleaded Mara.

"I told you to get from my sight! Now do as you're told!"

Maybe there was still time to find Henri too. Salace knew he needed him to keep the household and the estate running smoothly. He snatched up his shirt, cursing the heat and closeness of Haiti.

The vulnerable ebony body crouched at his feet. The onyx eyes were wide, looking up at him in timid adoration. The soft lips were parted so invitingly. Salace could see the black breasts hanging heavily from her slender ribs. Her whole attitude begged for attention, no matter how cruel that attention might be.

"You're a wicked little temptress," he murmured, driving the polished toe of his boot into the softness of her belly.

"Oh, sah ..." moaned Mara, moving sinuously sideways under the none-too-gentle persuasion of the boot. "Oh, monsieur, I wants nothing more than to please you."

A sly smile made the pale features less harsh as his long fingers halted in the task of buttoning the fine cloth of his shirt.

"Will you do anything, Mara?" he asked slowly. "Will you do anything to please me?" The wicked eyes regarded the girl with sombre curiosity. The aristocratic fingers fell slowly to his groin, stroking the swiftly returning hardness there. The girl quailed, seeming to grow smaller and more enticingly fearful. Salace liked her submissiveness. The alluring breasts seemed even more pert. The buttocks arched invitingly. The wide, frightened eyes shone with barely hidden excitement.

"Anything!" she hissed.

Salace's expression was vulpine as he gave the matter some thought. "Let me see now," he said slowly, pronouncing each word with careful enunciation. "Let me see." He frowned, letting his gaze linger upon each part of her cowering nakedness. The frown was replaced by a curious smile, terrifying in its ingenuousness.

"Humility was always so very eager to please," he said

at last, his eyes growing misty with the memory. "Could you become like her? Could you become like my Humility?" He knew he'd always had a cruel streak, but what he felt at that moment was something more; something devilish. Yes, that's what it was - devilish.

The pounding headache seemed to recede as he reached this conclusion, and a feeling of power flooded his tensed body. He felt he could do anything ... be anything.

Mara shrank away, shuffling backwards. Salace tutted angrily.

"My Humility would place her hands on her head," he said, his voice full of menace. "And she would look at me shyly from under those adorable lashes and say: 'Whatever pleases you, milord'. Say that for me, Mara, and place your hands on your head."

The girl looked up at him and hesitantly did as she was bid.

Salace sat upon the bench. "Stand before me, Mara," he commanded, "and we shall try again." He watched as the girl rose to her feet on legs which were far from steady. "Apart," he said huskily, slapping the tender inner sides of her thighs. "Nicely apart, and thrust that pretty little sex forward and upwards." He grazed the upper limit of the crisp curls which formed her bush to show her exactly what he required. "Humility always knew exactly what I needed from her, almost without me having to ask."

He watched her hands move obediently to her head, and watched the wriggle of her hips as she tried to please him by offering the fullness of her sex for his approval.

"That's nice," he said with a contented sigh. "That's very nice. I can see now how I stimulated you with the paddle. I can see the inner lips of your sex, all swollen and inflamed, glossed with your love sap." He nodded to confirm the pleasure he felt. He stroked the warm slickness of her sex.

"Oh, monsieur ..." Mara's exclamation was almost reproving and he looked up at her, his expression dark with annoyance. The long fingers suddenly closed on the wet, tender flesh.

"You feel humiliated?" he rapped. "Embarrassed by what I say and by the intimate touch of my fingers? Humility never did! No matter how intimate was my touch, she made no murmur of complaint."

The very tip of an index finger rubbed her clitoris, which arched from the flushed folds. He knew the girl was trying very hard not to anger him by giving even the slightest hint of rebuke.

"You're very wet, Mara," he said. "I like that. I like that very much."

"If it pleases you, milord."

"Ah," he sighed happily. "You're learning nicely."

Allowing his fingers to slide backwards to the deep, warm valley between her buttocks, he dipped into the wetness at her anus. She did not flinch or murmur, not even when he probed both her anus and her frontal opening with separate fingers, driving them in fully. "Yes, you're learning very nicely. My cock is once again fully erect inside my breeches. It's ready to impale one or other of these deliciously inviting orifices."

"Oh, yes, milord," she whispered huskily.

Salace's expression suddenly darkened yet again. His inconsistent moods were alarming. "But because I now know how to tease you, I shall not give you the benefit of my beautiful organ until I return." The fingers withdrew and picked up a cravat which lay on the bench by his side. "In the meantime I shall bind you helpless with this. Humility never complained at such treatment," he warned, "and I expect the same good behaviour from you."

Mara looked mouth-watering; her lovely eyes wide and shining with unshed tears, her spread legs trembling with both fright and need.

"But because I know you have never been trained as Humility has, and because I know you are unused to such exciting little games," he continued, stroking upwards to the enticing swell of her breasts, "I shall leave you in much more comfort than ever Humility experienced." He smiled, and the smile was more threatening than ever was his frown. "Lie on the bed with your legs open and your arms behind your back - wrists together."

Mara was genuinely frightened of the Vicomte now. She hesitated slightly, and glanced anxiously at the open window. "I can never be like Humility. Never!" A new-found strength surged through her athletic legs, and she leapt across the room, sprang nimbly through the window, and out onto the long verandah.

Salace looked with disinterest after the retreating figure. "Has the world gone utterly mad?" he asked of the empty room. The pounding in his head returned. His aquiline nostrils flared. There hung a sinister smell of death. He moved to the window and looked out upon the moonlit undergrowth and jungle beyond. An orange glow came from the direction of the cane fields, and reflected in his eyes. Thick smoke spiralled up into the night sky. The animals and insects had fallen silent. A macabre stillness hung heavily over the scene. Slowly and silently a mass of dark figures emerged from the trees, all appearing to carry makeshift weapons of one kind or another. At the front of them was Henri.

"You," said Salace with suppressed anger, but no real surprise. He stepped out onto the verandah and leaned over the rail, his hands gripping the weathered wood until the knuckles glowed white through the pale skin.

Shadowy features and hate-filled eyes stared up at the Vicomte.

CHAPTER FOURTEEN

Born aloft by four naked slaves, Humility shuddered in the bonds which chafed her flesh. In unison the slaves chanted as they reached the moonlit clearing. The rhythm of their chanting was in tune with the pulsing vibrations which soared through her tortured body.

Love sap, warm and creamy, seeped about the embedded hilt of the knife; a knife which seemed to be a living creature, slowly awakening, throbbing, becoming thicker, moving within her like the serpent so painstakingly carved upon the ivory handle.

Humility's own body responded quickly. Her clitoris jerked in swift spasms, gathering sensations to it, drawing on her life force. She felt detached from her surroundings. Her mind soared beyond the clearing while her abused body gloried in both pain and pleasure.

The clearing was crowded, full of dancing, sweating figures, all naked or almost naked. The women shimmied, arching gracefully, thrusting out their full, shapely breasts, their dark skin gleaming in the moonlight. The men were naked and their cocks reared up proudly, like ceremonial staffs, swaying and bobbing as they danced. Drums beat a relentless and unearthly rhythm.

Humility's arms were bound behind her head. Her legs were held out wide by the slaves who carried her. Fear numbed her mind while her sex glowed with the sensations given by the provocative knife.

"At last!" boomed a voice from the edge of the clearing.

"Our sacrifice has deigned to grace us with her presence."

Humility was set down upon the dusty ground. Her feet were kicked apart. She didn't dare look down, but she knew the broad blade of the knife glinted between her outstretched thighs. Just as she didn't dare look down, she also didn't dare raise her eyes to look upon Baron Samedi. The thick darkness of her lashes formed a fringe which shielded her from the visage of the god of death. The night was growing unbearably hot and humid. Specks of ash and tiny glowing embers drifted through the clearing. She had seen the sky glowing over the tops of the dense trees, but was totally disorientated, and could not determine the fire's direction.

Gradually, very gradually, she felt the light tickling of tiny feet as the ants, attracted by the sweetness of the molasses, began to climb the long shapeliness of her slender legs.

"We are so happy to see you here, my darling girl!" boomed the Baron. "Does not my precious knife delight your wanton sex flesh? Do you feel the undeniable throbbing of the serpent?"

The ants nipped Humility dreadfully, but she bit her lip and made no sound of pain or protest. The tone of the Baron's voice blended with the rhythm of the drums and the pulsing of the talisman within her. Even the acute pain of a scorpion's sting was softened by the highly charged mood in the clearing.

"See how proudly she stands!" continued the ominous shadow of the Baron, spreading his arms wide to encompass the whole of the heaving congregation. "See how beautiful she is! She is a perfect sacrifice!"

The shadow which was the Baron was still at the edge of the clearing, framed by the dense unmoving undergrowth. He was powerful. He was magnificent. He was splendidly male. Humility could already feel his severe touch on her breasts and thighs. She held her breath and closed her eyes. His voice was overwhelming, surrounding her and increasing in intensity with the beat of the drums. The rhythmic stamp of feet upon the dusty ground and the passionate cries of the Baron's worshipers combined to make the throb of the knife within her seem even greater.

"Will she be so proud," continued the Baron, "when she feels the fire of my loins, and accepts the molten heat of my seed?"

Humility opened her eyes and stared bravely at the shadow. Her arms were locked tightly behind her head. Her beautiful face was pale, even in the flickering of the fire and the light of the full moon. Her breasts and thighs were tender and flushed from the many tiny insect bites. What remained of the molasses glistened in the orange glow. Suddenly, and without Humility being aware of any movement, the large shadow loomed over her, reaching out to brush a stray tendril of hair from her cheek with unexpected gentleness.

"She does not flinch when I touch her," said the Baron to his followers without turning his head. He smelt of decay, and Humility could just see his lifeless eyes, bloodshot and red about the rims. Features became clearer as she focussed. The ghostly pale skin was pulled taut over the sculptured ridges of his cheekbones. The face was nothing as she expected. What did she expect? Dark, native features? Whose soul had Baron Samedi stolen? Whose empty body did he inhabit?

Pleasure washed again from the knife hilt, making her gasp at the strength of it.

"Another orgasm, my pretty?" mocked the Baron. "They weary you, do they not? They drain you beyond all imaginings. Any lesser girl would be unconscious by now, ready to be sacrificed to the ultimate." He laughed, a great

189

echoing bellow rising above the beat of the drums and the stamping of the feet. Long fingers held her trembling chin, lifting her face up to his. His open lips met hers, and they kissed passionately.

This was no goat, thought Humility. This was no beast who would kill her by supernatural means. This was a man. He was tall and broad, and his presence reminded her of the Vicomte. He had the same loving but cruel kiss. The touch of his fingers upon her face had the same warmth, the same firmness. For a surreal moment she *was* in the arms of the Vicomte.

"She is ready!" the Baron suddenly pulled away and announced. "Take her to the altar!"

Obtrusive hands grasped Humility's aching body, lifting it high. She was passed amongst the baying crowd. Fingers pinched and groped surreptitiously. She felt the unforgiving stone rough against her thighs, belly and breasts as she was laid facedown upon an unelaborate altar. Her forehead rested at its edge. Her wrists were untied and her aching arms flopped to her sides.

A shiver of trepidation ran through her as she awaited the Baron's next order. Hands held her down. Someone gripped her thighs and forced them apart. The touch was cruel, vicious, and uncaring, but it made her sex throb about the ivory shaft of the knife. Fingers entwined in her hair, and her head was lifted and drawn back, arching her neck uncomfortably and opening her mouth. She closed her eyes again.

"Good," sighed the Baron as he traced a fingertip around her soft lips. "A deliciously welcoming orifice. Who shall have the pleasure of filling this place first?"

The clearing was much quieter now; the dancing feet were stilled, the chanting had stopped, and only one drum thumped a slow, haunting beat. All eyes were on the helpless sacrifice.

An apprehensive murmur rose from the gathering. Humility realised they were wary of her. To them she was dangerous - evil. The Baron had doubtless fuelled their superstitions by telling them frightening untruths about her.

"Perhaps you, my dear Paolo?" encouraged the Baron.

By straining to the left Humility could see a slender young man being guided towards the altar by the Baron. He appeared to be no older than she was herself. His hair was red-gold and his skin was lightly freckled; evidence of a very mixed ancestry. His eyes were wide with suspicion.

The single drum fell silent.

The Baron laughed, throwing his head back to release a great bellow. "Why so, my dear chap?!" He continued to trace the succulent curves of Humility's lips, and then pushed his long fingers between them, letting them lie upon the warm moistness of her tongue. Unwittingly, after so many years of training with the emir, she sucked gently, pampering the slowly thrusting digits. "You see how eager she is?" he whispered enthusiastically, pulling the spellbound Paolo ever closer. "She loves her mouth to be filled. And she is trained to keep her delightful little teeth well clear of any flesh which slips between them."

Humility felt the sinister shadow of the Baron drape across her. She felt his lips brush her brow, and forgot for a moment the never-ending sensations between her outstretched thighs.

The shadow slipped away, and was replaced by Paolo's bursting erection, which nudged into her cheek. The helmet swayed across her open lips.

"No more hesitation!" ordered the Baron from somewhere. "Thrust your manhood between the lips which await it so hungrily!"

The lone drum beat again.

"I am sorry," moaned Paolo, bending over Humility as he inched his long thickness into her unprotected mouth. "Do not be angry with me."

Humility tasted the bitterness of his pre-issue on the back of her undulating tongue. She so wanted to tell the young man that she adored the taste of him; that she loved the feel of his finely stretched maleness; that she could barely wait for his precious semen to flood down her waiting throat - but his irregular movements gagged her.

The roughness of the altar felt warm against her body. It was as if this, too, was a living, breathing creature, like the hilt of the knife inside her. The slab of stone seemed to caress the tender flesh of her belly.

The young man suddenly stiffened and forced his groin hard against her flushed face. His lower belly pressed firmly against her forehead. He bucked without control, and she gratefully swallowed the warm cream he spilled into her.

"She shows such gratitude, my followers," crowed Baron Samedi. "See how she arches that lovely body to drink down all of Paolo's offering. Who will please her next?"

Paolo staggered from the altar, holding his still rigid penis in his hands, his eyes agog. "She *is* a witch!" he groaned. "I gave her my all, yet still my cock is full!"

The Baron's scornful laughter filled the clearing, rising above the sombre beat of the drum. "Then feel free to use her as you wish to satisfy your lust again, my young friend."

"No!" stammered Paolo. "She's evil!"

"Come ..." he urged the younger man. "Come closer." He signalled with a nod of his head, and Humility was grabbed and turned over by many eager hands. She was held with her torso raised at a slight angle, the back of her head resting against the muscled belly of the Baron. She could feel his splendid phallus pulsing against her shoulder. She watched a hand cupping and lifting her breasts, and knew it was his. Her nipples hardened beautifully, and then she watched, mesmerised, as the Baron reached out, gripped Paolo's bursting erection, and pulled him close to her side.

Both Humility and Paolo groaned as the Baron started milking the younger man.

"She has such exquisite breasts," the Baron whispered. "Do you not agree, my young friend?"

Humility watched Paolo try to answer, but the words hid somewhere in his throat, and he could only nod like an imbecile.

"Come, feel them."

Paolo reached forward and hypnotically squeezed the soft flesh offered to him by the Baron. He shuddered as the fist pumped him harder and faster. A bead of sweat dripped from the tip of his nose. He should not allow another male - be it god or human - to touch him so intimately, but the magic of the moment and the sight and feel of the beautifully submissive girl held before him were too much to deny. He stiffened and groaned, and his creamy offering suddenly arched into the air and splattered onto his hands and her breasts. It seeped into her cleavage, and he massaged it into her erect nipples.

"Bravo!" applauded the Baron with a thick chuckle.

Humility closed her eyes and allowed the many hands to return and lift her once again onto her front.

"She seems so contemptuous," Humility heard her tormentor, and knew there was much more yet for her to endure. "She has too much spirit and not enough respect. How would you suggest, my dear followers, we show her the error of her ways?"

The drumbeat slowed and softened.

"More scorpions!" offered a spiteful voice from the rear of the throng.

"Slit her throat and have done with it!" spat another.

"We can feed her to the fish at daybreak!"

"The snake!" hissed a woman, barely hiding a sadistic chuckle.

Humility felt tears seep from her tortoiseshell eyes. Why were they all so anxious to see such horrible things done to her? Was all of this at the suggestion of the Vicomte? Was his spite so great that he wished to see her dead?

"The snake?" echoed the Baron slowly, as though contemplating something especially pleasing. "Do you hear that, Humility? They wish you to be submitted to the snake."

"The snake! The snake! The snake!" From all around the clearing the words were chanted in a steady rhythm which blended with the thump of the drum.

Humility shivered desperately despite the heat of the tropical night. Not knowing exactly how Baron Samedi's followers craved to punish her was perhaps worse than the punishment itself would be. Was she truly to be fed to some terrible creature? To be eaten slowly or ingested whole by a hideous serpent?

There was a sudden change of mood; solemn and menacing.

"Get her up on her knees," ordered the Baron.

Uncaring hands lifted Humility's pliant body, positioning her beautifully rounded buttocks high, and displaying the blade which still projected from her to all those who gathered so eagerly about the altar. Humility felt the smooth skin of her breasts abraded by the rough stone, chafing her nipples to tightly erect buds. With her rear valley so exposed and her pierced sex so flushed and eager she should have felt humiliation, but she did not. The way she felt, she supposed, was much to do with the knife's mysterious magic.

"The snake." Baron Samedi's sibilant whisper sent an

icy chill up Humility's spine. An expectant hush fell across the arena. Everybody waited. A cloud passed over the moon, plunging the stilled figures into deeper shadow. The jungle vegetation surrounding the clearing seemed to close in upon the tableau.

Humility closed her eyes, waiting bravely and passively for whatever horrors the snake might bring. Fear reduced her concentration, her sex suddenly lost its grip about the ivory hilt, and the knife clattered noisily to the altar.

"Naughty!" she heard the Baron admonish. She clenched and raised her bottom even higher, tense in her apprehension. Her shy rose-hole pulsed fearfully.

"No matter," Samedi decided. "At least you'll be more easily accessible for the finale of the ceremony."

Humility gasped, tears of confusion blurring her vision. She pressed her cheek to the stone altar for comfort.

"Let our sacrifice worship the beauty of the snake," she heard the god of death whisper. A hand gripped her hair, lifted her head, and a threatening voice close to her ear ordered her to watch the Baron.

He was towering above her, his arms outstretched and hands raised in homage. Something lay, thick and powerful, across his upturned palms, and draped almost to the ground. Humility moaned fearfully.

"See how sinuously it moves, my pretty one," the Baron purred.

Something, Humility didn't know what, made her sway and grind her uplifted buttocks, and part her thighs a little to allow her gaping sex to pout. She shook her head and lifted her eyes to focus upon the thing held aloft by her tormentor. She felt her lips soften, her tongue sliding slowly across them. She felt her breasts tremble excitedly. She saw eyes, beady and emotionless, piercing deep into hers. She saw a mouth open to display white fangs, needle sharp and curved, while a forked tongue flicked between them. She clamped her eyes tightly against the awful vision, and felt tears squeeze down her cheeks.

The Baron sniggered. "Look again, my precious little one!" he urged.

"No!" Humility tried to choke back the disrespectful cry, but it forced its way from the depths of her soul.

"I command you!" roared the Baron. "Do not anger me further! Look up to my hands!"

"Look! Look! Look!" came the chant from the worshipers.

Humility raised her head and opened her eyes with terrible reluctance. At that moment the moon slipped from behind the clouds, spilling silvery light into the clearing and upon the beast lying across the Baron's palms. She would have laughed at her own stupidity had she not felt so ashamed by her lack of courage. The beast which had filled her with such dread was nothing more than a rope! It was grey and lifeless, the strands twisted to form a thick handle at one end and frayed to a taper at the other. Her voluptuous body relaxed. Filled with absolute relief and without thinking, she strained up against the strong fingers in her hair and kissed the tip of the Baron's majestic penis. She brushed them lightly down the thick length and felt the crispness of his black curls tickle her face.

"No! No, you wicked temptress!" he roared. "You do not escape your punishment quite so easily!"

Humility watched him hand the rope to a henchman who stood to his side.

"The snake demands that you suffer!" announced the Baron for all to hear. "It demands that you feel the sting of the lash upon your brazen buttocks!"

The congregation murmured its agreement. The drumbeat stopped again.

Instead of apprehension, Humility felt her bottom prepare itself, opening and softening, and transferring sheer delight to her swollen clitoris. With a resigned sigh, she waited.

There was a violent hiss as the rope swept down through the muggy air, and a dull thud as it bit into Humility's exposed bottom. She jerked forward. Her breasts swayed. She bit her lip to suppress the scream that threatened to erupt from within. The sadistic throng mumbled its satisfaction.

"Harder!" the Baron instructed.

Another hiss preceded the next swipe and she rocked forward again under its cruel impact. A second strip of searing heat crossed her buttocks, and she longed to massage the pain away.

"See how she enjoys the snake," purred the Baron as he moved slowly around to survey her beating from every angle. "See how her juices flow; lustrous little pearls beading the plump and pretty lips." The breathless compliments betrayed his excitement, and through her turmoil Humility wondered how he managed to contain himself.

"Again!" he urged. "Why have you stopped? Give the snake to me, I shall make that pretty bottom glow in earnest!"

Leaning forward he kissed along the graceful length of her neck. He traced a trail across the sweep of her shoulders with the tip of his tongue. Humility quivered beneath the sensual touch. "Is my darling girl afraid of what I might do next?" he whispered hoarsely. He leaned in further, enveloping her with his sultry body. She could hear his laboured breathing, smell his male musk, and feel his overpowering nakedness. Her stomach knotted with inexplicable delight. Something which was neither human or animal brushed unexpectedly against her wet sex. The touch of it made her hold her breath. It was warm and rough ... It was the rope.

"Yes, my sweet," he gloated. "It is the snake."

The coarse intruder prodded at her sex, experimentally probing inside. Humility bore back upon it, eager to feel more of the strange sensation. She heard the Baron chuckle, and the hank of rope was withdrawn, leaving her feeling empty and disappointed. The warm cloak of him lifted, leaving her exposed to the night air. She sensed, rather than heard or felt, bodies changing position. A gentle hand stroked and soothed her burning buttocks. She held her breath again and waited.

Another hiss swept through the still air and the snake bit down upon her quivering flesh once again. Tears meandered down her cheeks and dripped from her chin, but she would not cry out; she must maintain her dignity.

"You see!" cried Baron Samedi, looking down and correctly interpreting the cocktail of emotions etched on her tear-streaked face. "You see how she glories in pleasures? She cannot get enough of this beating! Would that all my offerings upon this altar were so eager!" He raised the snake once more, and then whipped it down to wrap the frayed end around the slender curve of her waist. Again she jerked forward in silence. She adjusted her position slightly; she dipped her back, tensed her buttocks, and lowered her breasts to ease the ache in her nipples against the rough stone.

"Do you enjoy the strange pain, my darling temptress?" teased the Baron.

She could hear his breathing, quick and intense. There was an urge, deep within, to feel him holding her in his arms; to feel the naked length of his sinewy body. She could not speak - could not answer.

"Here ... drink." The Baron held a bowl to her lips and

tipped a rich red wine down her throat. She immediately swooned and her vision blurred briefly. Panic seized her; What had he done? Had she been poisoned? Her body felt heavier and her fingers and toes tingled, but the sensations were not altogether unpleasant. In fact, a comforting peace quickly permeated her whole being, and she relaxed and floated contentedly.

Suddenly she tingled, and saw sparkling dust motes in the silver and orange moonlight. The motes fell upon her, and where they fell there was warmth and sensations like nothing else she had experienced. Moonstone powder!

Like a silent shadow the Baron leapt onto the altar. He knelt behind her glistening haunches, his face raised to the moon, and he saluted it with a lupine howl. "It is now, my followers!" he howled. "Are you ready?!"

A smooth erection nudged at Humility's entrance, slipping into the slick folds, caressing them, taunting them.

Figures writhed about the dusty floor of the clearing. A tall woman straddled a man, impaling herself upon his upstanding root, while another man stood over her, demanding his penis be sucked. She looked ecstatic, her breasts rising and falling as she panted heavily. Elsewhere a macabre black mass of sweating and heaving bodies entwined and twisted.

"The sacrifice will die! The sacrifice will die!" The dreadful words were chanted in a rhythm which matched the squirming followers of Samedi.

Humility felt her body pulsing to the same rhythm, felt the Baron open her, and felt him sink slowly into her. She welcomed his warm hardness, just as she had welcomed the pain of the snake.

"The sacrifice will die!" The phrase drummed in her ears.

The lovely darkness of her features was hidden by her tumbled palomino hair. Her breasts, too, were occluded from view by her kneeling position on the altar. She should, she knew, have been humiliated by it; her bottom raised high and her sex impaled by the hugeness of the Baron. But she was proud! She was proud to be at the mercy of such a powerful creature - whether it be man or beast!

"I, Samedi, impregnate you!" He pounded against her without consideration, and his groin slapped wetly against her rolling buttocks. His monstrous erection filled and stretched her beyond belief. Humility clutched the edge of the altar desperately. She worked hard to match and ride the almost frenzied assault, and winced at the savage fingers which clamped her shoulders and wrenched her back onto the waiting spear time and time again. She was drenched in shimmering perspiration.

At last, when she felt she could take no more, the Baron stiffened and knelt tall and still. "It is done!" he roared, and Humility felt her insides swamped with his priceless seed.

CHAPTER FIFTEEN

Dark figures huddled in the disused slave quarters at the edge of the Fairweather estate. Their conversation was intense and occasional angry words cut the gloom of the long hut. They could hear the distant roar of the fires and the shouts of men struggling desperately to contain them.

From the deep shadow at the far end came an exhausted cry of pain, the sound of laboured breathing, and the whistle and crack of a bullwhip.

"Merde!" came a coarse growl. "Must we take you to the very edge of death before you talk, girl?"

A muffled sob was the only answer, accompanied by a

clink of metal as the captive tried to ease the chains which held her in bondage.

"Why are you so loyal to this white man, Clea?" Henri whispered softly into her tawny ear, lifting the midnight curls to murmur into the dainty shell. Her slender arms were stretched to their limit and held by tight iron manacles which cut into the soft flesh of her wrists. Lacklustre eyes stared sightlessly at the big slave, but suddenly flashed hatred.

"He's a good man," she managed at last. It was no more than a croak, for her throat was parched.

Henri laughed and the others joined him. The noise filled Clea's mind and made her head ache.

"Good man?" Henri stood tall, grinning into the gloom, seeking the attention of his companions.

"A white man, good?" echoed a tall cadaverous Negro who bore the scars of many cruel whippings upon his bare back. "No white man is good!" he snarled. "None! They're a scourge upon this earth!"

"But they will make us our fortune, Essick!" said Henri with a knowing chuckle. Essick grunted without conviction.

Clea tensed in her chains, throwing back the thick midnight tresses and holding her fine features proudly. Her breasts were bared by the flail of the long bullwhip at Henri's side, her gown hanging in thin shreds. "Jonas Fairweather is a good man, I tell you," she said more clearly. "Just like his grandfather before him." She heard the crack of the bullwhip and held her breath, awaiting the vicious pain. She had no hope of escape, for the men had shackled her at wrist and ankle. Her spent body was on fire, striped with the vivid marks of the whip. "If you'd only give him a chance," she pleaded. "He could make this island a paradise for us all."

Henri stood before her and stroked her chin. He held it gently, lifting it and forcing her to look directly into his dark eyes. Too weak and too tired to fight against his caress, Clea returned his gaze.

In different times she would have smiled coquettishly at the former slave, slanting her mahogany eyes and parting her soft lips in mute invitation. When Old Masta was in charge of Sans Souci she would go deliberately to meet Henri at the border between it and the Salace place. Then she had been safe, sheltered by the patronage of old Mr Fairweather.

"Do you love the new white man?" asked Henri.

Tears brimmed in Clea's eyes, and she was unable to wipe them away. They fell hot and salty down her cheeks. For what seemed like hours he asked the same question over and over, punctuating it with the lash of the cruel bullwhip. She shuddered as his broad lips brushed the cheeks dampened by tears. Strangely, she felt her sex become soft and moist between her spread thighs.

"Can a whore truly fall in love?" he goaded. His mouth swooped down to capture hers before she could react. It was a demanding mastery, but the words stung her as much, if not more, than the lash. Their lips parted, but she felt a caress beneath the torn shreds of her gown. A featherlight stroke upon the tender inner surface of her spread thigh. She wanted to retort angrily to his unfair question; wanted to strike out with clenched fists.

"I've always loved you, Henri, you know that," she murmured. "We grew up together, did we not?"

The surreptitious caress reached the pliancy of her sex, pressing the plumpness of the labia, squeezing them tightly until she wanted to cry out.

"In chains!" hissed Henri with unbridled anger. "We grew up together in chains! Thanks to the white bastards!"

"And was it really so terrible for us, Henri?"

"Not for you, perhaps!" he spat. He opened her sex and drove his fingers without consideration into the silky wetness. "You, the old man's whore! But for me ...?!" He seemed unable to help himself as he left the question hanging in the air. He had to claim her lips again with hungry kisses which left her breathless and gasping for air. Her sex, too, craved more of him. No matter that his cruel use of the bullwhip had all but flayed her; no matter that he had demeaned her with cruel words. She hungered to feel the hugeness of his cock opening her out, splaying her where she hung in her chains.

"What you doing, Henri?" Essick's thin voice cut through the heavy, humid air.

"Yeah, are you taking what's ours to share?" added a small tough man called Elmo. He'd earlier taken great delight in snapping the shackles around Clea's wrists and ankles. She could still feel the pain of his sadistic bite on her left breast. She peered into the shadows, seeking him out.

"Mind your business!" snapped Henri. He drew Clea's yielding body towards him, bowing it in its chains. He wore a pair of his satin livery breeches, and she felt the bulge of his manhood against her thigh. The feel of it made her sex hungry; made it pulse. Her muscles screamed from the strain of her imprisonment.

Henri chuckled confidently, his breath whispering against her cheeks. "Yes, Clea," he murmured, "I know how much you want me. But I want you to beg me to fuck you. I want you to beg like a good whore should."

Clea shuddered. The chain links chinked and rattled, one against the other. Henri's words hurt her, but did not quench her longing.

"And me," added Elmo. "If she truly is a whore she can

take us all - one after the other!"

"Aye! One after the other!" The group of men shuffled closer, moving from the shadows, muttering eagerly. Some had already bared their cocks, hefting them out of the tattered homespun trousers which clothed the lower parts of their bodies.

"Do you hear that, Clea?" whispered Henri, his full lips moving the silky blackness of her hair as he spoke. "Do you see how much you've inflamed these poor men?"

Clea hung her head and let her slim body hang in the chains. She was weary - she'd had enough. She yearned for sleep to come and claim her. It seemed an age since she'd left Jonas to try and stop this uprising.

"Are you thinking of the white man, Clea?" asked Henri. She was vaguely aware that the big man had bared his manhood before her. It was magnificently erect and silky, swaying against her belly as he held her shoulders and allowed his hands to drift down to the fullness of her breasts, cupping them and supporting their weight. The hands were firm, the skin warm and dry, making her close her eyes with the beauty of his caress.

"No, Henri," she managed. "I think only of you. I came to find you ... please believe me. I wanted to do something to stop the bloodshed. I didn't want you to get hurt."

The other men drew closer, muttering ever more angrily. Clea could feel their heat and smell their musk.

"We don't want the bloodshed stopped!" shouted Elmo. "We only want revenge!"

Turning to him with eyes suddenly bright and full of spirit, Clea struggled against the unrelenting chains. "And who is going to supervise the work on the plantations when you kill the white men?" Her voice was level and firm. Despite her helplessness and the pain she tried to add reason to the fire of the rebellion.

"We're the ones who toil and die in the fields!" Essick's words were full of venom.

"When we're in charge we'll eat white man's food," said Elmo. "We'll dine at his table ..."

"But who'll labour in the fields?" said Clea as calmly as she could. "Who'll harvest the cane -?"

With lips softly pressing the upper slope of a breast and then brushing up the length of her neck, Henri finally stilled her words with a kiss in which her tired soul could easily melt. She slumped again in the chains, quivering as she felt his persistent globe open her soft folds. It slid up and down her welcoming valley, glancing irresistibly over the inflamed tip of her clitty as it moved. Henri's kisses, coming one after the other, left her feeling totally confused.

"Please let me down, Henri," she begged. Her own lips brushed his tight curls as he bowed his head to kiss the inflamed marks of the lash which lay across her breasts.

"No," he denied her. "How can I really know where your loyalties lie, Clea? I'll do nothing to jeopardise my men."

The caressing attentions made her weak with sensual delight, and she felt her juices flow from her depths. Had she not been chained she would have collapsed at his feet.

"Doesn't that tell you who has my loyalties?" she whispered hoarsely. "When my sap flows so freely over your cock? Isn't that sufficient for you?"

Henri thrust forward, holding her firmly by grasping her buttocks under the tatters of her gown. Sighing in her submission, Clea willingly took his full, hard length, feeling the silky turgidity slide in to the very hilt.

"But you've been to his bed!" growled Henri, roughly prying her wonderfully pliant buttocks apart.

Clea gasped. How did he know? How could anyone

possibly know that she and Jonas had coupled on Old Masta's bed? The shock made her insides tighten convulsively around Henri's cock. A grunt was the big man's only reaction.

"How ... how ...?" Clea stammered. The wonder of Henri's fucking took away all logical thought and she was rendered speechless for the moment. The atmosphere in the hut became suddenly stifling, and the sounds and mood of the other men became increasingly intense. Her rear bud was opened by a thick finger, and the sensation increased the urgency caused by Henri's fucking.

"Elmo - spied - on - you -" Henri panted in unison with each slow stab of his hips.

"Aye," leered the nasty little man. "I see how eagerly you go to the white man's bed - like a whore!"

Clea cast a fearful glance over her shoulder at Elmo. Her stomach churned as she saw his feverish eyes and watched the swift rubs he gave his excited cock. "But - ooh," she sucked in stagnant air and bit her lip as Henri rutted deeper than before. "But - Old Masta's room - ooh - is on the upper floor!" she managed to protest. The helplessness of her predicament seemed increased by this revelation. The chains, the roughness of Henri's plundering, and the smarting pain left by the lash, all seemed greatly increased by Elmo's intrusive knowledge of her intimate moments with Jonas.

"And I'se a great tree climber," he chuckled. "I seen everything!" His hands rubbed lewdly up and down his erection and his black eyes gleamed in the depressing gloom of the hut. "I seen you pull Old Masta's whip from under the bed!" He forced a hand between the two sweating bodies and pinched the place where he'd earlier left his mark; the mark of sharp teeth. "You so eager to let him whip you, girl, you didn't see me! Dat's why you

206

here!"

Fresh tears of defeat washed down her cheeks, but she couldn't help but secretly welcome Henri's more vigorous thrusts and the plunging of the finger into her rear.

"You taking her front and rear!" rasped Essick. "T'ain't fair!" A bony hand grasped her shoulder. It was Essick, Clea knew without turning to look. His touch made her cringe. Henri grunted in her ear as she felt another hand fumbling against her buttocks, and then the intruding finger was pulled from her rear passage. It was replaced by a cock which nudged blindly against her, demanding and as rigid as iron. She knew that Essick was intending to make good what he considered unfair.

"Yes," she encouraged and writhed between the two men. It wasn't that she desired Essick in any way at all - she had always loathed him, but she knew the only way she could hope to escape from these madmen with her life was by going along with everything they wanted. "Yes!"

"Let her down, Henri!" demanded Elmo roughly. "Her mouth done nothing but pour out words. I got something better for it to do!" He chuckled and tugged at the manacles at her wrists, enjoying making her whimper at the painful bite of the unyielding iron.

"Wait," grunted Henri. "I'm almost there!"

Clea could feel him pulsing and flooding inside her, and twisted in the metal restraints as he thrust at her with less and less control. Feeling strong fingers pinching her nipples with tantalising possessiveness she too reached an ecstatic climax. She arched her elegant back and rolled her head on Essick's shoulder. Her black hair shimmered and stuck to her perspiring forehead. Hands mauled her buttocks and squeezed them tightly around the column of flesh which speared her anus. Her rear passage rhythmically squeezed and milked it appreciatively.

"Let her down, get her on the floor!" croaked Elmo desperately. "You ain't the only bastards who want some fun!"

"Dat true!"

"Yeah!"

"Give us a go at her!"

Hands, many of them, were stroking her damp nakedness, and countless unfamiliar voices intruded into her waning consciousness.

Henri sighed and pulled his thickness from her. Essick whispered disgusting obscenities into her ear. She felt him reach a shuddering pleasure, and then felt him flood her rear with his unwelcome seed.

She felt her aching limbs being released at last, and she fell gratefully forward into Henri's strong arms. Someone ripped what remained of her gown from her poor body, and she felt it flutter uselessly to the dirt floor. She lifted her head and stood as proudly as her exhaustion allowed. The men inched around her like a dirty pack of scavenging animals. Elmo was the dangerous one, she knew. She had to defuse his aggression. She sought him out from their sweating mass, and beckoned him with her eyes and a barely noticeable yet highly sensual lick of her lips.

"She beggin' for it!" he crowed, grabbing her arms and throwing her to the floor. Henri did nothing to intervene.

Clea, knowing that compliance was her only chance of survival, allowed him to pin her down without resistance or complaint. She knew she must convince them all that she was theirs to make use of as they wished. Her mind span as the nasty Elmo fumbled with her numb body. She had to survive this ordeal; she had to save Jonas.

Another man squatted, his knees planted either side of her head, and slapped his semi-erect penis against her cheeks and slightly parted lips. She could taste the bitter saltiness of his slight discharge. "Dat what you want, girl?" she heard him ask. She nodded, looking up at him from beneath his muggy groin. He was lighter than the other men, almost the same colour as herself, but his penis was darkly flushed and suffused with blood. He spoke to her softly, but she no longer heard his words, and then he eased her neck up slightly so that her chin lifted, her face tilted back, and her juicy lips peeled open. Darkness crept over her. She closed her eyes as he pressed forward, and his cock slid inevitably into her vulnerable mouth.

She felt Elmo tug her legs open, cup and lift her bottom from the floor, and thrust into her without ceremony. "You were sure eager to have dat white man!" she heard his muffled gloat. "No mistake about dat! I see ev'ry moment of his taking you! Ev'ry stroke of dat lash you so anxious to taste!"

Clea squirmed beneath the weight of the two men. She could hear the slapping of Elmo's groin against the undersides of her thighs and buttocks as he bucked against her. She sucked desperately on the penis lodged in her mouth and throat, willing the men to finish. She felt countless hands on her breasts, and stomach, and legs.

"Oh yeah, Clea," she heard, but wasn't sure now who was goading her. "You a very willing little whore. I'll bet it came hard for Old Masta when he had to die." Elmo pumped his hips with vigorous stamina. Clea whimpered around the flesh grinding into her mouth. "I'll bet it came real hard on him when he had to bequeath you to his grandson!"

"Get on with it, Elmo!" urged another voice. "We ain't got all day! We all wants a piece of her!"

"Yeah! Get on with it you selfish bastard!"

These comments brought a grunt of anger from Elmo, and Clea felt his cock lurch wildly inside her. "I'se comin'!" he cried at last, arching his back in agonised ecstasy. "I floodin' this girl good and proper, jest like she wants!"

Sucking on the other man Clea urged him to give up his store of issue. Her tongue lapped into the tiny pore, rimming the salty fluid from him. He too gave a sudden growl of delight and her mouth filled with his thick ejaculation.

"'Bout time," grumbled one of the waiting throng. "My cock's throbbin' fit to burst!"

Clea sighed. Her sexual hunger was increased rather than diminished by the men who roughly took her one after the other. They turned her over and filled all available orifice's. They twisted her into an array of uncomfortable yet highly arousing positions and satisfied their lust on her. Thoughts of revolt increased their fervour. Their cocks were as hard as iron bars, hot and throbbing eagerly.

Clea loved every lewd moment.

After what seemed like hours they left her exhausted and aching - but alive.

Henri held her in his protective arms, brushing his lips over her perspiring face. She drank in the sweetness of his gentle kisses. She wouldn't blame him for what had happened.

CHAPTER SIXTEEN

"All hail to Papa Zaca." Humility said in a low, wary voice. Saluted as a goddess after lying with Baron Samedi and surviving the venom of his semen, she now drew upon the last vestiges of her waning strength to get her through this new ordeal. The words were intoned from a parched throat. They were words she had been taught to repeat over and over to appease the god of the cane fields, to make the soil fertile again after the fires. The fires had been all-consuming, terrifying in their energy, as if the wrath of some dreadful deity had been unleashed upon Haiti.

Smoke from the stubble of the fields rose in grey wraiths, twisting like knarled vines between the lushness of the tropical growth. The wraiths weaved in and out of the jungle like living, breathing spectres, and their choking odour clung to and invaded everything.

Humility shuddered in her cruel bonds. She was naked and bound to a tall stake. Her hands were tied above her head, and her breasts thrust between the biting fibres of the tight bindings. Despite her terrifying predicament, her nipples were erect and sensitive, and her sex tingled with suppressed excitement.

"All hail to Princess Humility!"

Despite the chants of adoration, she felt very much alone. She may be considered a princess again, but she had never felt so utterly lonely. Sadness made her bow her head humbly. The worshipers chanted rhythmically. They knelt upon the ground in the heat of the noon sun, their foreheads respectfully lowered to the charred dust.

Humility leaned back against the wooden stake. It creaked as she relaxed her weight. She allowed her eyelids to fall, shutting out the brilliance of the light. A heavy trickle of sweat ran slowly through the deep valley between her breasts, falling to the narrow dip of her waist. It pooled for a moment, shimmering in the glaring light and gathering substance, before trickling to the lushness of her silky bush. A light breeze soothed her skin.

More drums beat slowly and hypnotically.

"All hail to Papa Zaca," she whispered. If the god of

the cane was to appear, she thought, why did he not do so? What was he waiting for? If she was kept out here in the open for too much longer, she would surely die. Her tethered wrists were numb from the tightness of the bindings that held her to the stake. Her ankles had lost all feeling also.

Minor priests appeared from the dark green forest. Their bodies were painted with fearsome designs. Brilliant coloured feathers served as head-dresses. In their hands they held gourds which they shook violently, and sharp knives which they brandished and which shone brilliantly in the shafts of sunlight which pierced the canopy of the jungle.

They cavorted insanely, splay-legged and thrusting their genitals in Humility's direction. These were enormous and magnificently erect. Every turgid penis was shining and glossed with some kind of oily lubricant. Humility's stomach churned and knotted at the sight of their splendour. A sound, a soft sigh, whispered from her dry lips.

The priests crossed the stretch of field from the fringe of undergrowth, their feet kicking up charred dust as they danced, and eventually formed a circle around their victim. She heard their harsh breathing and saw the mad glint in their eyes.

"Take her down," ordered the one who stood directly in front of her and appeared to be the most senior; he looked older than the others, and was daubed with the most brilliant and bizarre designs. "We must position her on the image of Papa Zaca."

Humility looked around the clearing with anxious eyes, wondering what on earth he could mean. Where was this pagan god whom the priests revered and trusted so unreservedly? "We must let her feel the sweet punishment of Papa Zaca," he said with a finality that chilled her.

What was the sweet punishment?! What were they going to do to her?!

"You have done well, Princess Humility," complimented the priest. "Do not fail us now." He stood before her, his stern expression increasing the harshness of the painted features, watching his helpers cut the ropes which bound her at wrists and ankles. He looked with no emotion at her sweetly swaying breasts as she was helped stiffly away from the stake.

Humility felt his coldness, and a rush of perverse agitation shook her body. Her limbs ached as the blood returned to them, and she fell limply into the countless hands which mauled and pulled and lifted her. They bore her high, blatantly probing around the tight darkness of her rear crevice, squeezing her buttocks and breasts, pinching her nipples, pawing her legs, and snaking about the slenderness of her waist and the flat plain of her belly.

"Papa Zaca's ancient phallus awaits the Princess!" announced the high priest with great ceremony.

The persistent clutches in which she was held, although unrefined, were not too unpleasant. Her limbs were spread and stretched, and she was laid upon a bed of sweet smelling herbs, the scent of which made her feel strangely languid and lethargic.

"Open her!" commanded the high priest, standing over Humility with his arms raised to the clear blue skies.

She gazed up at him as the others adjusted her position and pulled her legs apart. She could see he was quite old. Her eyes followed as he moved slowly around to stand at the foot of the soft bed of herbs, between her spread feet. Hands released her and the other priests edged back. The drums died, and the worshipers fell silent. Humility held her breath, and defiantly returned his stare.

Lowering himself with surprising agility, he knelt between her thighs and slowly reached forward with knarled fingers to lightly stroke her firm breasts. Although he said nothing, Humility somehow understood his demands, and obediently stretched both arms above her head. He stroked the sensitive skin of her armpits, and then ran his fingertips down her exposed flanks. The touch made her shudder and moan softly. One of the tormenting hands came to rest in the hollow of her belly, and the other crept back up to cup and mould her left breast. She continued to hold his stare, although her courage was rapidly draining away. She realised this was an inspection; the old man was confirming her suitability for the great Papa Zaca. The silence unnerved her. His coldness unnerved her. She wanted this ordeal to be over, but the high priest seemed less inclined to rush things.

"I am ready," she whispered, wanting to bring the proceedings to a conclusion, whatever the outcome. Her heart pounded violently in her bosom, and she knew he could feel it. He looked pleased.

"How do you know?" he said at last. "How do you know you are ready? You don't know what we intend to do to you."

Humility peeped sheepishly through her cleavage at his erect organ. It rose up from his curling mass of greying pubic hair and pulsed like a resting creature. She shuddered with a mixture of apprehension and desire at the sight of it, and the thought of the delights it could bring.

"It is not for you to decide when you are ready, you are not worthy!" he was still talking dramatically, loud enough for all to hear. "You will obey all and speak only when spoken to, until we decide you are ready to be offered to Papa Zaca. Do you understand?"

Humility nodded timidly, and squirmed in spite of herself as he teased and pinched her nipple. The high priest nodded, and hands once again clamped onto her ankles and held them firmly. Her wrists were gripped and pulled above her head again. Something was about to happen, she knew. Another priest knelt by her side and smoothed her damp hair from her forehead. The touch felt somehow familiar, but her attention was focused on the two priests who now crouched on either side of their elder and anointed his rigid erection with fresh oil from a wooden bowl. They touched him with undisguised reverence, and carefully massaged the perfumed oil into his length. A cushion of lush woven leaves was pushed beneath her bottom, and used to adjust the height of her hips. The elderly priest nodded again and all activity stopped. His two attendants slipped silently away, and he looked down upon his victim for what seemed an eternity. Eventually both his hands moved deliberately to Humility's sex, and peeled her open without ceremony. She gasped at the crude touch, but she knew the fingers were instantly coated with her juices.

The priest kneeling by her side leant close and brushed her cheeks with confusingly tender kisses. "Do not resist, Humility," he breathed softly. "Do everything that is demanded of you."

She did know that touch and that warm voice! The priest pulled away slightly and she recognised him beneath the swirling colours of paint. She shuddered with relief. She opened her mouth to speak, but could only gasp again as two fingers slid slowly inside her molten vagina. Her eyes fluttered shut and she relaxed under the experienced caresses. Her head lolled dreamily to one side, and the hypnotic voice whispered again in her ear.

"This is my father, Humility." She knew he was talking

215

of the elderly priest whose fingers were expertly coaxing her to a sexual intensity she had rarely experienced before. "Give yourself freely to him, Humility. Deny him nothing. Let him prepare you for your destiny with Papa Zaca."

A thumb flicked her clitoris, and the strong hands which imprisoned her limbs were required to grip even tighter to restrain her. Strong hands closed over her perspiring breasts and squeezed and massaged them beautifully.

"Will you give yourself totally, Humility? Will you accept whatever befalls you?"

Humility panted and shuddered beneath the wonderful hands. She strained to raise her hips, and she filled her lungs to push her breasts up into the tantalising palms which covered them. Her fear was replaced by undiluted pleasure. "Yesss …" she swooned. "I will accept …"

The early afternoon sun heated her blood, and the murmuring of the onlookers and the watching priests lulled her into a dream-like state. Lips nuzzled into her pubic hair, and a snaking tongue joined the thumb in tormenting her swollen bud. A finger pressed rudely against her rear opening, her muscle relaxed, and the inquisitive digit popped inside. She tried hard to remain still; she understood now that the weakness of wantonness angered and insulted these men.

The lips and tongue disappeared, leaving her hanging on the crumbling edge of an explosive orgasm. "It is nearly time," she heard dreamily before the words drifted away on the warm breezes which floated over the island from the sea. She didn't know who uttered them, nor did she care. "She is almost ready."

She opened her eyes slightly, and peered between the strong hands that still milked her breasts, and over her raised belly, at the man who knelt between her parted thighs. As he leaned closer and guided his oiled penis to her entrance, she rolled her head to the side again and buried her face in her shoulder. The whispered encouragement came close to her ear once more, but she heard none of it. She held herself rigid, determined not to cry out her delight, as the slick globe stretched her open and then filled her with one precise lunge.

"Whatever happens, you *must* do as I tell you."

Humility was floating as the column of flesh pistoned into her, but she knew the whispering voice was trying to tell her something important; something to help her; she had to listen.

"For your own sake, Humility, do nothing to anger us or Papa Zaca."

Fingers found her chin and turned her face, and lips that she knew claimed hers passionately.

"Henri!" she panted breathlessly when the kiss ended and the lips drew away. "It *is* you!"

"Oui, ma petite."

"But - but I don't understand."

Heavy balls slapped and grazed against her bottom-cheeks.

"The Vicomte, he was possessed!" A feeling of nausea swept over her as she tried to remember. "He planned to kill you. He would rather that than allow anyone else to have you!"

Humility was aware of a sharp intake of breath, and then she felt the cock which impaled her pulsate and ejaculate with little warning. The high priest immediately got to his feet, and stood looking down upon his spread-eagled victim with contempt, his penis coated with their combined juices, and already wilting. "Now!" he bellowed. "Impale her upon the phallus of sweet punishment in sacrifice to Papa Zaca!"

Humility was hauled to her feet and held by Henri and

another priest. She dared not utter a word of complaint at the rough handling; she was terrified by the portentous words of the high priest, despite the close proximity of Henri. He'd said that if she obeyed them and did as instructed no harm would come to her. But there was a new excitement sweeping the field; a fervent lust amongst the group of priests and worshipers.

The drums began again, and there was a strange menace to their beat. The worshipers started a new and macabre chant. Four more painted priests walked slowly towards the gathering carrying an ancient stone statue. It was crudely carved, but was quite obviously intended to depict a male. Humility's eyes opened wide with fear and apprehension. She glanced from the high priest to Henri for some clue as to their intent, but both were staring with undisguised adoration at the approaching effigy.

Papa Zaca was seated. Its face was dark and brooding. The eyes, although blank, were somehow cruel and the mouth was open, the lips drawn back as if a howl of anger was about to burst forth. The chest was broad and muscular, the waist and hips were slender - but the most startling feature was the penis.

This was fashioned, not from stone, but from raw sugar cane. It was a bundle of thick fresh stalks sharpened to vicious points. It rose up tall and stiff from the stone loins of the seated pagan god.

Humility's legs buckled at the sight and the sickening dread which churned in her stomach. Her head span as the hands which held her urged her forward towards the terrifying statue. The drums grew louder. The chanting grew louder. She tried to strain against the force which inched her towards her horrendous fate, but it was hopeless.

"Henri, please ..." she panted desperately. "Please help

me."

"Remember what I said, Humility. Be brave. Accept this."

Humility's head and shoulders slumped in resignation. These people were insane. There would be no mercy. She glanced fearfully at the peeled sugar cane. She could feel it, in her mind, driving into the soft flesh between her thighs, tearing through her sex and violently piercing her innards. "Henri," she cried softly. "Why?"

"Sssh! Not another sound! Show some respect before Papa Zaca!"

"But, I've already been punished unjustly," she protested. "Remember that, Henri. I was punished by Baron Samedi."

"But you survived!" he snarled, his mood suddenly intensely malevolent. "I was unable to reach you because of the fires! But by some evil witchcraft you still managed to survive!"

"It wasn't witchcraft … I'm not a witch. You now that Henri. Please - !"

"How then?!" he growled angrily; he was afraid this whining offering risked bringing the wrath of Papa Zaca upon them all. "If not by witchcraft, and without my help, then how did you survive?! No sacrifice has ever survived Baron Samedi before!"

"He was not a demon - he was a man," she whispered sadly. "He was a man, just as you are, Henri … It was the Vicomte."

"He was possessed!" Henri snarled. "Possessed by the god of death. Everyone knows that. Everyone knows that's how Baron Samedi survives." He paused, a look of sly evil twisting his features. It was the look of madness.

"What do you mean? Where is the Vicomte?"

"He is dead. I killed him, Humility!"

"You -"

"With my own hands - and it felt *good*!!"

"No … you can't have," Humility felt dizzy with fear and confusion. "It was him! He was Baron Samedi!"

"Salace was already dead I tell you! I killed him after he sent you to the Baron!"

"No -"

"He burned the fields to avenge Fairweather and me. He wanted you for his own. He wanted your love, but knew it could never be; that your love lay elsewhere. I killed him!"

"This can't be true. I -"

Henri held up his hand to silence her. "Enough of this. Papa Zaca grows impatient."

"Please don't do this, Henri - I thought you loved me."

Humility thought she detected a momentary glimmer of affection in his eyes.

"Not any more …" He turned to the waiting priests. "Impale her! Let her feel the pain of the Sweet Punishment!"

Humility was too weary and too distressed to offer any further resistance; it was hopeless. Without a sound she allowed the priests to grip her arms and thighs and lift her into a sitting position. Her eyes closed and her chin fell to her chest as she resigned herself to a terrible fate. The hands which held her squeezed cruelly.

"Accept this woman as our sacrifice, Papa Zaca!" she heard Henri bellow insanely above the excited buzz. "Let her blood be spilled upon these fields to bring forth fertility!"

Humility shivered uncontrollably. She saw herself impaled and slowly dying upon the stakes driven deeply into her flesh. She saw her blood spilling over the effigy of Papa Zaca as he was borne across the smouldering fields. She saw herself, drained of life, alone upon the throne-like idol; a sacrifice to encourage the new harvest.

"Now!" screamed Henri, his arms raised skywards and his head thrown back.

"No!"

Humility heard the shout, and slowly realised it hadn't come from her arid lips. Her eyes opened. She searched desperately for its source.

"Stop what you're doing! Let her go!"

It was Jonas, a heavy sword held aggressively in one hand and a dagger in the other. Beside him stood Harry Dawkins, and emerging from the jungle behind them were many crewmembers from the Don Cortez, all equally armed. Humility's spirits soared at the sight of Jonas, and the sight of the crew gave her renewed strength and hope. "Jonas," she murmured, not wanting to believe her eyes for fear her imagination was playing cruel tricks and the image would disappear as quickly as it had appeared. She was thrown to the ground by the surprised priests. Her arms felt unsteady as she tried to lever herself up.

There was an eerie lull, and then the field was suddenly filled with screaming voices and running figures. Humility surged with strength. Her heart pounded in her chest. Her pulse raced as she dashed and dodged through the mass of fighting men to the dark shelter of the trees. She hid in the enveloping undergrowth and waited fearfully for the terrible confrontation to end. She held her head in her hands, and tried to close her eyes and ears to the terrifying sights and sounds of the fight. She dared not consider the consequences of Henri and his followers emerging victorious.

After what seemed an eternity, the horrific noises of the battle subsided and Humility sensed somebody was close-by. She slowly opened her eyes, and saw a pair of dusty boots just inches away. Rich red blood dripped intermittently onto the toe of one of them. Her gaze travelled apprehensively up a pair of buckskin breeches, over a broad and heaving chest, across which ran an angrily jagged slash, and into the clear periwinkle eyes of her beloved Jonas.

As she whispered his name and he crouched down to enfold her in his muscular protection, Humility knew her young life was about to change direction yet again, but that from hereon in she would have a say as to the course it took.